THE BEAST IN THE RED FOREST

Sam Eastland lives in the US and the UK. He is the grandson of a London police detective.

The Beast in the Red Forest

SAM EASTLAND

ff

FABER & FABER

First published in 2014
by Faber and Faber Ltd
Bloomsbury House
74–77 Great Russell Street
London WC1B 3DA

Typeset by Faber and Faber Ltd
Printed and bound by CPI Group (UK) Ltd, Croydon CR0 4YY

A CIP record for this book
is available from the British Library

ISBN 978–0–571–28146–6

2 4 6 8 10 9 7 5 3 1

THE BEAST IN THE RED FOREST

(Postmark: Elizabeth, New Jersey. March 4th, 1936.)

(Return Address: none)

To:
The United Brotherhood of Steelworkers, Branch 11, Jackson St,
Newark, New Jersey, USA

Boys, I am leaving today!

My bags are packed and I'm bound for a new life in Russia. I have a guarantee of work, housing and school for my two kids as soon as I walk off the boat. They are practically begging for skilled craftsmen over there, while here in America there are over 13 million unemployed. As you know, there are members of our New York City Chapter currently living with their families in abandoned buildings down on Wall Street. We are fighting each other for handouts at the bread lines. Last month, I sold, for the price of one dollar, all the medals I won fighting in the Argonne Forest back in the Great War.

Come to Russia, boys. That's where the future is. I realise that leaving home is hard, and starting a new life is even harder, but I know you are as tired as I am of being chewed up and spat out and begging for what we know is ours by right. Aren't you sick of staying up late nights and worrying if you will make the rent this month, or else be thrown out into the street?

The Soviet Trade Agency has an office in Manhattan. Each step of the way, they help those who are searching for a new beginning. Thousands of Americans are arriving in Russia every day and they are being welcomed with open arms. They don't care if you are black or white, as long as you're ready to work. Moscow has its own English-language schools, an English-language newspaper, and even has a baseball team!

I hope I will see you all again soon in the great new country Mr Joseph Stalin is building, with the help of men and women just like you and me.

Yours sincerely,
William H. Vasko

Western Ukraine
February 1944

Captain Gregor Hudzik remarked to himself, as his shovel chipped through the frozen ground, how many of the skeletons still had rosary beads entwined about their wrists.

South of the town of Tsuman, in western Ukraine, on a dirt road between the villages of Olyka and Dolgoshei, lay the ruins of a place called Misovichi. Its population had never been more than a few hundred. They were farmers, tanners of leather and brewers of rough alcohol, known as *samahonka*, which had achieved some notoriety in the region. Their unremarkable but steady way of life changed forever when, in late 1918, a soldier named Kolya Yankevitch returned to Misovichi after serving in the army of the Tsar. Soon after reaching home, Yankevitch fell ill with the Spanish influenza virus which, in the years immediately following the conflict, killed more people than the Great War itself had done. The virus spread through the town. Few were spared. The dead were buried in the woods, in mass graves dug by men and women who were themselves soon laid to rest in those same pits.

By the time the epidemic had run its course, disappearing as suddenly as it had arrived, there was no one left in the village of Misovichi.

Fearing that the disease might still be lurking in the beds of those who had perished, in their faded portraits on the walls and in the drawers of battered cutlery, the houses and their contents were left to rot. Whole shelves of books, their pages bloated with the damp and covers powdered green with mildew, remained abandoned. Floorboards buckled. Ceilings sagged and then collapsed, spilling beehives choked with honey and wooden chests containing baptismal cups, confirmation documents and wedding dresses into the rooms below. The streets and alleyways of Misovichi became rivers of wildflowers.

No one spoke of the town any more, as if the place had been washed from the memories of everyone who lived in the nearby villages of Borbin, Milostov and Klevan.

Almost everyone.

A local man named Gregor Hudzik had been thinking about the people of Misovichi, and the mass grave in the forest where they had all been laid to rest.

Hudzik was a farrier by trade. At one time, his business had made him one of the wealthier men in Borbin. He had travelled from town to town, as far away as Rovno and Lutsk, with an anvil, bellows, tongs and hammers on his cart. But there was more to being a farrier than simply shoeing horses all day long. He had to be a listener as well. People talk to a man who only comes by once a month in ways they never would if they saw him every day. Patiently, he listened to their fears and hopes and disappointments. Lovers and mistresses. Lies and betrayals. No detail was ever too small that someone did not choose to let him know. In silence, Hudzik endured their stories of self-pitying vanity, which was how he came to know that a good portion of the wealth of Misovichi lay glimmering in the jaws of its inhabitants.

By the time the war broke out in '39, Hudzik had been shoeing horses for over twenty years. At first, he imagined that his work prospects might even improve, but one day in the summer of 1941, he was stopped on the road by a column of Red Army soldiers as they retreated from the invading German army. They moved in a rabble of barely functioning trucks, spent horses towing overloaded wagons and men shambling along barefoot, their poorly made boots having long ago fallen apart.

They promptly confiscated his wagon, his horses and all of his supplies. They even took his shoes away from him.

When Hudzik, sobbing with impotent rage, asked what he should do now with his life, the leader of the column offered to bring him along. Or else, Hudzik was told, he could take his chances with the German army, who were, by then, only a few kilometres down the road.

Realising the true nature of his predicament, Hudzik agreed. His shoes were returned to him, along with his horse and his cart, now loaded down with wounded soldiers, and he joined the retreating Red Army.

Arriving in Kiev one week later, Hudzik was formally enlisted as a farrier in the Red Army. He was given a uniform and the rank of sergeant.

At first, it had all seemed like a cruel joke to Hudzik but, in time, he came to understand that this twist of fate had probably saved his life.

Both of his horses died in the winter of that year. The first stepped on a Russian landmine when it slipped its tether one night and wandered out into a field. The second froze to death in the town of Pozhaists and was immediately hacked to pieces for food. The cart wore out in the spring of 1942. With iron-rimmed wheels yawing on their axles, it finally collapsed beneath the weight of a thousand horseshoes which Hudzik was transporting from a foundry to a supply depot.

As he stared at the ruin of his cart, and the tangled heap of horseshoes strewn across the road, it seemed to Hudzik that the last link to his home had finally been severed.

Taking it as a sign that he would never get back there alive, Hudzik sat down by the side of the road, put his head in his hands and wept.

This event was witnessed by a famous journalist, Vasily Semyonovich Grossman, who wrote a story about it for the Red Army newspaper, *Krasnaya Zvezda*. In the article, Grossman transformed the shambles of Hudzik's wagon wreck into a symbol of the Red Army's heroic struggle. They even took Hudzik's picture, which showed a luckless creature, formed of mud and soot, with matted hair and staring eyes and the paths of tears like war paint daubed across his cheeks.

If it hadn't been for that photograph, Hudzik's grim prediction might well have come true. But in the halls of the Kremlin, his battle-weary face did not go unnoticed.

Soon afterwards, Hudzik received a medal, promotion to the rank of captain and orders of transfer to the Headquarters staff. From then on, he was no longer a driver of carts and a shoer of horses in the front line. That job passed to other men, who went on to die in great numbers, their mildewed bones lying jumbled with those of the horses who perished alongside them, unburied on the Russian steppe.

In 1943, when Russia went on the offensive, Hudzik found himself heading in the direction of his home in western Ukraine. Soon he even began to recognise places and names on the map. The closer he came, the more he began to think about what would become of him when the war ended. His horses, his wagon and his tools were all gone now, scattered across the length of Russia. Hudzik knew he would have to begin again, but to start from scratch required capital, and how on earth was he to come by wealth like that?

That was when Hudzik realised that it was time to pay a visit to the graves of Misovichi.

On a cold, clear morning in February of 1944, Hudzik's column halted twenty kilometres east of Rovno, only an hour's walk from Misovichi.

Knowing that it would be several hours before his absence was noticed, Hudzik slipped away, carrying his rifle and a shovel.

The mass grave was not difficult to find. It stood nestled in a grove of willow trees, only a stone's throw from the road.

After locating the site, Hudzik propped the gun against a tree, hung his coat upon a broken branch, took up the shovel and began to dig. Under the snow was a layer of hard frozen ground about a hand's length deep. He almost broke his shovel blade getting through it, but beneath that layer of ice-clogged dirt the ground was only crystallised with frost and cleaved away with much less effort.

The bodies lay close to the surface. No coffins had been used. Some of the skeletons wore clothing, but most were only wrapped in bed sheets. The dead had been stacked so deeply that even when the hole Hudzik had dug came up to his chest, there still seemed to be more layers below.

His first hour's digging earned him more than twenty golden teeth, which he wiggled loose from the jaws and placed in a small leather bag around his neck normally reserved for loose tobacco. He marvelled at how much precious metal had been hammered into the mouths of those same people whose claims of poverty, when it came time to pay their bills, he had silently learned to despise.

As he stared into the dirt-filled eye sockets, twisting them from side to side while he searched for the glint of metal, the faces of those men and women he had known in Misovichi passed before his eyes with the flickering uncertainty of an old film tripping off its spool.

Steam rose from the sweat on Hudzik's back as he cast aside ribs and shoulder blades and pelvises still scabbed with cartilage. The musty smell of the bones hung in the air around him.

Once, he stopped his digging and listened, in case anyone might be coming. But there was only the harmless droning of a plane high above the clouds. Hudzik had spent most of his life in these forests and he had always been able to sense, more than hear, when something wasn't right. Nobody could catch him by surprise. Not in this place.

Hudzik went back to work, widening the hole in which he stood. All around him, the white sticks of bones jutted from the dirt and he chipped them away with the blade of his shovel.

Suddenly he stopped and raised his head.

Somebody was out there.

Cautiously, Hudzik set aside the shovel and glanced towards his rifle, still leaning against a tree at the edge of the grave site. He looked around, but saw no one. Neither could he hear anything out of the ordinary; just the wind in the tops of the trees and the breath rustling from his lungs. Just when Hudzik had almost convinced himself that his mind was playing tricks on him, he saw a figure coming down the middle of the road from the direction of Misovichi.

Hudzik was baffled. No one lived in Misovichi. No one even used this road any more. It crossed his mind that maybe he was looking at a ghost.

The stranger was a civilian, a short-brimmed soft cap tilted back on his head, revealing a clean-shaven face. He was dressed in a short brown canvas coat with two large patch pockets at the hip and a double row of buttons down the chest. The coat was undone and, underneath, he wore a leather belt and a holster. Slung over one shoulder was a canvas bag with leather straps whose contents, judging from the way the man carried it, appeared to be quite heavy.

Although the man was clearly young, all youth had been purged from his eyes, replaced by a long-staring blankness in which Hudzik recognised the lurking nightmares of all that this man had endured.

Probably a partisan, thought Hudzik. There were many of them in this region and it wasn't always easy to tell which side they were fighting for.

Hudzik ducked down, anticipating that this man must be at the lead of a patrol. To his surprise, however, nobody else appeared. The man was entirely on his own and seemingly oblivious to everything around him.

What is he doing here, wondered Hudzik. People from the forest never walk in the middle of the road like that, as if afraid of the wilderness which surrounds them. They keep to the shadows at the side, knowing that the wilderness protects them. How can a man so alone be so confident? It made him nervous that he couldn't find the answer.

Standing absolutely still as the man walked by no more than twenty paces away, Hudzik felt a surge of confidence that he might indeed go unnoticed.

Then, just as the stranger drew level with Hudzik, he suddenly stopped and turned.

In that moment, Hudzik realised that the man had known about him all along. Standing up to his chest in the hole, with skulls and rib bones and the crooked dice of vertebrae strewn all around him, Hudzik knew that there could be no words to talk his way out of the trap he had made for himself. The blood seemed to drain from his heart. Once more, he glanced at his rifle, leaning against the tree.

The stranger followed his gaze.

Hudzik waited, knowing that he would never get to his weapon before the man drew his gun. All he could do was wait there helplessly, while the man decided what to do.

Slowly, without a word, the stranger turned away and continued on down the road. He soon passed out of sight.

Only when the sound of footsteps had faded from his ears did Hudzik begin to feel safe again. His shoulders slumped as he breathed out, leaning heavily upon his shovel, as if the strength had been sapped from his veins. Hudzik wondered if he should go back. Will this be enough, he asked himself, as he clenched the leather bag around his neck? Maybe just a little while longer. A little more gold. What good is it doing them now? And then I will leave them in peace and never come back. Never. Almost certainly never.

Hudzik returned to his digging and was pleased to find that the next skull he turfed up had been fitted with two golden teeth. With a grunt of satisfaction he twisted them out, the sound like a stalk of celery being snapped in half, and slipped them into the leather bag.

It was then that he heard, directly behind him, the faint rustle of somebody drawing in breath. Terrified, he froze. 'Who's there?' he whispered, too afraid to look.

There was no reply, but Hudzik could still hear the breathing.

Slowly Hudzik turned, shielding his face with the blade of the shovel, and found himself looking at the stranger.

The man stood at the edge of the hole, a pistol in his hand, its barrel pointed squarely at Hudzik's face.

'Did you find what you were looking for?' asked the stranger.

Slowly, Hudzik peered from behind the shovel. 'Yes!' he answered hoarsely, seizing on the shred of hope that he might be able to buy his way out of this predicament. 'There's plenty for both of us.' In spite of his terror, he managed to bare his teeth in a smile. 'Plenty,' he said again.

With a dull clang, a bullet punctured the rusty metal, passed through Hudzik's right eye and smashed through the back of his head.

For a moment, the man stared at Hudzik, lying at the bottom of the hole. Then he hauled out the body, stripped off Hudzik's uniform and put it on himself. He rolled the paunchy white corpse back into the hole, tossed in the rifle, his own clothes and the shovel, before kicking the dirt back into the hole until no trace of the farrier remained.

Carefully, he brushed the dirt from his sleeves, retraced his footsteps out of the graveyard and kept on walking down the middle of the road.

Moscow
The Kremlin

Major Kirov stood at attention, his gaze fixed upon the blood-red wall behind the desk of Joseph Stalin.

For the past several minutes, Stalin had been ignoring the presence of the major. Instead, he carefully examined several files laid out in front of him – although whether Stalin was actually reading them or simply taking pleasure in making Kirov nervous, the major couldn't tell.

By the time Stalin finally set aside the documents, the sweat had soaked through Kirov's shirt.

Stalin sat back in his chair and raised his head, yellow-green eyes calmly appraising the man who stood before him. 'Major Kirov.'

'Comrade Stalin!'

'Has there been any word from Pekkala?'

'None, Comrade Stalin.'

'How long has he been missing now? Two years, isn't it?'

'And three months. And five days.'

*

Pekkala had been born in Lappeenranta, Finland, at a time when it was still a Russian colony. His mother was a Laplander, from Rovaniemi in the north. At the age of eighteen, on the wishes of his father, Pekkala travelled to Petrograd in order to enlist in the Tsar's elite Chevalier Guard. There, early in his training, he had been singled out by the Tsar for special duty as his own Special Investigator. It was a position which had never existed before and which would one day give Pekkala powers that had been considered unimaginable before the Tsar chose to create them.

In preparation for this, he was given over to the police, then to the State police – the Gendarmerie – and after that to the Tsar's Secret Police, who were known as the Okhrana. In those long months, doors were opened to him which few men even knew existed. At the completion of his training, the Tsar gave to Pekkala the only badge of office he would ever wear – a heavy gold disc, as wide across as the length of his little finger. Across the centre was a stripe of white enamel inlay, which began at a point, widened until it took up half the disc and narrowed again to a point on the other side. Embedded in the middle of the white enamel was a large, round emerald. Together, these elements formed an unmistakable shape and it wasn't long before Pekkala became known as the Emerald Eye. Little else was known about him by the public. His photograph could not be published or even taken. In the absence of facts, legends grew up around Pekkala, including rumours that he was not even human, but rather some demon conjured into life through the black arts of an Arctic shaman.

Throughout his years of service, Pekkala answered only to the Tsar. In that time he learned the secrets of an empire, and when that empire fell, and those who shared those secrets had taken them to their graves, Pekkala was surprised to find himself still breathing.

Captured during the Revolution, he was sent to the Siberian labour camp of Borodok, the most notorious in the entire Gulag system, located deep in the forest of Krasnogolyana.

There, they took away his name. From then on, he was

known only as prisoner 4745.

As soon as Pekkala arrived at the camp to begin his thirty-year sentence for Crimes Against the State, the camp commandant sent him into the wilderness as a tree marker for the Gulag's logging crews, fearing that other inmates might learn his true identity. The average life of a tree-marker from Borodok was six months. Working alone, with no chance of escape and far from any human contact, these men died from exposure, starvation and loneliness. Those who became lost, or who fell and broke a leg, were usually eaten by wolves. Tree-marking was the only assignment at Borodok said to be worse than a death sentence.

Everyone assumed he would be dead before the end of winter, but nine years later, Prisoner 4745 had lasted longer than any other marker in the entire Gulag system.

Provisions were left for him three times a year at the end of a logging road. Paraffin. Cans of meat. Nails. For the rest, Pekkala had to fend for himself.

He was a tall man, broad-shouldered, with a straight nose and strong, white teeth. His eyes were greenish-brown, the pupils marked by a strange silvery quality, which people noticed only when he was looking directly at them. Streaks of premature grey ran through his long, dark hair and his beard grew thickly over windburned cheeks.

He moved through the woods with the help of a large stick, whose gnarled head bristled with square-topped horseshoe nails. The only other thing he carried was a bucket of red paint for marking the trees which were to be cut. Instead of using a brush, Pekkala stirred his fingers in the scarlet paint and daubed his print upon the trunks. These ghostly handprints were, for most of the other convicts, the only trace of him they ever saw.

Only rarely was he seen by those logging crews who came to cut the timber. What they observed was a creature barely recognisable as a man. With the crust of red paint that covered his prison clothes and the long hair maned about his face, he resembled a beast stripped of its flesh and left to die which had somehow managed to survive. Wild rumours surrounded him – that he was an eater of human flesh, that he wore a breastplate made from the bones of those who had disappeared in the forest, that he wore scalps laced together as a cap.

They called him the Man with Bloody Hands. No one except the commandant of Borodok knew where this prisoner had come from or who he had been before he arrived. Those same men who feared to cross his path had no idea this was Pekkala, whose name they'd once invoked just as their ancestors had called upon the gods.

In the forest of Krasnagolyana, Pekkala had tried to forget the world he left behind.

But the world he left behind had not forgotten him.

On the orders of Stalin himself, Pekkala was brought back to Moscow to serve as an Investigator for the Bureau of Special Operations. Since that time, the Emerald Eye had maintained an uneasy truce with the man who had once condemned him to death, but after his last mission, which took him deep behind the German lines, Pekkala had disappeared and was now presumed to have been killed.

*

'But you, Major Kirov, are convinced he's still alive.'

'Yes, Comrade Stalin,' he replied, 'until I see evidence that convinces me otherwise.'

'The fact that his personal effects were removed from a body on a battlefield has done nothing to persuade you. Some might consider that as ample proof that Pekkala is no longer with us.'

Those effects consisted of the Inspector's identity book, as well as his brass-handled Webley revolver, which had been a gift from Tsar Nicholas II. They had been recovered by a Soviet Rifleman named Stefanov, the last survivor of an anti-aircraft crew which had been whittled down to almost nothing by the fighting around Leningrad. After wandering for days in German-occupied territory, he had at last reached the safety of the Soviet lines, only to be ordered to accompany Pekkala as a guide back to Tsarskoye Selo, site of the Tsar's summer residence and the very battleground from which he had recently escaped.

The purpose of Pekkala's mission had been to determine the whereabouts of the priceless inlaid panels of the Amber Room, the greatest treasure of the Romanovs, last seen hanging on the walls of the Catherine Palace.

Initial attempts by palace curators to remove the panels and transport them to safety east of the Ural mountains had met with failure. The glue which held the amber fragments in place was over two centuries old and had become too fragile to be moved. In desperation, since the German army's advance threatened to overrun Tsarskoye Selo at any moment, the curators resorted to hiding the panels under layers of wallpaper and muslin cloth. Their gamble that the Germans might believe the amber had already been evacuated was reinforced by a broadcast made on Soviet State Radio, whose signal was constantly monitored by the Germans, that the amber was now safely in Siberia.

But locating the panels was only a part of Stalin's orders.

If the amber had indeed been discovered, Pekkala had been

instructed to destroy the contents of the room with explosives, rather than allow the panels to be transported back to Germany.

According to Rifleman Stefanov, by the time they reached Tsarskoye Selo, the panels had not only been discovered but were already being loaded into a truck for transport to the rail junction at Wilno. From there, Pekkala learned, the amber was due to be transported to city of Königsberg, where Hitler had decreed that it should remain until such time as the panels could be installed as part of the permanent collection in a vast art museum he had planned for the Austrian city of Linz.

Hoping to intercept the truck before it reached the railhead, the two men travelled all night through the forest of Murom and rigged a dynamite charge at a bridge on the edge of the forest.

At dawn, two vehicles appeared, one of them an armoured car, which was destroyed in the ambush.

Rifleman Stefanov had described to Major Kirov how he and Pekkala then came under fire from several German soldiers travelling as armed escorts for the convoy. None of the soldiers survived the gunfight which followed and Pekkala ordered Stefanov to head back towards the Russian lines while he himself prepared to destroy the panels.

After reaching the shelter of a wooded slope, Stefanov stopped to wait for Pekkala to catch up. That was when, he reported to Kirov, he saw a huge explosion from the place where the truck had been stopped. After some time had passed, and Pekkala did not appear, Stefanov became worried and returned to the site of the explosion.

What he found was a man lying dead in the road, his body consumed by the explosion. From the charred remains, Stefanov retrieved Pekkala's personal effects and presented them to Kirov upon his arrival in Moscow.

'Comrade Stalin,' said Kirov, 'that corpse was too badly burned to be identified. There's a chance that it might not have been the Inspector.'

'Surely, if that were true,' argued Stalin, 'then Pekkala would have surfaced by now. And yet, in spite of your best efforts to locate him, the man is nowhere to be found.'

'I might have had more success,' Kirov replied frustratedly, 'but for the fact that every case to which I've been assigned since he disappeared has kept me here in Moscow, the one place I'm certain he is not!'

'What makes you sure of that?'

'Why would he come back here, when doing so would put his life in danger?'

'In danger from whom?' demanded Stalin.

Kirov hesitated. 'From you, Comrade Stalin.'

For a while, Stalin did not reply.

Kirov's words seemed to sink into the red carpet, into the red velvet curtains, into the hollow walls, behind which hidden passages snaked from room to room inside the Kremlin.

In the long silence, Kirov felt an invisible noose tightening, the bunched fist of the knot pressing against the back of his skull.

Finally, Stalin spoke. 'Why would you say such a thing, Major Kirov? Pekkala carried out his orders, even if he himself was unable to return to Moscow. Such conduct might be deserving of a medal, if I could ever have persuaded him to accept it.'

'But you have left out one thing, Comrade Stalin.'

'And what is that?'

'In the radio broadcast which reported that the panels had been safely removed to Siberia, you also declared the Amber

Room to be an irreplaceable State treasure.'

'True,' Stalin admitted quietly, 'but what of it?'

'As you are surely aware,' explained Kirov, 'such a decree meant that the Amber Room was not allowed to be destroyed under any circumstances. And having made such a declaration, Comrade Stalin...'

It was Stalin who finished the sentence. 'I would not want the world to know that I was also responsible for its destruction.'

Kirov knew he'd gone too far to turn back now. 'Pekkala was to be sacrificed. He must have known that from the moment you gave him the order.'

To Kirov's surprise, however, Stalin did not explode into a fit of rage, as he usually did when confronted. Instead, he only drummed his fingers on the desk, while searching for the words that might make sense of such a contradiction. 'What you are saying may well have been the case when I sent Pekkala on the mission back in 1941. But things have changed since then. We no longer stand on the brink of destruction. After the defeat of the German 6th Army at Stalingrad, the tide began to turn. Since then, the Allies have taken North Africa and are making their way up through Italy. Soon, their forces will begin an advance through northern Europe. It is only a matter of time before the German army is crushed between the pincers of our advancing forces. What happened to the Amber Room has now been eclipsed by the victories of the Red Army. But what happened to Pekkala has not. It is he who has proved to be irreplaceable, not the amber which I sent him to destroy. Since he went away, I have watched cases grow cold, and criminals slip away into the darkness, because only Pekkala could have caught them. Nevertheless,' Stalin leaned forward, sliding his hands across the desk, 'the fact that we have seen no trace of

Pekkala since he disappeared obliges any reasonable man to conclude that he has finally vanished for good.'

'Then you are calling off the search?'

'On the contrary,' replied Stalin. 'I never claimed to be a reasonable man.'

'Then what are your orders, Comrade Stalin?'

'Find Pekkala! Scour the earth if you have to! Bring me that shape-shifting troll! From this point on, until the Inspector is standing here in front of me or else his bones are heaped upon this desk, you are excused from all other assignments.'

Kirov smashed his heels together in salute, then made his way towards the outer room, where Stalin's secretary Poskrebychev was busily stamping documents with a facsimile of his master's signature.

'Major!' exclaimed Poskrebychev, as Kirov entered the room.

Lost in thought as to how he could possibly accomplish Stalin's orders, Kirov only nodded and moved on. He had just reached the end of the hall, and was about to descend the staircase which would take him eventually to the exit where he had parked his car, when he heard someone calling his name.

It was Poskrebychev again.

The stout little man, with his wispy garland of hair clinging to an otherwise bald head, was shuffling urgently towards Kirov in his slipper-leather shoes, which he wore as he moved noiselessly around his office, in order not to disturb Comrade Stalin.

'Wait!' said Poskrebychev, as he came to a halt in front of Kirov, sweat beading on his forehead even after such a mild exertion. 'I must have a word with you, Major.'

Kirov looked at him questioningly. He had never seen Poskrebychev outside of his office before. It was almost as if the secretary could not survive in any other atmosphere, like a goldfish scooped out of its bowl.

Hesitantly, Poskrebychev took another step towards Kirov, until the two men stood uncomfortably close. Slowly, Poskrebychev reached out and clasped the flap of Kirov's chest pocket. As if hypnotised by the texture of the cloth, he began to smooth the material between his thumb and first two fingers.

'What's wrong with you, Poskrebychev?' Kirov blurted out, pushing him away.

Poskrebychev glanced nervously around, as if worried that someone else might be listening. But the hall was otherwise empty and the doors nearest to them were closed. Behind them, the sound of clattering typewriters would have drowned out even a loud conversation in the hall. In spite of this, Poskrebychev now moved even closer, causing Kirov to lean precariously backwards. 'You should pay a visit to Linsky,' he whispered.

'Linsky? You mean Pekkala's old tailor?'

Poskrebychev nodded gravely. 'Linsky can help you, Major, just as he helped Pekkala.'

'Yes, I'm well acquainted with Pekkala's choice of clothing and, trust me, Poskrebychev, he is the one who needs help in that department. So you see, even if I did want a new uniform, which I don't, I can assure you that I wouldn't go to Linsky!' As Kirov spoke, he pressed the pocket flap back into place, as if worried that his wallet might be missing.

'It's just a little friendly advice.' Poskrebychev smiled patiently. 'Even the smallest detail should not be overlooked.'

He's gone mad, Kirov thought to himself, as he watched Poskrebychev return to his office, slippered feet whispering across the polished stone. The man is completely insane.

(Postmark: Nizhni-Novgorod, October 14th, 1936.)
Passed by Censor, District Office 7 NKVD
Ford Motor Plant
Worker's Residence Block 3, 'Liberty House'
Nizhni-Novgorod, Soviet Union

To:
The United Brotherhood of Steelworkers, Branch 11,
Jackson St,
Newark, New Jersey, USA

Boys, you ought to see this place!

I am now working at the Ford Motor plant, just like the one in Rouge River back home, and run by an American who used to work there – Mr Victor Herman. The only difference is that here in Russia, I don't have to worry all the time about being fired, or having the shift bosses give me the high hat and knowing I have no choice but to take it. I have a house, just like they promised, as well as hot water and a roof that doesn't leak. My wife is happy in our new, rent-free home and my daughter and my son both go to the local school, where they speak English. We even have our own newspaper now. It's called the Moscow News.

It's everything I hoped it would be and then some. I work hard but I get paid on time and if I get sick, there are doctors who will treat me for free. On the weekends, we play ball or else there are clubs for us, where we can play cards and relax.

In case you think that all the good jobs have been snapped up already, I'm here to tell you that there are still plenty of spots to be filled. This whole country is on the move. They are building bridges, planes, railways, houses, everything you can think of, and they need skilled workers like yourselves. So come on over! Don't wait another day. Armtorg, the Russian company that operates out of New York, can help get you all the emigration papers you need, or else there's Intourist, who can get you over here on a tourist visa. Trust me, though, once you've set foot in the Soviet Union, you won't want to go back.

Your new friends are waiting for you.

And so is your old pal,

Bill Vasko

After driving back across the city, Kirov climbed the five flights of stairs to his office. With movements made unconscious by years of repetition, he unlocked the door, strode across the room and slumped into his battered chair by the stove.

The silence seemed to close in around him as he stared at Pekkala's empty desk.

Stalin's orders had done nothing to raise Kirov's confidence. His stubborn belief that Pekkala might still be alive had lately begun to seem less like faith and more like pure delusion. Surely, he thought, if Pekkala was out there somewhere, he would have found a way to let me know. Why can't I accept that he is truly gone?

The answer lay in a single detail, to which Kirov had been clinging since the day he heard that Pekkala was dead. It wasn't what Rifleman Stefanov had found on the burned corpse. It was what he hadn't found – the emerald eye.

Kirov felt certain that, even if Pekkala had been forced to leave behind all of his other belongings, he would never have parted with the eye. The gold badge had been the Inspector's most prized possession; the symbol of everything he had accomplished since the Tsar first pinned it to his coat.

When questioned about it, the Rifleman had insisted that no such badge was on the body, leading Kirov to suspect that Pekkala might have faked his own death and gone into hiding.

Since the day Kirov had set eyes on the crumbled remains of

Pekkala's identity book, and the heat-buckled ruin of the Webley, the question of the missing badge had swung back and forth inside his brain with the relentless ticking of a metronome. But Kirov was no closer to answering it now than he had been at the beginning.

If it hadn't been for Elizaveta, he would long since have gone out of his mind.

*

Kirov had first met Elizaveta Kapanina just before Pekkala departed on his last mission. She worked as a clerk in the Records Department at NKVD headquarters. Their office was located on the fourth floor, and required such a trudge to get there that most people simply left their requests for documents with the secretary on the ground floor and stopped back the following day to collect the files which had been brought down for them. But those flights of stairs were not the only reason people stayed clear of the fourth floor. The director of the Records Department, Comrade Sergeant Gatkina, was a woman of such legendary ferocity that, for many years, Kirov had heeded the advice of his NKVD colleagues and kept clear of the fourth floor.

But the day had come when Pekkala had insisted that certain documents be found immediately. With no choice but to ask for them directly, Kirov made the trek to the fourth floor. He had no idea what this Sergeant Gatkina looked like, but by the time he reached the metal grille at the entrance, behind which the thousands upon thousands of NKVD files slept in dusty silence, Kirov had conjured something nightmarish into the forefront of his mind.

Cautiously, he rested the weight of his hand upon a little button protruding from a bell set on the counter. But he lowered his palm

25

so slowly that the bell hardly made a sound at all. To remedy this on the second attempt, Kirov struck it smartly with his fist. The bell gave a jarring clang and jumped from the counter as if the force of his blow had brought it to life. The bell tumbled to the floor, clanging even louder than before. Before Kirov could stop it, the bell had rolled across the narrow corridor and down a flight of stairs to the third floor landing, ringing all the while with a demented clatter that seemed to echo throughout the entire headquarters building.

By the time Kirov had retrieved the bell, a figure was waiting at the grille.

Kirov could only make out the face of a woman, but he felt certain this must be the fearsome-tempered Sergeant Gatkina. As he drew closer, however, Kirov realised that if the person who smiled at him through the black iron bars was indeed Sergeant Gatkina, then the rumours about her equally fearsome appearance were surely untrue. She was slight, with freckled cheeks, a round chin and dark, inquisitive eyes.

'Comrade Gatkina?' he asked nervously.

'Oh, that's not me,' replied the woman, 'but would you like me to fetch her?'

'No!' blurted Kirov. 'That's all right. Thank you. I'm here to pick up a document.' He rummaged in his pocket for the scrap of paper on which Pekkala had written the file number. Clumsily, he poked the crumpled document under the bars.

'People don't usually come up here,' remarked the woman, as she tried to decipher Pekkala's writing.

'Really?' Kirov did his best to look surprised. 'I can't imagine why.'

'What happened to the bell?' asked the woman. 'It's missing.'

'I have it right here.' Hastily, Kirov put it back on the counter.

'That is Sergeant Gatkina's bell,' whispered the woman.

'She has her own bell?'

'Yes.' The woman nodded.

For the next few moments, the two of them stared at the miniature silver dome, as if the dents might suddenly flow together, like mercury, and become smooth once again.

It was the clerk who finally broke the silence. 'I'll just fetch your documents, Major,' she said, as she spun on her heel and vanished into the paper labyrinth of the Records Office.

While he waited, Kirov paced back and forth between two closed doors at either end of the landing. He began to wonder how it was that he had never seen this woman before, in the canteen or the lobby or on the stairs. She must be new, thought Kirov. I would have remembered that face. And he began to calculate how he might find his way back here more often and how it might be possible to learn her name and to lure her out from behind those prison-like bars.

A few minutes later, a figure appeared at the grille.

'That was quick!' said Kirov cheerfully.

'What happened to my bell?' said a gravelly voice.

Kirov's guts lurched as he focused in on a solid and putty-faced matron, with a thatch of grey hair densely bristling her scalp. The collar of her tunic was tightly fastened, and the skin of her neck overflowed it like the top of a Kulich Easter cake. Wedged between her knuckles was a hand-rolled *machorka* cigarette, whose acrid smoke enveloped her so thickly that the woman's whole arm appeared to be smouldering. So this is Gatkina, he thought.

'My bell,' repeated the woman.

'It fell down,' Kirov struggled to explain. 'I picked it up. There's no harm done.' To reinforce this statement, he stepped over to the counter and gave the bell a cheerful whack but instead of a deafening ring, it responded only with a dull clunk of metal on metal.

'Why are you here?' demanded Sergeant Gatkina. She seemed to be questioning his very existence.

At that moment, one of the side doors opened and the dark-eyed girl appeared. 'I have your document, Major!'

'Thank you!' muttered Kirov, as he hurriedly plucked the dull grey envelope from her hand.

'Is something wrong?' she asked.

It was Gatkina who answered, her voice rumbling like a furnace. 'He has ruined the bell.'

'Comrade Sergeant!' gasped the young woman. 'I did not see you there.'

'Evidently.' Gatkina replied contemptuously. She fitted her lips around her cigarette, and the tip burned poppy red as she inhaled.

'I must go,' Kirov announced to no one in particular.

The young woman smiled faintly. 'Just bring it back when you're done, Major . . .'

'Kirov. Major Kirov.'

This was the moment when he had planned to ask her name, and where she was from and whether, by chance, she might join him for a glass of tea after work. But the smooth and seamless flow of questions was interrupted before it had even begun by Comrade Sergeant Gatkina, who proceeded to stub out her cigarette upon the counter top, using short, sharp, stabbing motions, as if breaking the neck of a small animal. This was accompanied by a loud, whistling exhalation of smoke through her nostrils.

'When you come back,' whispered the young woman.

Kirov leaned towards her. 'Yes?'

'Make sure you bring another bell.'

Kirov did return, and it was not until this second visit that he learned the name of the dark-eyed woman. And he had been going back ever since, slogging up those stairs to the fourth floor. Sometimes it was on official business, but usually not. That pretence had long since been set aside.

It took him an annoyingly long time to find another bell exactly like the one he had destroyed, but he did track one down eventually. And when he handed the replacement to Sergeant Gatkina, she placed it on her outstretched palm and stared at it for so long that Kirov felt certain he must have missed some crucial detail of its construction. Setting it on the counter, Gatkina struck it with her clenched fist and before the sound had died away, she hit it again. And again. A smile spread on her face as she pummelled the new bell, deafening everyone in the room. Satisfied at last, she ceased her attack and allowed the noise to fade away into the stuffy air. The ceremony concluded with the old bell being presented to Major Kirov as a memento of his clumsiness.

By this sign, Kirov came to understand that his presence would be tolerated from now on, not only by Sergeant Gatkina but also by the other inhabitant of the Records Office, Corporal Fada Korolenko, whose small head perched upon her pear-shaped body in a way that reminded Kirov of a Matryoshka doll.

Together, Kirov and these women formed a tiny and eccentric club, whose meetings took place within a small, windowless space used to hold buckets of sand for use in the event of fire. Placed along the walls, these buckets formed a border around the room, their grey sand spiked with Sergeant Gatkina's cigarette butts. In the middle of the room, Kirov and the ladies perched on old wooden file boxes, drinking tea out of the dark green enamel mugs which were standard issue in every Soviet government building, every school, hospital and train station café in the country.

Running into Elizaveta that day had been one of the luckiest moments of his life. With her, he sometimes even managed to forget the gaping hole in his life which had been caused by Pekkala's disappearance.

But Kirov always remembered by the time he returned to his office, and he would find himself as he was now, staring across the room at Pekkala's empty desk. It almost seemed to Kirov as if the Inspector was actually there, silhouetted in some grey and shadowed form. Kirov steadfastly refused to believe in ghosts, but he could not deny the prickling sensation that sometimes he was not alone. This left him with the distinct feeling that he was being haunted by a man who might not even be dead.

In spite of his stubborn convictions, as far as Kirov was concerned, if anyone had figured out how to transform himself into a wandering spirit, it would be Pekkala, for the simple reason that he had never been completely of this world in the first place.

Evidence of this was the Inspector's utter disregard for even the most basic creature comforts. Although Pekkala had a bed, he usually slept on the floor. His meals, when he remembered to eat them, were always taken at the dingy, sour-smelling café Tilsit, where customers sat at long, bare wooden tables, surrounded by a haze of tobacco smoke. Seemingly impervious to temperature, he wore the same clothing every day of the year, no matter what the weather was outside: corduroy trousers, a deep-pocketed waistcoat and a thigh-length double-breasted wool coat made from material so heavy that it would have been better put to use in the manufacture of curtains or carpets.

Kirov had abandoned any hope of unravelling the mystery of why the Inspector lived the way he did.

And if Stalin is right, thought Kirov, as he strode across to the window and looked out over the rooftops of the city, I must now devote my energy to solving the riddle of his death.

Catching sight of his own reflection in the glass, Kirov thought back to his bizarre encounter with Poskrebychev in the hallway of the Kremlin. Until Poskrebychev mentioned it, he hadn't even considered buying a new tunic. But now, as Kirov surveyed his shabby appearance in the glass, he realised that the man had a point.

The cuffs of Kirov's tunic were frayed and stained. Both elbows had been patched and the inside of his collar, polished by sweat, had turned from olive brown to a slick, gun-metal grey. Washing did little to help, except to shrink the cloth and fade what was left of its original colour.

Given the shortage of materials since the German invasion back in June of 1941, the idea of requisitioning a new uniform had simply been out of the question. As a result, the clothes he wore now were more than two years old and he had used them almost every day. But now that war aid was flowing in from the United States – everything from tanks to clothing to cans of blotchy pink meat commonly referred to as 'The Second Front' – the stranglehold on such items was slowly beginning to loosen and tailors like Linsky could find the raw materials to carry on their trades.

Kirov had previously convinced himself that he could perhaps get another year out of his present set of clothes. But if a man like Poskrebychev can notice the defects, he thought, then maybe it is time, after all.

And although Kirov hated to admit it, Linsky was a good tailor. It wasn't his fault that Pekkala ordered him to make garments that were as much of a throwback to a bygone age as the Inspector himself seemed to be. Kirov took great pleasure in reminding Pekkala that Linsky was best known as a man who made clothes used for dressing corpses laid out at funerals. It only made sense that a man like Linsky should have ended up as tailor to the Emerald Eye, especially since Pekkala's own family had been undertakers back in Finland.

Kirov's good-natured mockery hid the fact that he was extremely self-conscious about his own appearance. He was tall, with a shallow chest and embarrassingly thin calves. His uniform cap made his ears stick out and his waist was so thin that he couldn't get his thick brown gun belt, its buckle emblazoned with a hammer and sickle, to stay where it should across his stomach. Most shameful of all to Kirov was his thin neck, which, in his own opinion, jutted from the mandarin collar of his tunic like the stem of some pale, potted plant. Since joining NKVD, he had only ever worn issue clothing. His natural frugality prevented him from actually paying for a uniform when he could get one for free, even if the issue clothes never quite fitted as they should.

Maybe it's time I listened to Poskrebychev, thought Kirov, as he climbed out of his chair. After all, I can't report to Comrade Stalin in clothes fit only for the battlefield. The thought occurred to him suddenly that it might have been Stalin himself who raised the objection, and Poskrebychev was just delivering the message. The idea made him queasy, as Stalin was not slow in punishing those who failed to heed his advice. Now there was no question in his mind. It was time for a new set of clothes. Kirov only hoped that, if by some miracle the Inspector was still alive, he never learned about this trip to Linsky.

Jangling the car keys in his hand, Kirov trampled down the stairs towards the street, bound on a mission to Linsky's.

(Postmark: Nizhni-Novgorod, June 14th, 1937.)
Ford Motor Plant
Workers' Residence Block 3, 'Liberty House'
Nizhni-Novgorod, Soviet Union

Boys, I am writing in haste. Whichever one of you opens this letter, I hope you will read it to the others. The truth is, I may need your help. My situation has changed recently. It's too much to go into right now, but the upshot of it is that I am sending my family back to America. I expect it will only be temporary, but they are going to need a place to stay and since my wife's family is spread out all over the Midwest, I figure it would be better for her and the kids to stay in a neighbourhood where she has friends like you. She's going to need a place to stay. You know Betty. She doesn't need much, and she'll be glad to earn her keep in whatever way she can. I wouldn't ask this of you if it wasn't real important. But I am asking you now. I expect she will be home again in a couple of months at the outside. Depending on how things go, I might be following her in a matter of days or it could be a matter of weeks, but I think it's best if she and the kids leave now. I don't know if you've heard anything from the others who came over, and by that I mean anything about me specifically, but if you have, then just remember that there's two sides to every story. I'll explain it all when I see you again, which I hope won't be too long from now.

Your old friend, Bill Vasko

The tyres of Kirov's battered Emka saloon popped rhythmically over the cobblestones.

Robotically, Kirov steered down one street and another as the chassis of the Emka swayed creaking on its worn-out springs. He wheeled past roadblocks fashioned out of torn-up railroad tracks which had been in place since the winter of 1941, when advance units of the German army Group Centre came within sight of Moscow and the seizure of the capital had seemed almost a foregone conclusion. Now those sections of rail, welded into bouquets of rusted iron, seemed to belong to a different universe from the one in which Russia existed today.

At last, Kirov pulled up to the kerb outside Linsky's. It was on a dreary street, so choked with ice and snow by midwinter that few vehicles would risk the journey. Even in summer, the tall buildings cleaved away the light except when the sun stood directly overhead.

As Kirov climbed out of the car, he paused and looked around. Apart from a man sweeping slush from the sidewalk with a large twig broom on the other side of the street, there was nobody around. And yet he had the feeling that he was being watched. This same sensation had come to him so many times since Pekkala disappeared that Kirov had begun to worry he might be growing paranoid. With gritted teeth, he scanned the windows of the buildings across the way, whose empty reflections returned his nervous stare. He looked up and down the street, but there was only the sweeper, his back turned to Kirov, methodically brushing the sidewalk. Finally, with a growl of frustration at his own fragmenting sanity, Kirov returned to his errand.

Linsky's window had not changed in all the years that Kirov had known about the existence of this eccentric little business. The intricate floral designs etched into the corners of the frosted-glass window belonged to a style more reminiscent of the nineteenth century than of the twentieth.

Inside, it was cramped and poorly lit, with scuffed wooden floors and a large mirror at one end. On the other side of the room was a platform on which clients stood when they were being measured for their clothes. The wall behind the platform was papered dark green and decorated with vertical pillars of ivy printed in gold and red. The effect was like that of a dense hedgerow, through which Kirov imagined he might push into a secret garden on the other side. Opposite the entrance was a large wooden counter, on which stood an ancient cash register with a brass plate identifying its maker as M. Righetti, Bologna. On either side of the register stood little trays of pins, loose buttons and a tattered yellow tape measure, coiled like a snake about to strike.

Behind this stood Linsky himself. He was a slight but well-proportioned man, with rosy cheeks, pale blue eyes and hair combed so flat that an ashtray could have balanced on top. He had thin, smirking lips, which gave him an expression of permanent disdain that Kirov could not help but take to heart.

'Comrade Linsky,' he said, as he removed his cap and tucked it smartly under his right arm.

'Major Kirov.' Linsky bowed his head in formal greeting. 'Comrade Poskrebychev mentioned that you might be stopping by.'

Kirov felt the blood rush to his face as he imagined the laughs they must have had at his expense. 'I had been meaning to stop by, anyway,' he muttered.

Faint wrinkles of bemusement appeared in the corners of the old man's eyes. 'Judging from the state of your clothes, Major, you have arrived not a minute too soon.'

Kirov's jaw muscles clenched. 'If we could just get started,' he said.

'Certainly,' replied Linsky. Opening a drawer in the counter, he pulled out a black box and rifled through the crumpled documents inside. A moment later, he withdrew a letter and handed it to Kirov.

'What's this?' he asked.

'The real reason you are here,' replied Linsky.

'The real reason? I don't understand.'

'But you are about to, Major Kirov.'

Cautiously, Kirov took hold of the envelope, opened it and removed the piece of paper it contained. As he read, his head tilted to one side, like a man who has suddenly lost his balance.

The typed letter was an order for a new set of clothes, specifically two pairs of brown corduroy trousers made of 21-ounce cotton, three white collarless shirts made of linen with mother-of-pearl buttons, two waistcoats made of dark grey Bedford cord and one black double-breasted coat made of Crombie wool and lined with navy blue silk. At the bottom of the page was a date, specifying when the clothes should be ready.

The breath snagged in Kirov's throat as he recognised the familiar patterns and materials. 'Are these clothes for Pekkala?'

'It would appear so,' answered Linsky.

'And this is from two weeks ago!'

'Yes.'

'So you have seen him!'

Linsky shook his head.

Kirov held up the piece of paper. 'Then where did this come from? Was it mailed to you?'

'Somebody slid it under the door.'

'So how can you be certain that these are for the Inspector? I admit I don't know anyone else who dresses like this, but . . .'

'It's not just the clothing,' explained Linsky. 'It's the cloth. No one but Pekkala would have requested Crombie wool or Bedford cord. Those are English fabrics, of which I just happen to have a small quantity. And the only person who knows that I have them is the person who brought them to me before the Revolution, when I ran my business out of the Gosciny Dvor in Petrograd! He left the cloth with me so that I could use it to make the clothes he wanted. And that is what I have done for many years, for Pekkala and for no one else. The measurements are his, Major. There can be no doubt about who placed the order. They are exactly the same as he has always ordered from me. Well, almost exactly.'

'What do you mean by 'almost'?' asked Kirov.

'The coat had some modifications.'

'What kind of modifications?'

'Little pockets, two dozen of them, built into the left inside flap.'

'What was the exact size of these pockets?'

'Four centimetres long and two centimetres wide.'

Too wide for a bullet, thought Kirov.

'And there was more,' continued Linsky. 'He also ordered several straps to be fitted into the right inside flap.'

'For what purpose? Was it clear?'

Linsky shrugged. 'The specifications were for double-thick

canvas straps so whatever things he intended to carry with them must have been quite heavy. It required reinforcement of the coat's entire right flap.'

'More than one strap, you say?'

'Yes. Three of them.'

'Did they correspond to any particular shape?'

'Not that I could tell. I puzzled over them for quite some time.'

'And did you make the clothes?'

'Of course, exactly as instructed.'

Kirov turned his attention back to the piece of paper in his hand. 'According to this, everything should have been picked up by now.'

'Yes, Major.'

'But you say you haven't seen Pekkala.'

'No.'

'Then where is the clothing? May I see it?'

'No, Major. It's all gone.'

'Gone?' Kirov's forehead creased. 'You mean somebody *stole* the clothes?'

'Not exactly, Major.' Linsky pulled back a dark blue curtain directly behind him, revealing a grey metal bar, on which hung several sets of newly finished clothes, waiting to be picked up by their owners. 'On the day before everything was due to be picked up I placed the garments here, as I always do with outgoing orders. But when I arrived here for work on the following day, the clothes were missing. The lock had been picked.'

'Did you report the break-in?'

'No. Nothing was stolen.'

'But you just told me you were robbed!'

'The clothing was gone, but payment for the order was left in a small leather bag, hanging from the bar where the clothes had been hanging.'

'And there were no messages inside?'

'Just the money.'

'Do you still have that leather bag?'

'Yes, somewhere here.' He rummaged in the drawer and pulled out a bag of the type normally used by Russian soldiers to carry their rations of *machorka* tobacco. The bags were made from circles of leather, which then had holes punched around the edges. A leather cord was threaded through the holes and drawn tight, forming the shape of the bag. The bag Linsky held out to Kirov was, like most bags of this type, made from soft, suede leather, since it was intended to be worn around the neck of the soldier, where the tobacco stood the best chance of staying dry.

'What type of payment was used?' asked Kirov. 'Gold? Silver?'

'Nothing so exotic, I'm afraid. Just paper notes. That's all.'

'Was anything written on them? There might have been a message.'

'I thought of that,' Linsky replied, 'but it was just a fistful of money, the likes of which you'd find inside the pocket of every person walking past this shop.'

'And all of this happened almost a week ago.'

'Five days, to be precise.'

'And why didn't you tell anyone until now?'

'I did,' answered Linsky. 'I told Comrade Poskrebychev the day after the clothes disappeared, when he came in to pick up a new tunic for himself.'

'Let me get this straight, Linsky. You don't trust me enough to let me know that Pekkala himself, with whom I have worked for over a decade, was, in all probability, standing right here in this shop when the whole world thinks he is dead and yet the only person in whom you choose to confide is Poskrebychev?'

Now Linsky leaned across the counter. For a moment, he did not speak, but only stared at Kirov, his pupils the colour of old glacier ice. 'Would you mind if I spoke plainly, Major?'

'I imagine that you're going to, whether I mind it or not.'

'There have only ever been a handful of people I trusted in this world,' said Linsky, 'and you and your Internal Security thugs killed most of them a long time ago. I do not question your loyalty, Major, only I find myself wondering with whom that loyalty ultimately rests. As for Poskrebychev, he and I have spoken about Pekkala many times before and I know he would do anything, just as I would, to help the Emerald Eye. I can only hope his instincts are correct and that you will use whatever help we can offer to guarantee Pekkala's safe return.'

'That much, at least, we can agree upon,' said Kirov, as he handed Linsky the leather tobacco bag.

Linsky held up his hands in refusal. 'Hold on to that, Major. Perhaps, one day soon, you can return it to our mutual friend. Now,' he gestured towards the platform on the other side of the room, 'if you would not mind standing over there, we can get you fitted for your new uniform.'

'Is that really necessary now?' asked Kirov.

Linsky glanced at him knowingly. 'Why else would you be here, Comrade Major?

*

After his brief conversation with Major Kirov in the hallway outside Stalin's office, Poskrebychev had returned to his desk and immediately resumed his rubber-stamping of official documents. But his hands were trembling so much that he kept smudging the facsimile of Stalin's signature. Eventually, he was forced to set it aside. He folded his hands in his lap and breathed deeply, trying to slow the tripping rhythm of his heart.

Ever since Linsky had confided in him, Poskrebychev had known that he could not go to Stalin with the news. As far as the Boss was concerned, Pekkala was either dead or soon would be if he ever reappeared. In spite of what Stalin had said to Major Kirov, Poskrebychev knew from experience that death warrants, such as had been issued for Pekkala, were rarely, if ever, rescinded. Only Kirov could help Pekkala now, and Poskrebychev's loyalty to the Inspector demanded that he pass along to the major what he had learned in Linsky's shop. But how? He couldn't place a call to Kirov. All of the Kremlin lines were monitored, even those originating from Stalin's own office. The same was true for telegrams and letters. Poskrebychev didn't dare go in person to the Major, in case he was observed along the way. If that happened, questions would be asked and those questions would end with his brains splashed on the wall of Lubyanka prison. Days passed as Poskrebychev struggled to find a solution. Valuable time was being wasted. Just when Poskrebychev was on the verge of despairing, Stalin had summoned Kirov to a briefing. Poskrebychev knew that this would be his only chance, but he couldn't just blurt it out there in the halls of the Kremlin, where ears were pressed to every door and unblinking eyes peered from each polished brass key hole. All he could do was to point the Kirov in the right direction and hope that the major did as he was told.

But now his mind was filled with doubts. He won't go, thought Poskrebychev. It would never occur to Kirov that I might know anything of value except those scraps of information which Stalin permits me to overhear from his office, like breadcrumbs swept from a table for a dog to lick up after a meal.

But this time it was different.

In spite of the risk, Poskrebychev did not regret what he had done, nor would he have taken such a risk for anyone except the Emerald Eye.

The reason for this was that he and the great Inspector shared a secret of their own which, if Pekkala had ever divulged it, would undoubtedly have cost Poskrebychev his life. But Poskrebychev knew without a shadow of doubt that his secret would be safe with Pekkala. The very fact that Pekkala had never used this knowledge as leverage against him, nor even mentioned it in passing, was what now compelled Poskrebychev to do whatever he could on behalf of the Emerald Eye.

It all had to do with a joke. Several jokes, in fact, all of them conjured by Stalin and unleashed upon his secretary. They amounted to three or four each year, and ranged from sawing the legs off Poskrebychev's desk to dismantling it entirely so that it collapsed on top of him when he opened the main drawer. There had been others, less inspired, such as the day Stalin's bodyguard, Pauker, threw him in a duck pond on Stalin's orders, after Poskrebychev had admitted that he could not swim.

When Poskrebychev described these events to the few friends he possessed, he was astonished and frustrated to discover that none of them actually believed him. Comrade Stalin would not engage in such behaviour, they told him. The Boss is too serious a man to be amused by acts of mere frivolity.

What their shuttered minds so stubbornly failed to comprehend was that these jokes, and the cruelty which lay at their core, revealed more about Stalin's true nature than anything which they might ever wring out of the pages of *Izvestia*.

If they could only have witnessed Pauker, describing to Stalin how, at the trial of Nikolai Bukharin, one of Stalin's most loyal followers, the accused man had begged the court to notify the Boss as he was led away to be shot, little realising that it was Stalin himself who had ordered the execution. With ape-like gestures Pauker acted out the scene, clawing at the walls and promising to make amends for crimes he had never committed.

Stalin enjoyed it so much that he ordered Pauker to tell the story twice. Each time Stalin wept with laughter, gasping for breath until finally he had waved everyone out of his office. For the rest of the day, fits of giggling exploded from the room as Stalin replayed Pauker's antics in his head.

But there was no laughter when, soon afterwards, Stalin ordered Pauker himself to be shot against the wall of Lubyanka.

After Poskrebychev's desk collapsed, and Stalin's crow-like cackling reached him through the scratchy intercom, something snapped inside him. Poskrebychev did something he had thought he'd never do. He took revenge.

Knowing the fastidiousness with which Stalin monitored his surroundings, Poskrebychev waited until Stalin left for a meeting, then crept into his master's office and began to rearrange the objects in the room. The chair. The clock. The curtains. The ashtray. He moved them only fractions of centimetres, so that the displacement of each object by itself would have gone unnoticed. But cumulatively, the effect was exactly as Poskrebychev had intended. When Stalin arrived at his office, he was driven almost to distraction by some nameless anxiety whose source he could not comprehend. After the Boss had left, Poskrebychev replaced everything exactly as it had been before, which only added to Stalin's consternation when he showed up the following day.

For a brief moment, Poskrebychev believed he had committed the perfect act of revenge. Then Pekkala emerged from a meeting in Stalin's office and, stopping at Poskrebychev's desk, very carefully moved the black box of the intercom a hair's breadth to one side. No words passed between them. There was no need. In that moment, Poskrebychev knew he'd been discovered by the only person, he now realised, who could possibly have figured it out.

This was the secret they shared, the value of it measured not only by the fact that it was safe, but that someone aside from Poskrebychev had enjoyed a laugh at the expense of Joseph Stalin. And survived.

Letter hand delivered to American Embassy, Spano
House, Mokhovaya St, Moscow.
Date: July 2nd, 1937

Dear Ambassador Davies,

My name is Betty Jean Vasko and I am a citizen of the United States of America. I came here to see you in person, but the secretary here told me you are away on a sailing trip and will not be back for some time. I asked him to forward this letter to you and he said he would see what he could do.

I am writing to you about my husband, William H. Vasko, who is a foreman at the Ford Motor Car Plant in Nizhni Novgorod.

We came to Russia last year so that my husband could look for work. He had been laid off from his job where we lived in Newark, New Jersey, and we had no prospects there at the time. We brought our two children with us because we didn't know how long we would be gone and we considered the possibility that we might settle here in Russia for good.

When we arrived, my husband quickly found work at the Ford plant and, for a while, things were pretty good. My husband was promoted to foreman of the welding section. We had a house, thanks to the company. We had food and we had a school for our children. Truly, Ambassador, the closest I have come to living the American Dream was right here in the Soviet Union.

But things have taken a turn for the worse and that is why I am writing to you now. Last week, Bill was arrested by Russian police at our home, just as we were sitting down to dinner. I do not know why this happened and the police did not give us a reason. They put him into the back of a car and drove away and I have not seen him since. And Mr Ambassador, that car was one of the same Fords my husband helped to make!

I went to the police station in Nizhni-Novgorod but they told me he wasn't being held there. They told me to go home and wait for a call, which I did. I waited three days, then four then five and finally I decided I would have to come to you to ask for help.

Ambassador Davies, please help me to find out what has happened to my husband and to secure his release because whatever they are saying he did, I swear he is innocent. As a citizen of the United States, I'm sure he must be entitled to representation by our government.

Thank you for taking the time to read my letter. Please hurry. I do not have a job as I have been home with the kids. I have no means of support except my husband's salary and do not know how much longer the factory will continue to allow us to remain in the housing they provide.

Yours sincerely,
Betty Jean Vasko

Immediately after departing from Linsky's shop, Kirov drove straight to NKVD Headquarters in Lubyanka Square. But instead of heading up to the fourth floor to visit Elizaveta, as he usually did, this time he made his way down to the basement to consult with Lazarev, the armourer.

Lazarev was a legendary figure at Lubyanka. From his workshop in the basement, he managed the supply and repair of all weapons issued to Moscow NKVD. He had been there from the beginning, personally appointed by Felix Dzerzhinsky, the first head of the Cheka, who commandeered what had once been the offices of the All-Russian Insurance Company and converted it into the Centre of the Extraordinary Commission. From then on, the imposing yellow-stone building served as an administrative complex, prison and place of execution. The Cheka had changed its name several times since then, from OGPU to GPU to NKVD, transforming under various directors into its current incarnation. Throughout these gruelling and sometimes bloody metamorphoses, which emptied, reoccupied and emptied once again the desks of countless servants of the State, Lazarev had remained at his post, until only he remained of those who had set the great machine of Internal State Security in motion. This was not due to luck or skill in navigating the minefield of the purges, but rather to the fact that, no matter who did the killing and who did the dying above ground, a gunsmith was always needed to make sure the weapons kept working.

For a man of such mythic status, Lazarev's appearance came as something of a disappointment. He was short and hunched, with pockmarked cheeks so pale they seemed to confirm the rumours that he never travelled above ground, but migrated like a mole through secret tunnels known only to him beneath the streets of Moscow. He wore a tan shop-coat, whose frayed pockets sagged from the weight of bullets, screwdrivers and gun parts. He wore this tattered coat buttoned right up to his throat, giving rise to another rumour; namely that he wore nothing underneath. This story was reinforced by the sight of Lazarev's bare legs beneath the knee-length coat. He had a peculiar habit of never lifting his feet from the floor as he moved about the armoury, choosing instead to slide along like a man condemned to live on ice. He shaved infrequently, and the slivers of beard that jutted from his chin resembled the spines of a cactus. His eyes, watery blue in their shallow sockets, showed his patience with a world that did not understand his passion for the gun and the wheezy, reassuring growl of his voice, once heard, was unforgettable.

The last time Kirov had seen Lazarev was to hand over the fire-damaged Webley belonging to Pekkala, and which had been brought back from the front line by Rifleman Stefanov as proof of the Inspector's death. The once lustrous bluing on its barrel had been peeled away by the intensity of the blaze that had devoured the body on which it had been found. The trigger spring no longer functioned. Empty bullet cases appeared to have fused in place inside the cylinder. It was lucky that Pekkala had fired all the rounds. If the cartridges had been loaded, they would almost certainly have exploded in the fire, destroying the weapon completely. Only the brass grips, peculiar to this weapon, seemed to have been unaffected by the blaze and the metal still glowed softly as it had done when Pekkala carried the weapon with him, everywhere he went.

Even though the weapon was so damaged as to be inoperable, regulations dictated that it still had to be delivered to the NKVD armoury for processing.

'Major!' exclaimed Lazarev, as Kirov reached the bottom of the stairs. 'What brings you down here to the bowels of the earth? From what I hear these days, your visits are usually,' he grinned and aimed a dirty finger at the ceiling, 'to the lair of Sergeant Gatkina.'

Kirov sighed, wondering if there was anyone in this building who did not know every detail of his romance with Elizaveta. 'I'm here,' he said, 'because I need some advice.'

'If it's anything to do with that charming young lady on the fourth floor,' remarked Lazarev, allowing his hands to settle gently upon the counter top which separated the two men, its surface strewn with gun parts, oil cans, pull-through cloths and brass bristled brushes, coiled like the tails of newborn puppies, 'then I'm afraid you have come to the wrong place.'

'I want to know why someone would have certain modifications made to an overcoat.'

'An overcoat?' Lazarev screwed up his face in confusion, sending wrinkles like branches of lightning from the corners of his eyes. 'I'm a weapons man, Major. Not a follower of haute couture.'

'That much I know already,' Kirov told him, and he went on to describe the loops and straps which Linsky had built into the coat.

Lazarev nodded slowly as he listened. 'And you think this has something to do with weaponry?'

'I believe it might.'

'What leads you to this conclusion?'

'The coat in question was made for Inspector Pekkala.'

'Ah, yes,' muttered Lazarev, 'the famous Webley.'

'But even I can tell that those straps weren't made for a revolver. I was hoping you could tell me what they are.'

'Does it really matter now?' Lazarev drew in a slow, rustling breath. 'Why can't you let a dead man rest in peace?'

'I would,' replied Kirov, 'if I believed that he was truly dead.'

Lazarev touched his fingertips to his lips, momentarily lost in thought. 'I always wondered if they'd really got to him. Since he disappeared, rumours have trickled down to me here in the basement, but it's hard to know which ones you can believe.'

'I must follow them all,' replied Kirov. 'There is no other way.'

'Well, I don't know if this will help you or not, Major, but I know exactly what those straps were made for.'

'You do?'

'A shotgun.'

Kirov shook his head. 'Perhaps I didn't make myself clear. You couldn't hide a whole shotgun under that coat. It's too short.'

'You could,' insisted Lazarev, 'if the gun had also been modified.'

'But how?'

'It's an old poacher's trick. Cut down the stock, saw off the end of the barrel. Rework the hinge so that barrel and stock can be quickly pulled apart and fitted back together. Hang the separate pieces in your jacket, gun on one side, ammunition on the other.'

'Shotgun shells,' exclaimed Kirov. 'Of course! That's what those loops would hold, but I doubt that Pekkala would have turned his talents to poaching ducks.'

'Not ducks, Major. My guess is that he's after bigger prey. Few weapons can do more damage at close range than a shotgun. It is hardly a weapon of precision, but as a blunt and lethal instrument, you'd be hard pressed to find something better.'

'That still doesn't explain what he'd be doing with it. We're in the middle of a war of rifles and machine guns and cannons and tanks. Who would choose a shotgun to fight against weapons like those?'

Lazarev did not hesitate. 'The answer is partisans. Think about it, Major. The coat you have described to me is not a piece of military uniform.'

Kirov agreed. 'Except for those modifications, it's the same kind of coat he always wore.'

'Now who wears civilian clothes and still carries weapons?'

'Some members of Special Operations. Pekkala for one.'

'And except for him, they all carry Tokarev automatics. But the only people out of uniform who are involved in the kind of close-quarter fighting where shotguns are turned into an anti-personnel weapon are partisans. Shotgun ammunition isn't regulated the way military ammunition is, because people still use it for hunting and the more they can hunt, the less they have to rely on the authorities to feed them. If you're looking for him, Major, you should begin your search among the partisans.'

'But there must be hundreds of groups scattered behind the German lines.'

'Thousands, more likely, and most of them in western Ukraine. Some groups have only a few dozen members. Others are almost as large as divisions in the army. There are bands of Ukrainian Nationalists, Poles, Jews, Communists, and escaped POW's. And they aren't all fighting the Germans. Some of these people are so busy fighting each other that they barely have time for the Fascists. And as far as the Germans are concerned, the whole lot of them should be finished off. They give out awards to their soldiers who fight against the partisans. The medal shows a skull with snakes coiled around it. That's how they think of the partisans; as nothing more than reptiles to be wiped off the face of the earth.'

'Stalin has ordered me to track down Pekkala, no matter where the journey takes me, but if you're right, Lazarev, then how on earth do I even begin searching for him?'

'For that, you'll need more clues than the one you have found in this coat, but if you do locate the Inspector, you may as well give this to him.' As Lazarev spoke, he opened a battered metal cabinet, removed an object wrapped in a dirty, oily rag and handed the bundle to Kirov.

Inside, Kirov was astonished to find Pekkala's Webley. The last time Kirov had seen this gun, it was little more than a charred relic. Now, with its fresh coat of bluing, the Webley appeared almost new. While Lazarev folded his arms and gazed on with satisfaction at his work, Kirov squinted down the barrel, then opened the gun, which folded forward on a hinge. He spun the well-oiled cylinder, and examined with approval the almost gilded finish of the solid brass handles.

'How did you do it, Lazarev?' gasped Kirov.

'For many months now, it has been my secret project.'

'And what did you plan on doing with it when you finished?'

'Exactly what I'm doing now,' he answered. 'Making sure that the Webley is returned to its proper owner.'

'So you didn't believe the stories, either?'

'About Pekkala's death?' Lazarev waved a hand through the air, as if to brush away the words he had just spoken. 'The day they can find a way to kill the Inspector, I'll hang up this coat and go home.'

'I will hand this to him personally,' said Kirov, tucking the gun inside his tunic, 'and it won't leave my sight until then.' He turned to leave.

'You are forgetting something, Major.'

Kirov spun around. 'I am?'

Lazarev slid a fist-sized cardboard box across the counter. A dog-eared paper label, written in English, listed the contents as fifty rounds of Mark VI .455 Revolver ammunition, dated 1939 and manufactured by the Birmingham Small Arms factory. 'Bullets for the Webley,' he explained.

'Where on earth did you find these?' asked Kirov.

'The British Ambassador here in Moscow had a rather expensive shotgun made by James Woodward on which the side-lock ejector had broken. Stalin himself referred the Ambassador to me, in order to see if the gun could be repaired. When I had completed the work, the Ambassador offered to pay me, but this,' he tapped the box of bullets, 'is what I asked for instead. You can tell Pekkala that there are plenty more where these came from. Now,' Lazarev held out his hand, palm up, like a man looking to be paid, 'before you leave, let's have a look at your own gun, Major Kirov.'

Kirov did as he was told, removing the Tokarev from its leather holster and handing it to Lazarev.

With none of the reverence he had shown to Pekkala's Webley, Lazarev took hold of the weapon. With movements so fast that they were hard to follow, he disassembled the Tokarev and laid it out in front of him. Over the next few minutes, Lazarev inspected the barrel to check for pitting, tested the recoil spring, the trigger and the magazine. Satisfied, he reassembled the gun and returned it to Kirov. 'Good,' said Lazarev.

'I'm glad you approve,' replied Kirov.

'I expect you'll need that where you're going. And I hope for your sake that you're right about one thing if you do ever find Pekkala.'

'What is that, Lazarev?'

'That the Emerald Eye wants to be found.'

Letter forwarded July 16th, 1937 by Samuel
Hayes, clerk at US Embassy Moscow, to poste-
restante Gotland, Sweden, awaiting arrival of
yacht 'Sea Cloud' on extended tour of Baltic
region.

Letter arrived Gotland August 2nd, 1937.

Forwarded to Grand Hotel, Oslo, August 10th.

Forwarded to Hotel Rondane, Bergen, September 1st.

September 30th, 1937, Hirtshals, Denmark. Yacht
'Sea Cloud'. Memo from Joseph Davies, US
Ambassador to Moscow, to Secretary Samuel Hayes,
Moscow.

The Ambassador has no comment on the matter of the arrest
of William Vasko or on the numerous other arrests of
American citizens which have allegedly taken place in recent
weeks. He is confident that any arrests are the result of crimes
committed and confident, also, that the Soviet authorities
were acting within their legal jurisdiction in these cases. Said
authorities will process these criminals according to their own
judicial system, at which time said authorities will notify the
Embassy. Until such time, no action should be taken that
could impede the forward momentum of US–Soviet relations.

Signed, p/p for Joseph Davies, Ambassador

Before leaving NKVD headquarters, Kirov climbed up to the fourth floor, where he found Elizaveta, Sergeant Gatkina and Corporal Korolenko in the fire-bucket room, just sitting down to tea.

Sergeant Gatkina slapped her hand upon the empty crate beside her. 'Perfect timing, Major,'

'I have some good news,' announced Kirov, as he took his place upon the rough wooden seat.

'A promotion, I hope,' said Gatkina. 'It's about time they made you a colonel.'

'About time!' echoed Corporal Korolenko.

Gatkina turned and stared at her. 'Must you repeat everything I say?'

Korolenko did her best to look offended, turning up her nose and looking the other way, as if suddenly fascinated by the wall.

'Well, no,' began Kirov, 'it's not a promotion. Not that, exactly.'

'Is it scandal?' asked Corporal Korolenko, unable to sustain her indignation. 'Because I love scandal.'

'Then find yourself some general to seduce!' grumbled Sergeant Gatkina.

'I might,' replied Korolenko, sipping at the scalding tea. 'I just might.'

'Spit it out, Major!' commanded Gatkina, oblivious to their difference in rank.

'It's about Pekkala,' explained Kirov.

At the mention of the Inspector, a tremor seemed to pass through the room.

'What about him?' asked Elizaveta.

'I've been given new orders by Comrade Stalin. I'm no longer tied down here in Moscow. I am to search for the Inspector, no matter where it takes me. He told me to scour the earth if I had to! And that is exactly what I intend to do. New evidence has surfaced. I can't talk about it. Not yet. But I can tell you that there's a chance, a good chance, that Pekkala might still be alive.'

For a while, there was nothing but silence.

'Tea break is over!' announced Sergeant Gatkina. 'Back to work, Korolenko.'

'But I've just sat down!' protested the corporal.

'Then you can just stand up again!'

Muttering, Korolenko left the room, followed by Sergeant Gatkina, who rested her gnarled hand gently on Elizaveta's shoulder. 'Not you, dear,' she said.

And then it was just Kirov and Elizaveta.

'What did I say?' asked Kirov. 'Why did they leave like that?'

Elizaveta breathed in slowly. 'Because they know I have been dreading the day that you would bring me news like this.'

'News that Pekkala . . . ?'

'Yes,' she told him flatly.

'But I thought you would be pleased!'

'Did it never occur to you that I might wish he would never come back?'

'Of course not!' replied Kirov. 'I don't understand you, Elizaveta.'

'Do you know that when Sergeant Gatkina heard you were working with Pekkala, she gave you six months to live?'

'Why would she do that?'

'Because of something everyone can see. Except you, apparently.'

'And what would this be?' he demanded.

'Death travels with that man,' she said. 'He is drawn to it and it is drawn to him.'

'And yet he has survived!'

'But those around him have not. Don't you see? He is like the lamb that leads other sheep to the slaughter.'

'That's ridiculous!' laughed Kirov. 'Listen to yourself.'

But Elizaveta was not smiling. 'The first time I looked in Pekkala's eyes, I knew exactly why the Tsar had chosen him.'

'And why is that?'

'Because of what he is.'

'Because of *who* he is, you mean.'

'No, that is not what I mean. If you go out there,' Elizaveta aimed a finger through the wall, 'in search of that man, I'm afraid you will never come back.'

'Even if that were true, what choice do I have? Stalin has given me orders!'

'To look for him, yes, but how hard you look is up to you.'

A look of confused disappointment passed like a shadow across Kirov's face. 'Even if I had no orders, you know what I would do.'

She nodded. 'And that is why I am afraid.'

*

With Elizaveta's words still echoing in his head, Kirov returned to the office.

Immediately, he set to work. After clearing everything off his desk, he laid out a map of Ukraine. Kirov's lips moved silently as he whispered the names of places he'd never heard of before. Bolshoi Dvor, Dubovaya, Mintsevo. The vastness of it overwhelmed him.

If Pekkala really is out there, thought Kirov, somewhere in that wilderness of unfamiliar names, then why did he come all this way to Moscow, only to vanish again without ever getting in touch?

Lost in his own mind, Kirov reached instinctively for his pipe and the dwindling supply of good tobacco which he kept in the drawer of his desk. The tobacco was stored in an old leather pouch, so old and frayed that blond crumbs sifted through its broken seams every time he picked it up. Remembering the new pouch given to him by Linsky, Kirov fished it out of his pocket. For a moment, he studied the leather, turning it over in his hand as if the wrinkles of its grain, which curved and wandered like the roads upon the map which lay beneath it, might offer him some clue as to its original owner. Finding nothing, he untied the cord which held the pouch together and turned it inside out, to make sure it was free of dust and grit before loading the pouch with tobacco.

That was when he noticed a small black symbol burned into the hide. It showed what looked like two commas, facing each other. Beneath the commas was a triangle, the tip of which nudged up between the brackets. Under the triangle were the numbers 243.

It was just a tanner's mark, the likes of which he had seen branded on leather saddles when his parents had run a tavern in a village called Torjuk on the road between Moscow and Petrograd.

Travellers arrived at all times of day or night, and it had been Kirov's duty to see to their horses, removing the saddles, brushing them down and feeding them before the travellers departed.

Almost every saddle had some kind of stamp in the leather, and sometimes several, placed there not only by the craftsmen who had manufactured the saddle but also by their owners. It had always seemed to Kirov that there were as many different stamps as there were saddles which he lifted from the backs of tired horses.

There was only one person he knew of who might have any idea how to trace such a symbol – a cobbler named Podolski. After the disappointment of his meeting with Lazarev, Kirov held out little hope that this tiny symbol might bring him any closer to Pekkala. But he knew he had to try, if only for the sake of thoroughness. With a groan, he rose to his feet and made his way back downstairs.

This time, Kirov did not take the car, but walked instead, striding across the city with his particular loping gait, the heel irons of his boots sparking off the cobblestones.

Podolski ran a shoe-repair business in a side street across from Lubyanka Square. His proximity to NKVD headquarters, and the fact that he specialised in military boots, meant that the personnel of Internal Security comprised almost all of his customers.

Unlike Linsky's front window, which at least contained the products of his trade, festooned though they were upon some of the ugliest mannequins Kirov had ever seen, Podolski's window display had nothing to do with shoes. The dusty space was strewn with old books, hats and odd gloves which Podolski had picked up off the street. This collection of orphaned relics was presided over by an old Manx cat who never seemed to move from its fur-matted cushion.

Just before he stepped inside the shop, Kirov paused and looked around. Once again, he had the feeling that he was being watched. But the side street was empty, and so was Lubyanka Square. No faces loomed from the doorway of NKVD Headquarters, or from the shuttered windows up above. And yet he experienced the unmistakable sensation of a stare burning into him, like a pinpoint of sun concentrated through a magnifying glass. I really am losing my mind, he told himself. If Stalin knew what was going on in my head, he'd tear up my Special Operations pass and have me thrown out into the street. If I could just talk to someone about it, he thought, but the only one who'd understand is Pekkala. I can't breathe a word of this to Elizaveta. She already thinks I'm mad for not giving up on this search. I love her, he thought. I just don't know if I can trust her. Not with something like this. Can you love someone and still not trust them? he wondered. Or do only mad men think these thoughts?

Podolski's shop smelled of polish, glue and leather. Rows of repaired boots, buffed to a mirror shine, stood on shelves awaiting their owners, while boots still in need of repair lay heaped upon the floor.

Podolski was a squat, broad-shouldered man, whose body looked as if it had been designed for lifting heavy objects. A pair of glasses hung on a greasy length of string around his tree-trunk neck. On his gnarled feet, he wore a pair of old sandals so thrashed by years of use and neglect that if a customer had brought them in, he would have refused to fix them.

'I just fixed your boots!' muttered Podolski, when he caught sight of Kirov. He sat on a block of wood which had been draped with a piece of old carpet, a hammer in one hand and an army boot grasped in the other. The boot was positioned upon a dingy iron frame which resembled the branches of a tree. The end of each branch had been formed into shapes like the bills of large ducks, each one corresponding to the size and type of shoe which Podolski was repairing. Clenched between Podolski's teeth were half a dozen miniature wooden pegs, used for attaching a new leather sole. When he spoke, the pegs twitched in his lips as if they were the legs of some small creature trying to escape from his mouth.

'I'm not here about my boots, Comrade Podolski,' replied Kirov. 'I've come because I need your help.'

Podolski paused, hammer raised. Then he turned his head to one side and spat out the pegs between his teeth. Lowering the hammer to his side, he allowed it to slip from his fingers. The heavy iron fell with a dull thump to the floor. 'The last time someone asked me for my help, I ended up fighting at the front for two years. And that was in the last war! Don't say you're calling me up again!'

Ignoring Podolski's outburst, Kirov handed him the piece of leather from the tobacco bag. 'Do you recognise that symbol?'

Without taking his eyes from the blurred scar of the brand mark, Podolski slid his fingers down the string attached to his glasses and perched them on the end of his nose. 'The numbers 243 are the date this leather was tanned. It means 'the second work quarter of 1943', so somewhere around June or July of this year. But the symbol,' he clicked his tongue, 'isn't one I've ever seen before. There are thousands of those symbols and they all look more or less the same. Trying to isolate just one of them would be like carrying water with a sieve.'

'That's what I was afraid of.' Already, Kirov regretted having left the comfort of his office.

'You'd have to go through the whole book,' said Podolski.

'A book?' asked Kirov. 'There's a book of these symbols?'

'A big book, but it would take hours to go through.'

'Where can I find it?' Kirov snapped impatiently.

With a groan, Podolski rose to his feet and made his way over to the window of his shop. 'I've got it here somewhere.'

'Find it, Podolski! This could be very important.'

'Patience, Major. Patience.' He paused to scratch the ear of his cat. 'You should be like my friend here. He's never in a hurry.'

'I don't have time to be patient!' replied Kirov.

Podolski lifted up a thick volume crammed with pulpy grey pages. 'Then good luck to you, Major,' he said as he tossed the book to Kirov, 'because you'll find thousands of those little brands in there.'

The volume thumped against Kirov's chest, almost knocking the wind out of him.

'It's probably in there somewhere,' continued Podolski, making his way back to the wooden block. Thoughtfully, he rearranged the piece of carpet before sitting down again. 'Unless it's not a Soviet brand, in which case, you are completely out of luck. Either way, I wouldn't know. I've never even looked in it.'

Kirov looked around for a chair, but there wasn't one, so he lowered himself down to the floor with his back against the wall and rested the book on his lap. He was just about to open it, when suddenly he paused. 'Why do you even have this book, Podolski, if you've never looked in it?'

'The government gave it to me. I told them I didn't want it, but they said it was the law. I have to own a copy, and so does anyone else who works with leather in this country.'

'But why?'

'All the leather I use for mending shoes and belts and whatever else comes through that door has to come from a State-approved tannery. Each tannery has its own symbol. They stamp the outer edges usually. You find them in each corner, in the parts of the hide that aren't of even thickness or have too many creases. They usually get thrown away as scrap or turned into laces or,' he skimmed the tobacco bag across the floor to Kirov, 'turned into trinkets like these. As long as one of those stamps is on the hide when I buy it, I have nothing to worry about. But if I get caught using leather which hasn't been approved, whether it's any good or not, then I'm in trouble. And given my clientele, Major, that's a chance I'd rather not take.'

'You mean you have to go through this whole book every time you buy a hide for fixing shoes?'

'All my leather comes from two or three local tanneries. I know their symbols by heart. One thing I can tell you, Major, wherever this came from, it's nowhere near Moscow.'

Kirov began leafing through the fragile pages.

Podolski went back to work, after carefully fitting a new set of wooden pegs between his teeth.

The tanneries were listed alphabetically, each one with a symbol marked beside it, and Podolski was right – there were thousands to sort through. After half an hour of staring at symbols, they all started to look the same. They seemed to jump across the flimsy paper as if the book held a nestful of insects. Kirov kept losing his focus, sliding away into daydreams, only to wake from them and realise that he had been turning pages without looking at them properly. He had to go back and look at them again.

'It's time for me to go home,' said Podolski. 'My wife will be wondering what's happened.'

'Patience, Podolski,' replied Kirov. 'Think of your cat.'

'He's not married,' grumbled Podolski. 'He can afford to be patient.'

Two hours later, just as Podolski was closing up his shop for the day, sweeping the floor for scraps of leather and tooth-marked wooden pegs, Kirov located the symbol among the tanneries beginning with the letter K. By then, he was so dazed that he had to stare at it for a while before he could be sure. 'Kolodenka Leather Cooperative,' he read aloud.

Podolski's broom came to a rustling halt across the floor. 'Kolodenka! Where the hell is that?'

'No idea,' replied Kirov, 'but wherever it is, that's where I'm going.'

'Then I hope it's some place in the sun.' Podolski propped his broom in the corner. Removing a small can of ground meat from the shelf above his head, he opened it with a key attached to its side. The lid peeled away in a coil like an old clock spring. Then he emptied the food into a bowl and placed it on the window sill for the cat.

The two men walked out into the dusk.

While Podolski locked the shop, Kirov glanced uneasily up and down the street.

'Are you expecting someone?' asked Podolski.

'I wish I was,' muttered Kirov. 'Then, at least, I could explain why I always feel as if I'm being watched.'

'You are being watched,' Podolski told him.

'But by whom?'

Podolski tapped the glass of his shop window, drawing Kirov's gaze to the Manx cat. With eyes as green as gooseberries, it stared clean through into his soul.

*

'You're going *where*?' demanded Stalin.

'To the village of Kolodenka in western Ukraine,' replied

Kirov. 'I believe that Pekkala may have been there recently, or somewhere near there, anyway.'

'And this is based on what?'

Kirov paused. He knew he could not tell Stalin the truth. To do so would be to sign the death warrants of Linsky and Poskrebychev. 'Unsubstantiated evidence,' he stated categorically.

At that moment, in the outer office, Poskrebychev muttered a silent prayer of thanks. As usual, he had been eavesdropping through the intercom system between his desk and that of Stalin. Relaying Linsky's message to the major had been the greatest act of faith that he had ever undertaken, and the days since then had been filled with terror at each unfamiliar face he encountered in the hallway, every noise outside the door of his apartment. Even the casual glances of people he passed in the street caused sweat to gather like a scattering of pearls upon his face. When Kirov had passed by on his way into Stalin's office, he had not said a word to Poskrebychev. Kirov didn't even look in his direction, which had caused Poskrebychev's heart to accelerate completely out of control, and to flutter about his chest like a bird trapped behind the flimsy caging of his ribs. As soon as Kirov entered Stalin's room, Poskrebychev had leaned forward and, with trembling fingers, switched on the intercom so as to hear every word of what he felt sure was his impending doom.

'In other words,' said Stalin, 'you have nothing to go on but more rumours.'

'That is correct, Comrade Stalin. Rumours are all we have.'

'How did you plan on getting to this place? Kodo . . .'

'Kolodenka. I took a look at the map and the nearest airfield is just outside the town of Rovno, only a few kilometres from Kolodenka.'

'Rovno.' A flicker of recognition passed across Stalin's face. 'That's partisan country.'

'Yes, and I believe it's possible that Pekkala has been living among them.'

'I suppose this should come as no surprise, given how much trouble they have caused us in that region.'

'Trouble?' asked Kirov. 'But the newspapers are filled with reports of their heroism in fighting behind the lines.'

Stalin barked out one sarcastic laugh. 'Of course we are calling them heroes! That sounds a lot better than the truth.'

'And what is the truth, Comrade Stalin?'

'The truth,' boomed Stalin, 'as always, is complicated. And people don't want complications. They want a simple narrative. They want to know who's good and who's not. Some of them have been fighting bravely against the Fascists, but others fought alongside them when the tide of war was flowing the other way. There are heroes among them and there are traitors as well. Deciding which is which has become very difficult. There is even a danger that some of them might turn their guns upon us, now that we are recapturing that corner of the country. The situation has become so serious that, just last week, I dispatched Colonel Viktor Andrich to Rovno, with the job of sorting out this mess. If anyone knows where Pekkala might be hiding, it is Andrich. I will see to it that you have letters of introduction, which will guarantee his full cooperation in your search. In the meantime, you may requisition whatever means of transport you might need to get you there. But you had better leave now, Kirov. If Andrich fails in his mission, a war could break out any day now between the Red Army and the partisans.'

Two minutes later, Kirov was striding down the hallway,

bound for the nearest airfield and the first plane he could find which might be heading west. Then he heard someone calling his name. Kirov spun around and realised it was Poskrebychev, galloping unevenly towards him. Poskrebychev's balance was offset by a bundle, wrapped in paper and tied with string, which he carried tucked under his arm.

'Not again,' Kirov muttered to himself. He had avoided even making eye contact with Poskrebychev on his way into Stalin's office. Given the risks both of them had taken in keeping information from Stalin, the less the two men had to do with each other the better, at least for the present. And now, here was Poskrebychev, bounding through the Kremlin and shouting out his name as if everyone in Russia knew their secret.

Poskrebychev skidded to a halt in front of Kirov. He tried to speak but was so winded that at first he could not even talk. Instead, he held up one finger, nodded, then bent over and rested one hand upon his knee while he struggled to catch his breath. In his other arm, he continued to clutch the package he'd brought with him. 'I have something for you,' he gasped, still staring at the floor.

'Something for me?'

Poskrebychev nodded, wheezing.

A woman passed by on her way to the records office, carrying a bundle of files. She eyed them suspiciously and then hurried on her way.

Kirov smiled at her and patted Poskrebychev on the shoulder, as if they were the best of friends. Then he lowered himself, until his lips were almost touching Poskrebychev's ear. 'What the hell are you doing?' he whispered, his teeth clenched in a skull-like grin. 'Are you trying to get us both killed?'

With a final gasp, Poskrebychev righted himself. His face was a liverish red. 'From Linsky,' he announced, shoving the parcel into Kirov's hands. 'Your new tunic, Major.'

Kirov had forgotten all about it. 'Well,' he said, flustered, 'I don't know how to thank you.'

'Just bring him back,' whispered Poskrebychev. 'That will be more than enough.'

```
Letter found November 1st, 1937, wrapped around
stone at entrance of US Embassy, Spano House,
Mokhovaya Street, Moscow.
(Postmark: none.)
```

Dear Ambassador Davies,

I sent a letter to you in July of this year, regarding the arrest of my husband, William H. Vasko, of Newark, New Jersey, by Russian police at our home in Nizhni–Novgorod, where he was employed as a foreman at the Ford Motor Car factory.

I came to the Embassy several times to see if you had replied to my letter, but was told by your secretary, Mr Samuel Hayes, that you had no comment on the matter.

I cannot believe this is true.

Ambassador, my husband has been missing for almost five months and during that time I have received no word as to his whereabouts or even the crime he is supposed to have committed. In August, my children and I were told to vacate our house in order to make way for a new family of workers and since then we have been living at a homeless shelter here in Moscow.

I would like to return to America but I have no money and our passports were taken from us when we first arrived in the Soviet Union. We were told we'd get them back but it never happened.

I now believe that we are being followed and I do not dare approach the Embassy in person.

Ambassador Davies, I appeal to you as an American citizen to help me and my son and daughter.

Sincerely,

Betty Jean Vasko

The following day, out of a gently falling rain, a two-seater Polikarpov UTI-4 roared down on to a grass strip runway which ran beside the railway tracks, a few kilometres northwest of Rovno. The Polikarpov, normally used as a training aircraft, had been pressed into service earlier that day when Kirov, in his perfectly fitted new tunic, had interrupted a young pilot's first day of flight instruction. Shortly after Kirov had transmitted instructions to the newly established Red Army garrison in Rovno that he would require transport upon his arrival, the Polikarpov had taken off towards the west, the pilot instructor still protesting loudly through the headphones and the student standing by himself on the runway, watching as the plane rose up into the clouds.

At the edge of the runway stood the ruins of a building which had once housed the ground controller. All that remained of it now was a silhouette of ash, and the smell of the damp, burned wood filled Kirov's lungs as he walked towards a mud-splashed American Willys Jeep, one of thousands sent to Russia as part of the Lend-Lease programme, which waited for him by the railway tracks. The rails, destroyed by the retreating German army, twisted into the air like giant snakes charmed from a basket.

The only thing that Kirov carried with him was a canvas bag with a wooden toggle closure, intended for an army-issue gas-mask. Its original contents had been disposed of, in favour of Pekkala's Webley, the box of bullets, a lump of half stale bread and a piece of dried fish wrapped up in a handkerchief.

The driver of the Jeep was a thick-necked man with a wide forehead and narrow eyes, his upper body cocooned in a *telogreika* jacket. The *telogreika*'s tan cotton exterior was faded by washing in gasoline, which soldiers at the front often used instead of soap and water. The white fluff of raw cotton used to pad the jacket peeked from numerous tears in the cloth.

'Welcome, Comrade Major!' said the driver. 'I am your driver, Sergeant Zolkin.'

Kirov climbed into the Jeep, dumping the bag on the floor at his feet. The seats smelled of sweat and old smoke. 'Do you know where I can find Colonel Andrich?'

'Yes, Comrade Major!' exclaimed the driver, a broad smile sweeping across his face. 'He is expecting you.'

Soon, the Jeep was racing along the muddy roads, its wipers twitching jerkily back and forth, like the antennae of an insect, smearing the raindrops from the windscreen.

'So you have come from Moscow?' asked Zolkin.

'That's right.'

'It has been a dream of mine to visit that great city.'

'Well,' said Kirov, 'perhaps you will get there some day.'

'I do not have long to wait, Comrade Major! You see, I have been loaned to you by Commander Yakushkin, who is in charge of the Red Army garrison here in Rovno. This Jeep belongs to him and so do I. Commander Yakushkin will soon be transferred to Moscow, and I will be travelling with him. Once I am there, I intend to fulfil my life's ambition, which is to shake the hand of the great Comrade Stalin.'

Although Kirov knew that the odds against that were slim indeed, he said nothing to dampen the sergeant's enthusiasm.

By now, they had entered the outskirts of Rovno.

As two white chickens scattered from beneath the heavy-lugged tyres of the Jeep, Kirov glanced at the abandoned houses, their thatched roofs slumped like the backs of broken horses. He wondered how long it would take to rebuild a village like this. Perhaps, he thought to himself, they won't even try. That was what had happened to his family's tavern after the opening of the railway between Leningrad and Moscow. Within a year or two, traffic on the old road almost disappeared. There weren't enough customers to keep the tavern open and they had to close. The building was left to rot. He had only seen it once since his family moved out, one winter's day as he rode past in a train bound for Leningrad. By then, the roof had collapsed. The chimneys, one at either end of the tavern, leaned as if swooning into the ruins of what had once been the dining room. Snow had swept up against one side of the building and the jagged teeth of broken window panes glittered with frost. He had found it strangely beautiful to see how the structure, once the centre of his universe, had surrendered to the gravity of seasons.

The meandering of his thoughts was interrupted as the Jeep came to a sudden halt, slewing almost sideways in the mud.

'What happened?' asked Kirov, who had barely saved himself from being thrown out of the vehicle.

Zolkin didn't reply. He left the engine running and launched himself from behind the wheel, drawing the pistol from his belt.

Seeing the gun, Kirov hauled out his Tokarev, jumped from the car and dived into the wide ditch, which was chest deep in water. The crack of the sergeant's gun was the last thing Kirov heard before he went under. A moment later, he popped to the surface, spluttering out a mouthful of the oil-tinted ooze. The gunfire continued, but Kirov couldn't tell what the driver was shooting at since his view was obscured by the wall of mud in front of him. He scrambled up the side of the ditch, one hand clawing at the dirt slope and the other still gripping his gun.

The shooting stopped abruptly and Kirov knew the man's magazine must be empty. He rolled on to his back and chambered a round in the Tokarev, catching sight of his cap floating upside down in the ditch water like a child's lopsided boat.

Cautiously, Kirov raised his head, ready to fight off the ambush into which he felt certain they must have driven. Instead, what he saw was the driver, standing in the middle of the road, the pistol tucked into his belt. In each hand, the man held a dead chicken. 'What on earth are you doing, Comrade Major?' asked the sergeant.

For the first time, Kirov became aware of the cold slime which filled his boots, the trickles of grit running down into his eyes and the taste of dirty water, rank and metallic in his spit. 'What am *I* doing?' he bellowed in reply. Then he sloshed back to the bottom of the ditch, retrieved his hat and squashed it on to his head. 'If this is how you drive a car,' he called out, 'I don't think you'll last long in Moscow! And what are you doing with those birds?'

'They're for you, as well, of course,' the driver told him, as he tossed the chickens into the back of the vehicle, splashing the seats with blood and feathers.

Kirov didn't reply. He returned to the Jeep, climbed in, and stared off down the road. Water seeped from his cap and trickled down the side of his face.

'I just couldn't pass up—' the sergeant began to explain.

'This was a brand-new uniform!' interrupted Kirov.

They finished their journey in silence.

Coils of smoke snaked upwards from the devastated centre of

the town, obscuring the powder-blue sky. From what Kirov could see, not a single home was left intact.

Slowly the Jeep made its way forward over broken glass and pieces of smashed stone. Here and there, work crews made up of German prisoners were clearing the rubble, pitching brick after fire-blackened brick into rusty wheelbarrows.

In what had once been the display window of a shop stood a mannequin of a woman, naked except for a helmet which someone had put on her head. With one arm extended, her crumbled plaster fingers seemed to beckon them, like a leper begging for charity.

In the middle of this bombed-out street, their progress was halted by a huge crater, at the bottom of which a 20-ton Russian T34 tank lay upside down. There was no way to get past on either side.

Kirov climbed out of the Jeep, shouldering the bag, which had escaped being soaked in the ditch. Leaving the Jeep behind, the two men continued on foot.

Memo from Samuel Hayes, Secretary, US Embassy, Moscow, to US Ambassador Joseph Davies, Hotel President, Paris, November 5th, 1937

Ambassador – I would draw your attention to the unfortunate situation of Mrs William Vasko who, you might recall, wrote to you earlier this year concerning the arrest of her husband, William Vasko, a worker at the Ford Plant in Nizhni-Novgorod. As you instructed, no comment was made concerning the arrest. Mrs Vasko and her two children, whom she believes are now under surveillance by Soviet police, are now living in a homeless shelter here in Moscow.

Mr Vasko is only one of hundreds of arrests of American citizens reported to have taken place this year. I believe the real number may extend into the thousands. The Soviet government has furnished us with no information regarding any of these cases and we have, at present time, no way of ascertaining the whereabouts of these people.

May I impose upon you, Ambassador, to employ your considerable influence with Comrade Stalin to open a window into this phenomenon, so that we might take steps towards affording to these citizens of our country the legal assistance which is theirs by right?

I need not tell you that, with winter already upon us, significant adverse publicity could be generated if word were to spread that American women and children were freezing to death in the streets of Moscow while no action was taken by our own Embassy.

Sincerely,

Samuel Hayes, Secretary, US Embassy, Moscow

In spite of the damage, Rovno still showed signs of life.

A woman with soot-smeared hands picked through a broken chest of drawers which had somehow found its way into the middle of the road. She plucked out neatly folded undershirts and handkerchiefs, laying some over her arm to take away. The rest, she folded up, dappling them with smoky fingerprints, and replaced inside the drawer.

In the next street, a boy wearing a pilot's leather flying helmet walked past them. Around his neck, he carried a belt of machine-gun bullets, like the sash of an Orthodox priest.

On a wide boulevard which cut through the centre of the town, a group of soldiers huddled around the wreck of a German aircraft. They were sawing off pieces of the aluminium wings and melting the metal over a fire. Once the aluminium had liquefied, they poured it into a mould shaped like a spoon which they had carved into a brick. Over this, they set another brick and bound the two together with wire. They had a production line of bricks stacked along the sidewalk, and dozens of new-made spoons were cooling in a bucket of water.

The plane was a German Focke-Wulf Fw 190, although little remained of it now. The propeller blades had been sheared off, along with the entire tail section, which now lay at the other end of the street. Bare metal showed through its camouflage paint, whose hazy black and green ripples resembled the pattern on a mackerel's back.

In the mangled cockpit, minus his flying helmet, sat the pilot, still strapped into his seat. His chin rested on his chest. His eyes were closed. He looked almost peaceful, except for the fragment of propeller, as long as a man's arm, which protruded from his chest.

They walked on, stepping over wooden beams puffed and blackened by the fires which had carbonised them.

At last, they stopped outside a house whose front door had been blown away, leaving only shards of wood attached. Now a piece of burlap sack hung in its place.

Zolkin pulled aside the burlap and gestured down a staircase, which leaned drunkenly sideways as it descended into the darkness. From somewhere down below came the clattering of typewriters. 'Colonel Andrich is down here.'

Leaving Zolkin to wait in his Jeep, Kirov descended the staircase. At the bottom, he entered a small room with a low ceiling where case upon case of rifles, grenades, land mines, canned rations and field telephones had been stacked against the walls.

In the centre of this room, two women faced each other across a single desk. They wore heavy, knee-length army-issue skirts and *gymnastiorka* tunics. The sound of tapping keys filled the air, punctuated by the rustle of carbon paper and the whiz and ping of the return arm being struck. Each was so absorbed in their work that they did not even glance up to see who had entered the room. The women smoked as they typed. Ash fell in amongst the keys.

'I am looking for Colonel Andrich,' announced Kirov.

Only now did the women look up.

'Through there,' said one, jerking her chin towards a narrow tunnel that had been dug through to the basement of the adjoining building, of which only a pile of wreckage existed above ground. Wires along the dimly-lit corridor were held up by bent spoons jammed into the bare earth roof.

At the end of this tunnel, Kirov emerged into a second basement where more munitions had been piled up in the corners. Some of these cases were open, revealing stacks of Mosin-Nagant rifles and PPSh sub-machine guns. Canvas slings twined around their polished wooden stocks like olive-coloured vines. Another box, made of zinc and lined with foil that had been torn away, contained hundreds of rounds of loose ammunition. The brass cartridges gleamed in the dim light of a candle burning on an upturned fuel drum in the centre of the room.

Kirov had never set eyes upon so much weaponry before. Mixing with the smell of dampness, gun oil, and new paint from the ammunition crates was the sharp musty odour of sweat, tobacco smoke and the marzipan reek of ammonite explosives.

Several men were also crammed into this space. The only one dressed in full military uniform was a Red Army officer, perched on a flimsy chair and swathed in a bandage which covered one side of his face. Blood had soaked through along the line of his jaw.

There were two others, each of them garbed in a mixture of military and civilian clothing. Straggly and unkempt beards ranged across their filthy, wind-burned cheeks.

Partisans, thought Kirov, fear and curiosity mingling in his mind as he studied the assortment of captured German boots, Russian canteens and civilian coats so patched and ragged they belonged more on scarecrows than on men. The partisans were festooned with weapons. Grenades, knives and pistols hung from their belts and cross-straps like grotesque ornaments.

The focus of their attention was a large, bald man wearing a grey turtleneck sweater, who sat at the back of the room at a desk which had been cobbled together from a door torn off its hinges and balanced on two empty fuel drums. The man's thick, dark eyebrows stood out sharply against his hairless face and his anvil-like hands lay flat upon the paper-strewn surface, as he if expected it all to be blown away by a sudden gust of wind. Beside the papers stood a candle in a wooden bowl and a civilian telephone, gleaming like a big, black toad upon the desk.

One by one, the men turned and stared at Kirov. The eyes of the partisans narrowed with contempt as they caught sight of the red bullion stars sewn to each of Kirov's forearms, indicating his status as a commissar.

'Colonel Andrich,' said Kirov, addressing the wounded officer.

But it was not the officer who answered.

'I am Colonel Andrich,' said the man in the turtleneck sweater, 'and you must be Major Kirov.'

Kirov slammed his heels together. 'Comrade Colonel!'

'I am quite busy at the moment,' said Andrich, 'so if you will excuse me, Commissar . . .'. Without waiting for an explanation from Kirov, the colonel turned his attention back to the partisans. 'As I was saying, we can protect you.'

'The only people we need protection from are yours!' replied a tall and sinewy man, whose sheepskin jacket was held tightly about his middle by a leather belt whose buckle bore the insignia of an SS officer, grey eagle and swastika surrounded by the words, 'Meine Ehre Heisst Treue' – My Honour is Loyalty. 'Who is speaking for us in Moscow? What about the Central Partisan Command?'

Andrich tried to reason with the man. 'Comrade Lipko, I have already explained to you that Partisan Central Command was abolished last month. As far as Moscow is concerned, the question of what should happen to the partisans has already been decided.'

'Not by us,' said Lipko.

'That's why I'm here,' Andrich's voice was filled with exasperation. 'Moscow has sent me as proof that you have not been forgotten. There is now a Central Staff of the Partisan Movement, with departments represented by the Army, the Party and by the NKVD. It's all under the direction of Panteleimon Ponomarenko. He is an expert on partisan issues.'

'Then why are we speaking to you?'

'Do not forget that I was once a partisan. For two years, I fought alongside you, until I agreed to return to Moscow and meet with those who are now deciding your fate, and the fate of all partisans.'

'That's right,' sneered the other partisan. He had a slightly upturned nose wedged into a square face and small, vicious eyes, like those of a wild boar Kirov had seen, gutted and hanging upside down outside the stable of his father's tavern. 'You went to Moscow, far from the guns of the enemy.'

To Kirov, it seemed that this conversation had already been going on for a long time, and also that it was getting nowhere. As if to confirm Kirov's assessment, Andrich raised his fist and smashed it down on the desk. 'But then I came back, Comrade Fedorchak! Because Moscow knew that you would only speak to someone who truly understood what you had lived through. And, for myself, I knew that we would need someone to speak for us, or else we'd face oblivion. Why else would I be here, in this basement full of bombs, instead of safe in Moscow?'

'And when it is over,' demanded Lipko, 'and we have been disarmed or else are lying dead somewhere out in the forest, what will you do then?'

'I will return to Moscow,' replied Andrich, 'to work with Central Staff. There, I will have direct contact with Comrade Stalin. Through me, he will hear your voices and will be aware of your concerns.'

'Central Partisan Command!' spat Fedorchak. 'Or Central Staff of Partisan Movement! What's the difference? Do you think that by changing your name, you can fool us into thinking that you are different people? You're all the same. You always have been. It's men like you who came here in the twenties, ordering the farms to be collectivised and telling us how bright the future looked. And how did that work out? Ten million dead from starvation! And if we did do what you're asking? If we laid down our weapons and disbanded, what then?'

'All partisans who are eligible would be immediately enlisted in the Red Army. They would receive uniforms, weapons, food and they would be paid.'

'What does it mean to be eligible?' asked Lipko. 'Who are those you don't consider eligible and what will happen to them?'

'I'll tell you,' answered Fedorchak. 'It's what all of us here already know.'

'And what is that?' asked Andrich.

'That former prisoners of war, who escaped from captivity and joined the partisans, are being sent straight to the Gulag. And the same thing goes for anyone who's not already a member of the Communist Party.'

'How do you answer that?' demanded Lipko.

Kirov glanced nervously around the room. From the looks on the faces of these partisans, it seemed to him that if the colonel didn't provide them with a satisfactory answer, they would finish this conversation with gunfire.

For a moment, it appeared that Andrich was at a loss for words. But then he breathed in, slowly and deeply, and at last began to speak. 'Not everyone's motives in joining the partisans have been as clear and pure as yours. There are men who collaborated with the enemy, who are *still* collaborating, and who must now answer for their crimes. If you imagined it to be different, then you are simply being naive. And you are also being naive if you do not consider the alternative to what I'm offering. What do you think that Red Army Command is going to do? Allow heavily armed gangs to roam about freely in the newly reconquered territory? No! They are making you an offer to join them and if you turn them down, they are going to come in here and wipe you out. You can't just turn around and vanish back into your secret lairs. They'll burn your forests to the ground. In a matter of months, you'll have nowhere left to hide.'

'The Germans made the same threats back in 1941,' remarked Fedorchak. 'Now they're gone and we're still here. Maybe we'll take our chances.'

'The Fascists gave you no choice except to fight them or to fight against each other,' explained Andrich, 'but what I'm offering you is a way to not only survive but to be remembered as heroes in this wretched war. Victory is almost in sight. Why not share in the return of everything we have been fighting for?'

'We did not fight so that everything could go back to the way it was before. We are fighting so that things might finally change. No more collective farms. No more forced conscription. No more arrests and executions simply to fill quotas set by Moscow. This whole countryside is one mass grave, and it's not just our enemies who have done this.' Now Fedorchak levelled a finger at Kirov. 'It's men like him as well.'

What have I walked into? wondered Kirov. The situation with these partisans is even worse than Comrade Stalin described.

'What you want is what I want as well,' Andrich pleaded with the men, 'and I have faith that those things will come in time. But what matters right now is that we stay alive.'

For the first time, his words were not met with angry and sarcastic replies. The partisans seemed to be listening.

Taking advantage of this lull in the negotiations, Kirov removed the envelope, now wet and stained with water from the ditch, containing his letter of introduction from the Kremlin. He held it out towards Andrich, the once crisp rectangle sagging over the tips of his fingers. 'Comrade Colonel, I have come directly from Moscow with instructions from Comrade Stalin.'

'Can't you see,' Andrich said drily, 'that I am already in the middle of following Comrade Stalin's instructions?'

'These are new instructions,' answered Kirov.

Slowly Andrich reached out, took hold of the envelope and weighed the soggy paper in his hand. 'Have you been swimming?'

Kirov opened his mouth to explain, but then thought better of it and said nothing.

Andrich opened the envelope, removed the letter it contained and glanced at it. 'You've come all this way to search for one man, who may or may not be living with the partisans?'

'Yes, Comrade Colonel.'

'In which Atrad does he serve?'

'Atrad?' asked Kirov.

'That is the name we give to groups of partisans.'

'The answer to your question, Colonel, is that I do not know.'

The colonel's breath trailed out impatiently. 'Do you know

how many bands are out there in the forests and the swamps?'

'No, Comrade Colonel.'

'Neither do I.' Andrich gestured at the partisans. 'Or they.' Now the dagger of his finger swung towards the officer in the chair. 'Not even this man knows and he has just arrived here today as my new intelligence liaison.'

The wounded officer attempted to nod in agreement, but the gesture was halted by the bandage wrapped around his head.

'But his intelligence is *useless* to me!' said Andrich, his voice rising to a shout.

Kirov imagined that the officer must have been grateful, at that moment, for the bandage concealing his expression.

'It is useless,' the colonel went on, 'because, like everyone else, he cannot tell me the number or location of the Atrads. In spite of this, Moscow has given me the task of negotiating with them. How can I negotiate, Comrade Major, if I don't even know who I'm negotiating with?' Without waiting for a reply, he went on. 'As you just heard me explain, if all partisans do not come in willingly and begin the process of demilitarising, they will find themselves at war with the same people who are currently trying to save them from extinction. The men you see before you are those I was able to track down, but I can't get that message to the others, can I, if I don't know where they are? So you see my predicament, Major.'

'Yes, Comrade Colonel.'

'And yet, Moscow would now like me to assist you in locating a single man who *might* be living with the partisans, even though neither you, nor I, nor God himself, knows where to find him?'

'Yes, Comrade Colonel.'

Andrich sighed angrily. 'I suppose you had better start by telling me his name.'

'Pekkala.'

The wounded officer turned to stare at Kirov. 'Pekkala, the Inspector? The one they call the Emerald Eye?'

'That's him,' answered Kirov.

'I heard he was dead,' said Lipko, scratching at the collar of his coat as if the fur was his and not stripped from the back of a goat.

'So did I,' added Fedorchak. 'A long time back.'

'I have reason to believe that he may still be alive,' Kirov assured them. 'Have either of you heard any mention of his name out there in the forest?'

'No,' replied Fedorchak, 'but that doesn't mean he isn't there. When people join the partisans, their real names are often kept secret, so that their friends and families, or sometimes the whole village where they lived, would not be put to death if their real identities were discovered.'

'So now,' said Colonel Andrich, 'you can see what you are really up against. To find a man who may or may not be dead, without a name, living among partisans no one can find, sounds to me like an exercise in futility.'

'He was a Finn, wasn't he?' asked Lipko.

'That's right. Why?'

'I heard a Finn was living with the Barabanschikovs.'

At the mention of that name, it grew suddenly quiet in the room.

'Who are these Barabanschikovs?' asked Kirov.

The partisans kept quiet, shifting uneasily in their corpse-robbed boots.

It was Andrich who replied. 'Let's just say, that if he's with the Barabanschikovs, then your task may be even more difficult.'

'But if you know *who* they are, then surely someone must know *where* they are.'

Fedorchak laughed. 'Oh, we know where they are, more or less. They're in the Red Forest.'

'I don't recall seeing that name on the map,' said Kirov.

'That's because it isn't there,' Fedorchak told him. 'The Red Forest is a name the locals gave to a wilderness south of here, where hundreds of maple trees grow. In the autumn, when the leaves turn red, the forest looks as if it has been painted with blood.'

Kirov looked anxiously from one man to the other. 'Will you take me there? It's still light. We could set off now.'

The partisans both shook their heads. 'That land belongs to Barabanschikov.'

'Then just point me in the right direction,' shouted Kirov, 'and I'll go myself!'

'You don't understand,' Lipko told him. 'No one in their right mind goes into the Red Forest.'

At that moment, the phone rang. Colonel Andrich picked up the receiver, pressing it against his fleshy ear. 'Damn!' he shouted and hung up.

'What is it?' asked Kirov,

'Another air raid.' The words were not even out of his mouth before they heard the rumble of multi-engine planes. The droning of the unsynchronised motors rose and fell. Kirov could tell they were German. Soviet bombers had synchronised engines, so that the noise they made was a steady, constant thrum, instead of this.

Soon after came the first deep shudder of explosions in the distance. The bombs were falling in clusters. Kirov flinched at each detonation. The floor trembled under his feet.

'This is the third time in two days,' muttered Colonel Andrich, staring grimly into space.

The next volley of explosions seemed to happen all at once. The building shook. A crack, like the path of a tiny lightning bolt, appeared in the ceiling above Kirov's head.

The lights flickered.

If one piece of hot shrapnel hits these crates, thought Kirov, we will be falling from the sky in pieces as small as rain.

The colonel swore and grabbed hold of the sides of his desk.

The next sound was like a huge flag billowing in the wind. The shock nearly dropped Kirov to his knees and panic washed through him at the thought of being buried alive.

The candle went out, and was followed by darkness so complete, it was as if they'd all been struck blind.

A dry, snapping boom shook the building.

That blast was followed by another, but this one was more distant than the last. As the seconds passed, bombs continued to fall, each one further away than the last.

It's over, Kirov thought to himself.

But, in the next instant, the room was filled with deafening explosions.

Kirov's first thought was that some of the loose ammunition must have exploded, but then he glimpsed the splashing light of a gun muzzle. Somebody had opened fire, but he couldn't see who held the gun. In the flickering glare, Kirov watched Fedorchak go down, his blood splashing in an arc across the ceiling.

Kirov turned to run, hoping to reach the stairs which led up to the street, when suddenly he felt a stunning blow to his side. The impact threw him against the wall. He stumbled and fell to the floor, gasping for breath. The whole upper part of his body felt as if it had caught fire.

The firing stopped and, a moment later, a sabre of torchlight punctured the dusty air.

Someone stepped over to the doorway.

Kirov heard a metallic rustle as the gunman slid an empty magazine from his pistol, letting it fall with a clatter to the floor. Unhurriedly, he replaced it with another, then chambered a round in the breech.

Kirov struggled to focus on the man, but his eyes were filled with smoke.

At that moment, there was a sound at the end of the excavated hallway.

The gunman aimed the beam of his torch down the tunnel, just as the two typists made a run for the exit.

The gun roared again, twice, three times, and the women fell in a heap at the base of the steps.

Spent cartridges clattered down. One of them bounced off Kirov's cheek, searing the flesh.

The gunman heard him gasp and suddenly the torch beam was burning into Kirov's face.

The man bent over him.

Blinded in the glare, Kirov felt the hot muzzle of the gun pressing against the centre of his forehead. Cordite smoke sifted from the breech. Kirov knew he was about to die. The clarity of that thought cut through the shock of his wounds, but where Kirov had expected to feel terror, there was only a strange, shuddering emptiness, as if some part of him had already shrugged itself loose from the scaffolding of flesh and bones that anchored him to the world. He closed his eyes and waited for the end.

But the shot never came.

The next sound Kirov heard was the soft tread of the man's boots as he made his way along the earth-walled passageway, stepped over the two dead women, climbed the stairs and was gone.

Kirov lay in the dark, unable to move, tasting blood at the back of his mouth and wondering why the gunman had left him alive. Perhaps, he thought, I am so badly wounded that he knows I'll be dead before help can arrive. Although Kirov knew he had been shot, he wasn't sure where he'd been hit. The pain had not yet focused and his whole body felt numb. Feebly, he dragged his fingertips across his chest, searching for a tear in his uniform where the bullet had gone in. But his strength began to fail him before he could locate the wound. A velvety blackness sifted through his mind. He struggled against it, but there was nothing he could do. The darkness seemed to overflow his skull and pour out through his eyes. His last conscious thought was that he might have been dead after all.

Memo from Joseph Davies, US Ambassador to
Moscow, Hotel President, Paris, to Secretary
Samuel Hayes, US Embassy, Moscow, November 21st,
1937
Following message to be forwarded through
standard unofficial channel via Kremlin to
Comrade Joseph Stalin.

Dear Comrade Stalin,

News has reached me of an unfortunate situation regarding
one of our citizens currently residing in the Soviet Union, a
Mrs William Vasko, who reports that her husband was taken
into custody while employed at the Ford Motor Car plant in
Nizhni-Novgorod. No word has been received of his
whereabouts for some time. Any word on this matter would
be greatly appreciated.

Yours etc. Joseph Davies, Ambassador

PS Your proposal to purchase cargo ships currently in the
process of being decommissioned by the US Navy is being
closely examined in Washington. I hope soon to be able to
deliver favourable news on the subject.

Kirov regained consciousness just as he was being wheeled into an operating room. He sat up suddenly, startling the nurses who were moving the gurney towards the surgery table. Ignoring their protests, he began to climb down, but when his feet touched the floor, he found that he could barely stand. It felt as if his bones had been removed.

One of the nurses took hold of Kirov's shoulder, trying to push him back, but Kirov, in his morphine-fuelled delirium, punched her on the chin and laid her out cold on the red linoleum floor. Then the other nurse attacked, kicking his shins with her blunt-toed shoes and pulling his ears while she called for the doctor.

Angry and completely confused, Kirov fought against the woman, staggering around until his legs gave out from under him. His head struck the floor with a crack.

From where he lay, Kirov noticed a pile of severed arms and legs heaped into the corner.

The face of a man appeared above him. He wore a white smock smeared with blood. 'You fool!' he shouted, as he pressed something cold and wet against Kirov's face. 'These people are trying to help you!'

A sickly sweetness, smelling like paint thinner, filled Kirov's lungs. 'Damn you,' he managed to say, before he tumbled back into oblivion.

Kirov woke with the sun on his face. His chest was covered with bandages and his bare feet poked out from under a grey army blanket.

He was by himself in a small room, which appeared to have been converted from some kind of closet. It had one window, against which the ice-sheathed branches of a tree tapped as they jostled in the breeze. The walls of the room were a pale brownish yellow, like coffee with milk that had been left in a mug and gone cold. The only thing aside from his bed was a collapsible chair in the corner.

Vaguely, he remembered hitting somebody. A woman. No, he thought. That can't be right. I would never have done such a thing.

Then he leaned over and threw up, surprised to find a bucket already waiting on the floor beside his bed. He groaned, still hanging almost upside down, and wiped his mouth on the sleeve of his hospital pyjamas. Although Kirov's sight was blurred, the sunlight melting into rainbows everything on which he tried to focus, he was relieved to see his boots standing at the foot of the bed, along with the canvas bag containing Pekkala's revolver.

As he lay back, Kirov noticed a movement on the other side of the room. A man was standing there, hidden until that moment by the glare of light pouring in through the window. 'Who's there?' he asked.

The man did not reply.

'Do I know you?' demanded Kirov.

The man walked towards him, still masked in the flare of the sun.

In that silhouette, Kirov thought he recognised Pekkala's

shoulders, like plates of armour slung across his back, but his vision was blurred and his mind kept skipping, like a needle jumping on a record.

The man reached out and Kirov felt the warmth of a hand pressed against his forehead.

'Sleep now,' whispered the stranger.

As if the voice compelled him, Kirov slipped from consciousness, wading out into the black lake of his dreams.

*

The next time he woke, it was evening.

A nurse was tucking in the blanket, her back turned towards him.

'Where am I?' asked Kirov.

'In the hospital,' the nurse replied, 'not far from Rovno, where you were wounded yesterday.'

'I dreamed I hit someone,' said Kirov.

Now the woman turned to face him. 'Is that so?'

Kirov gasped as he caught sight of her black eye.

'I must have had that dream as well,' said the woman.

'Forgive me,' muttered Kirov.

'In time, perhaps,' she told him

'There's something else I dreamed,' he said, 'or thought I dreamed, at least.'

'What was it?'

'A man, standing right over there by the window.'

'I was on duty all afternoon, and nobody came into the room apart from me. But don't think you're going crazy. They gave you morphine for the pain. That stuff can play tricks with your mind.'

'I saw him, too,' said a voice.

Kirov glanced towards the doorway, where a man sat in a wheelchair. He had lost both his legs halfway down the thigh and one of his arms at the bicep. With his one remaining hand, he steered the chair by gripping one of the wheels.

'Return to your room, Captain Dombrowsky,' commanded the nurse. 'Leave this man alone. He needs his rest.'

Grinning but obedient, the man manoeuvred himself back into the hallway and creaked away back to his bed.

'Don't pay any attention to him,' said the nurse. 'His limbs aren't the only things he's lost. The Captain was transferred here from another hospital right after the Germans pulled out. He made such a nuisance of himself at the other place that they passed him over to us. And now we're stuck with him.'

'How did I get here?' asked Kirov.

'Some soldiers brought you in. They found you in a bunker after the air raid. They said you had been in a gunfight, but against whom they didn't know.'

'I don't know, either,' said Kirov. 'Someone just started shooting. How are the others?'

'You are the only survivor,' replied the nurse. 'When the soldiers carried you in, you were covered in so much blood that I thought they'd wasted their time. Turns out, it wasn't all yours. The soldiers told me that, apart from you, they found three men, all of them dead. Two were obviously partisans. The third man had a Soviet identity book, but was wearing civilian clothes. They didn't tell me his name.'

'That must be Colonel Andrich,' said Kirov, 'but there was also a Red Army officer in the bunker with us. Did they find him, too?'

The nurse shook her head. 'Whoever he was, it sounds like

that's the man who shot you and your friends.'

'And there was a driver. He waited outside during the meeting. How is he?'

'No one mentioned anything about a driver. He might have been killed in the air raid.'

At that moment, the doctor walked in. It was the same man who had dosed Kirov with ether when he tried to get down off the gurney. The doctor's apron had been cleaned, but still showed the marks of blood stains in the cloth. Without any smile or greeting, the man unclipped a chart from the foot of Kirov's bed. Still glancing at the chart, the doctor reached into the pocket of his white hospital coat, removed something about the size of a cherry stone and tossed it on to the bed. 'Major, you're a lucky man,' he said.

Kirov squinted at the object, which had landed on the blanket just above his chest. It was a bullet, or what was left of one. Kirov stared at the gnarled mushroom of lead and copper.

'The bullet must have ricocheted,' explained the doctor, 'which explains its deformed shape. By the time it hit you, the force was almost spent. We removed it from under your collar bone. If the round had been going any faster, it would have torn away your shoulder blade.'

A shudder passed through Kirov as he thought of the bullet ripping through his skin.

Seeing Kirov's discomfort, the nurse picked up the piece of lead and tucked it into the pocket of his tunic, which was now draped over a chair in the corner of the room. 'I really don't know why you hand those things out,' she told the doctor.

The doctor smiled. 'A reminder to be more careful next time.'

'I really should be going,' said Kirov. 'You see, I came here from

Moscow to find someone.' As he struggled to sit up, he felt a dull, tearing sensation across his chest and slumped back with a groan.

'Be patient,' warned the doctor. 'Even for a commissar, will-power alone is not a cure. You'll be back on the street soon enough. In the meantime, allow my nurse to make your life miserable for a few days. It's the least you can do after punching her lights out yesterday.'

'I have already apologised.'

'Knowing her,' said the doctor, as he replaced the chart, 'I think it might take more than that to earn forgiveness.'

When the doctor had gone, the nurse finished tucking in the bed. 'Don't pay any attention to him,' she told Kirov. 'He likes to stir up trouble.'

'So you won't be making my life miserable?'

'When the morphine wears off,' she assured him, 'your life will be miserable enough without my help.'

And she was right.

In the long, sleepless night which followed, blinding flashes of colour exploded behind Kirov's eyes and pain rose from the fading haze of morphine, shuddering through his body as if some cruel phantom was prising at his joints with screwdrivers. He listened to the Morse-code tap of the branch against the window and the whimpering of soldiers whose amputated limbs still ghosted them with agony. The more Kirov listened, the louder the noises became, until he had to press his hands against his ears or else be deafened by them.

Kirov had no sense of having slept, or for how long, but in the morning he woke bathed in sweat, to the sound of a creaking wheel as Captain Dombrowsky steered himself into the room. 'The nurse told you I was crazy, didn't she?'

98

'More or less.' Kirov's throat was dry. He wished he had something to drink.

'Do you know what those nurses call me behind my back?' asked Dombrowsky. 'Their name for me is Samovar, because that's what I look like with no legs and only one arm. To them, I am nothing more than a glorified teapot. Maybe I'm insane, but I know what I'm talking about.'

Kirov fixed him with a bloodshot stare. 'And what *are* you talking about, Dombrowsky?'

'About the man you saw. He appeared out of nowhere, like a ghost, right when the nurses were changing their shifts. He went straight to your room and as he walked he made no sound. No sound at all.'

'What did he look like, this man?'

'He was tall.'

'That's all you can tell me?'

'He wore an old-fashioned coat, of a kind I haven't seen since before the Revolution.'

Maybe I wasn't hallucinating after all, thought Kirov.

The nurse appeared in the doorway. 'What did I tell you, Captain?' she scolded. 'Now leave Major Kirov in peace! And stay away from the stairs! I saw you this morning, and you were much too close to the edge. If you try going down in that wheelchair, you'll kill yourself.'

'I'm going! I'm going!' Meekly, Dombrowsky wheeled himself away, but as he passed by Kirov's bed, he turned his head and winked.

*

That night, Rovno was bombed again. This time, it was the out-skirts that received the full force of the destruction. Above the burning houses, the sky turned pink as salmon flesh and, at the hospital on the other side of town, shockwaves caused the win-dows to tremble like ripples in a pond.

Kirov drifted in and out of sleep. The fever had broken and now his discomfort centred on the livid purple scar beneath his collarbone. He found it difficult to lie in any one position for long and each time he moved, the pain would jolt him awake.

With a moan, Kirov rolled on to his back. His eyes flickered open and the darkness took shape around him – the light bulb in the ceiling, the crack in the bottom left pane of the window, through which he saw the sky punctuated by the flash of high ex-plosives in the distance.

That was when he realised there was someone standing right beside his bed.

This time, there could be no doubt.

It was Pekkala.

For a moment, Kirov was too stunned to speak. Even though he had believed all along that the Inspector could have survived, he had always been guided more by faith than certainty. Now, at last, Kirov's mind was no longer shackled by doubt. 'I knew it!' he shouted. 'I knew they couldn't kill the Emerald Eye!'

Pekkala responded by slapping his hand over Kirov's mouth. 'Quiet!' he hissed. 'Are you trying to wake the dead as well as the living?'

Kirov blinked at him in silence until Pekkala finally removed his hand.

'How did you know I was in Rovno?' asked Kirov.

'The clues I left with Linsky,' explained Pekkala, speaking so matter-of-factly that it was as if no time at all had passed since the two men parted company. 'I knew they'd lead you here eventually.'

'So you really were in Moscow!'

Pekkala patted his new coat. 'And I did not leave Moscow empty-handed.'

'But why did you wait so long?'

'I came as soon as the German army pulled out of this area,' explained Pekkala. 'Before that, it was not possible to travel.'

'But why leave clues for me to follow you out here?' demanded Kirov. 'Why didn't you simply come to the office?'

'You were being watched,' explained Pekkala.

'Watched?' Kirov remembered the feeling of uneasiness which had pursued him almost to the point of madness. 'By whom?'

'From the look of them,' answered Pekkala, 'I'd say they were NKVD Special Operations.'

'Our own people?'

'Stalin knew that his best chance of catching me was if I came back to look for you. That's why he had you followed.'

Now it all began to make sense. 'And why every assignment I've been given since you disappeared has kept me in Moscow. He wanted to make sure you could find me.'

'But Stalin grew tired of waiting. That's why he finally allowed you to leave the city, hoping you'd lead him to me.'

'All this time,' Kirov muttered angrily, 'I have been nothing more than bait in a trap.'

'There's a way around every trap,' said Pekkala, 'and my way around this one was Linsky. For several days, I had been shadowing the same people who were following you. They had staked out the office, your apartment, even your friend Elizaveta. But they had no one watching Linsky. I knew he would recognise who placed the order, even if I didn't leave a name. I gambled that, as soon as Linsky realised I was still alive, he'd find a way to get in touch with you, and for you to pay a visit to a tailor would not arouse the suspicions of NKVD. In the meantime, I couldn't stay in Moscow. It was too risky. So I left behind that tobacco pouch, trusting that the tanner's mark inside would lead you here to Rovno.'

'There was one other clue, Inspector.'

'Oh, yes? And what was that?'

'Your pass book and your gun were found on that body at the site of the ambush, but the emerald eye was missing.'

A faint smile creased Pekkala's lips as he turned down the lapel of his coat. By the light of bombs exploding in the distance, the emerald-studded badge winked from the darkness.

'I came here to find you, Inspector, but I should have known you'd track me down instead.'

'As soon as news reached me of a tall, skinny NKVD officer who had just arrived by plane from Moscow, I set out to meet you. Unfortunately, I was too late to prevent what happened. Can you describe the man who opened fire in the bunker?'

'It was dark,' explained Kirov. 'There had just been an air raid and the electricity had gone out. But I know who it must have been, even if I didn't see him pull the trigger. The nurse here told me that they recovered three bodies from the bunker. One was Andrich and the other two were partisans. The only other man in that room was a Red Army officer. With a bandage wrapped around his face, he looked as if he'd just been wounded, but I realise now that it was only a disguise. Andrich said the officer had just arrived from headquarters, so he might have been carrying forged papers as well as a stolen uniform. Inspector, do you have any idea why this happened?'

'There are many blood feuds between the partisans,' answered Pekkala. 'It may be that you and Andrich were simply caught in the crossfire. Or it may be that Andrich himself was the target.'

'But why would anyone want to murder the colonel? After all, he was negotiating a ceasefire.'

'Perhaps,' answered Pekkala, 'because Andrich might have succeeded. He was the only man Moscow trusted who could speak to the partisans. When Andrich's division was annihilated back in '41, he took to the forest and joined the partisans, rather than surrender. Two years later, Moscow made contact with his group by dropping leaflets over the forest requesting someone who could act as a representative for the partisans. Andrich volunteered. He knew that somebody would have to speak for the partisan groups still active in this area. The partisans are sick of fighting, whether it's against the Germans or each other. They just can't find a way to stop. There is too much hatred among them.'

'Why are they killing each other?' asked Kirov.

'Some groups originally sided with the Germans,' explained Pekkala, 'who used them to hunt down other partisans or to commit atrocities against Ukrainian civilians. When the Germans began to retreat, many of those who had taken up arms against the Ukrainians became victims themselves as old scores were settled. This has been a war within a war, Kirov, more bloody than anything I've ever seen before. Andrich knew that the only way the killing would cease was if all sides learned to trust each other. It might have worked, too, if Andrich hadn't been murdered. And the fact that those two partisan leaders also died will only make the situation worse. Those men were all supposed to be under Soviet protection when the attack occurred. If

Andrich was indeed the target, then the killer must have known that murdering him would destroy any hope of peace between the partisans and the Red Army. The faith which Andrich worked to build has now evaporated, just as Stalin knew it might. That's why he recently ordered a brigade of counter-intelligence troops to be transferred to the Rovno garrison.'

The Soviet Counter-Intelligence Agency, known as SMERSH, had been formed by Stalin the previous year as a specialised task force with the NKVD and was responsible for crushing any acts of rebellion in the newly reconquered territories of the Soviet Union. Ruthlessly, they sought out enemy agents who had been recruited by Germany's spy organisation, the Abwehr, under the control of Admiral Canaris, as well as those partisans, civilians and former POWs, who might have collaborated with the Germans during the years of occupation. Within six months of coming into existence, Counter-Intelligence troops had massacred tens of thousands of Russians, for crimes as vague as selling apples to German soldiers, allowing them to drink from a well or for having been captured in one of the vast encircling attacks that wiped out entire Soviet divisions in the first days of Operation Barbarossa.

The brigade that had been sent to Rovno fell under the Counter-Intelligence Agency's Anti-Partisan Directorate. This brigade had originally been led by the notorious Commander Danek, whose excesses stunned even the most hardened NKVD members. But Danek had recently been killed under suspicious circumstances. It was rumoured that he had met his end at the hands of one of his own people, although nothing had been proven. The man who took his place, Commander Yakushkin, had been Danek's right-hand man throughout the war. Since taking control of this SMERSH brigade, Yakushkin's methods had proved to be even more cold-blooded than those of his former master.

'Stalin said nothing to me about SMERSH,' remarked Kirov.

'Why would he?' asked Pekkala. 'Stalin may be hoping for peace, but he is also preparing for war. Commander Yakushkin had orders to wait and see if the partisans could be persuaded to lay down their arms peacefully. But Yakushkin knows only one thing and that is the art of butchery. Now that Andrich is dead, Yakushkin and his troops will soon begin the process of wiping out every partisan band in the whole region. The partisans may disagree with each other about many things, but even the bitterest foes among them will unite against a common enemy, especially if the alternative is annihilation. SMERSH have now become that enemy. The result will be the deaths of countless soldiers and partisans, along with any civilian who gets caught in their path. The only way to prevent it is to prove to Yakushkin that he is being drawn into a plot designed to pit him against the partisans, which would only end in their mutual destruction. Even a killer like Yakushkin doesn't want that, but first I must persuade him. To accomplish this, Major Kirov, I am going to need your help.'

Kirov opened his mouth to reply, but Pekkala cut him off before he could speak.

'Think carefully before you answer. Do not forget that Stalin has a price upon my head. That's why I came here in the middle of the night, so that you can still return to Moscow if you choose, and pretend this meeting never took place.'

'There's no need for that, Inspector. The situation has changed. Whatever charges Stalin laid against you have been dismissed. You are forgiven. Stalin told me so himself. He needs you back, Inspector!'

Pekkala was not convinced. 'One thing I have learned about Stalin is that the man does not forgive. All he does is to postpone his vengeance, but hopefully it will be long enough for me to track down this assassin.'

'And of course I will help you to do it, Inspector, just as soon as I can get out of here!'

'Is now soon enough?' asked Pekkala.

'Now?' echoed Kirov. 'Well, I suppose I . . .'

'Good!' Pekkala walked over to the doorway and peered down the hall. He listened carefully. Satisfied that no one was coming, he beckoned to Kirov. 'Hurry! There is much to be done.'

'But can't this wait until morning? Why do we have to leave now?'

'It's quite simple, Kirov. When the shooting started in the bunker, you were only an innocent bystander, but as soon as this assassin learns that you are intent on hunting him down, he will come back to finish what he started.'

'I'll just put some clothes on!' whispered Kirov, as he lowering his feet uncertainly to the floor. He wasn't even sure if he could walk, but a few minutes later, dressed in his still-muddy uniform and with the canvas bag slung over his shoulder, Kirov slipped past the night duty orderly, who had fallen asleep at his desk. Making their way through the deserted kitchen, which reeked sourly of cabbage and boiled fish, the two men made their way out into an alley behind the hospital and set off towards Rovno, where fires from the air raid still painted the low-hanging clouds.

'You might need this,' said Kirov, handing over a new Soviet identity book. 'NKVD made you a replacement, since your last one was burned to a crisp. Fortunately, your picture was still on file. It's the only one known to exist!'

The pass book was the size of a man's outstretched hand, dull red in colour, with an outer cover made from fabric-covered cardboard in the manner of an old school text book. The Soviet State seal, cradled in its two bound sheaves of wheat, was emblazoned on the front. Inside, in the top left-hand corner, a photograph of Pekkala had been attached with a heat seal, cracking the emulsion of the photograph. Beneath that, in pale bluish-green ink, were the letters NKVD and a second stamp indicating that Pekkala was on Special Assignment for the government. The particulars of his birth, his blood group and his state identification number filled up the right-hand page.

Most government pass books contained only those two pages, but in Pekkala's, a third page had been inserted. Printed on canary yellow paper with a red border around the edge, were the following words:

THE PERSON IDENTIFIED IN THIS DOCUMENT IS ACTING UNDER THE DIRECT ORDERS OF COMRADE STALIN.

DO NOT QUESTION OR DETAIN HIM.

HE IS AUTHORISED TO WEAR CIVILIAN CLOTHES, TO CARRY WEAPONS, TO TRANSPORT PROHIBITED ITEMS, INCLUDING POISON, EXPLOSIVES AND FOREIGN CURRENCY. HE MAY PASS INTO RESTRICTED AREAS AND MAY REQUISITION EQUIPMENT OF ALL TYPES, INCLUDING WEAPONS AND VEHICLES.

IF HE IS KILLED OR INJURED, IMMEDIATELY NOTIFY THE BUREAU OF SPECIAL OPERATIONS.

Although this special insert was known officially as a Classified Operations Permit, it was more commonly referred to as a Shadow Pass. With it, a man could appear and disappear at will within the wilderness of regulations that controlled the state. Fewer than a dozen of these Shadow Passes had ever been issued. Even within the ranks of the NKVD, most people had never seen one.

'I never thought I'd need another one of these,' said Pekkala, as he slipped the pass book into the inside pocket of his coat.

'I have brought you something else as well,' said Kirov, handing the bag to Pekkala.

'I didn't realise that we would be exchanging gifts,' remarked Pekkala, as he undid the wooden toggle on the flap and reached into the bag. Feeling the familiar coolness of the Webley's brass grip against his palm, a look of confusion spread across his face. He withdrew the weapon from the bag and stared at it, as if he did not quite believe what he was seeing. 'Wasn't this destroyed in the fire?'

'Oh, it was. Believe me. I'd have said it was a hopeless task, trying to repair that gun.'

Pekkala glanced across at Kirov. 'Then how . . . ?'

'The miracle of Lazarev.'

'Ah.' Pekkala nodded slowly. 'That explains it.'

'It was he who helped me to understand those strange modifications Linsky made to your coat.'

'I wondered if you would figure that out,' said Pekkala, as he pulled aside the flaps of his coat, revealing a sawn-off double-barrelled shotgun, just as Lazarev had predicted. On the other side, tucked neatly into the loops fashioned by Linsky according to Pekkala's cryptic instructions, were two rows of shotgun shells.

Kirov nodded at the bag in Pekkala's hands. 'There's a box of bullets in there as well.'

'And a nice piece of fish!' exclaimed Pekkala, as he scrounged the dried meat from the bottom of the bag. With a grunt of satisfaction, he tore off a strip with his teeth and chewed away contentedly. 'I must say,' Pekkala said with his mouth full, 'this is quite a treat.'

If a lump of old fish counts as a treat, thought Kirov, I wonder what Pekkala has been living off, out there in the forest. He knew that, in all likelihood, he might never know. The past would be consigned to the catacombs, deep inside Pekkala's mind, surfacing only when he called out in his sleep, chased across the tundra of his dreams like a man pursued by wolves.

From the office of Comrade Joseph Stalin,
Kremlin to Ambassador Joseph Davies, US Embassy,
Mokhovaya Street, November 23rd, 1937

Ambassador –

On behalf of Comrade Stalin, I acknowledge receipt of your letter regarding Mr William H. Vasko. In view of the sensitive situation and as witness to the unbreakable bonds between our two great nations, Comrade Stalin has instructed me to inform you that he has assigned Inspector Pekkala, of the Bureau of Special Operations, his most capable investigator, to personally undertake an examination of this case. Comrade Stalin adds that he looks forward to your favourable news regarding the purchase of American cargo ships.

With great respect,

Poskrebychev

Secretary to Comrade Stalin

*

Memo from Joseph Stalin to Pekkala, November
23rd, 1937

Find out what is going on here and report back to me as soon as possible. William Vasko is being held at Lubyanka, prison number E-151-K.

*

From Inspector Pekkala, Special Operations, to
Henrik Panasuk, Director, Lubyanka, November
23rd, 1937

You are hereby ordered to suspend all interrogation of prisoner
E-151-K, William Vasko. He is to be transferred to a holding cell
pending investigation by Special Operations.

As Pekkala strode along, Kirov struggled to keep pace. 'Where are we going, Inspector?' he asked.

'We must return to the place where you were shot. Valuable evidence may be lost if we do not move quickly, and we must take advantage of the mistakes this assassin has made.'

'What mistakes, Inspector?'

'Leaving you alive, for one! By doing so, he left a witness to his crime.'

'But Inspector, that was no mistake.'

Pekkala stopped in his tracks. 'You mean he knew you were still breathing?'

'Yes, Inspector. He saw me lying there. I was wounded, but still conscious.'

'Why didn't you shoot him?'

'Everything had happened so quickly that my gun was still in its holster. I couldn't get to it. I was completely helpless. I was certain he would finish me off, but he didn't.'

'Then he was sending a message,' remarked Pekkala. 'The question is, to whom?'

'That day in the bunker,' said Kirov, 'when I asked the partisans if they had seen or heard of you, they spoke of rumours that a Finn was living among the Barabanschikovs, but both of them refused to take me to the Red Forest.'

'They call it the country of the beast,' replied Pekkala. 'And they avoid it at all costs.'

'So if nobody goes there,' asked Kirov, 'how on earth did you find them?'

'I didn't,' answered Pekkala. 'They were the ones who found me.'

*

After ambushing the truck that contained the stolen panels of the Amber Room, Pekkala knew that if he carried out his orders and destroyed them, Stalin would allow the blame to fall upon him, rather than accept responsibility himself. By liquidating Pekkala as soon as he returned to Moscow, Stalin would ensure that no word of the mission was ever traced back to the Kremlin.

Reluctant as he was to destroy the panels, Pekkala was certain that if he refused to carry out the order, Stalin would only send another to take his place, and another after that until the grim task had been completed.

Standing amongst the casualties of the battle, who lay strewn across the road amongst spatters of congealed arterial blood, Pekkala realised that he had no choice except to complete the mission, and then to fake his own death, before going into hiding.

After placing his Webley and pass book on the body of a soldier killed in the attack, he removed a flare gun from the driver's compartment of the truck which had been halted in the ambush. Then he unlatched a 20-litre fuel can from its mountings on the running board and doused the vehicle, as well as the body he had chosen. He poured the last of the fuel on to an armoured car which had been escorting the convoy and which lay upside down in a gulley, its muffler pipes skewed out like antlers on the carcass of a deer.

When everything was ready, Pekkala gathered up a rifle from among the weapons which lay scattered on the ground, then fired one flare into the truck and another into the armoured car.

As a wall of boiling orange flame rose up from the explosions, Pekkala sprinted for the shelter of the trees. It would not be long before the vast column of black smoke was spotted by a squadron of German cavalry who had been sent into the forest to pursue him.

Pekkala kept moving until sunset, when he came upon a cluster of houses which had recently been destroyed. The cavalry had been here. Empty cartridges from Mauser rifles littered the ground. Pekkala went to drink from the well in the centre of the compound, but when he threw down the bucket on its rope, he heard it strike against something hard. As he peered into the darkness, he saw a pair of bare feet floating upside down just below the surface of the water.

Travelling mostly at night, he pressed on through the swamps, wading hip-deep in the tar-black water past peeping frogs whose ball-bearing eyes glinted amongst the reeds. When exhaustion overtook Pekkala, he struggled to dry ground, covered himself with leaves and slept while mist drifted around him like the sails of phantom ships.

In his restless dreams, Pekkala saw himself caught and hanged by the men who were hunting for him now. The grotesque image swung like a pendulum from darkness into view and into darkness once again.

When turquoise banners trailed across the evening sky, Pekkala rose up from his shroud of leaves and continued on his way.

For weeks, Pekkala headed south, keeping to the forests, deserted valleys and roads so seldom travelled that they had all but been reclaimed by the wilderness from which they had been cut. All this time, he was pursued by an enemy whose numbers seemed to grow with every day. From hiding places in the bramble undergrowth, Pekkala watched them riding by, the hooves of their horses sometimes no more than an arm's length away.

These cavalry men were used to open country, not the stifling confines of the forest and he realised they, too, were afraid.

Ultimately, it was the sheer size of their force which proved to be Pekkala's greatest ally. He learned to watch for the dust kicked up by their horses and he listened to the plaintive wail of bugles calling from one squadron to another as they meandered lost among the alder thickets. After dark, he glimpsed the orange tongues of their campfires and when it rained and they could make no fires, he smelled the bitter smoke of Esbit cooking tablets used by German soldiers to heat their rations.

Only once did Pekkala come close to being caught, one night when he almost stumbled into one of their encampments. Their shelters had been sturdily built with pine-bough roofs and camouflage rain capes covering the entrances, on either side of a stream. Their horses had been tethered to a nearby tree.

Slipping into the water, Pekkala gritted his teeth against the shock of cold. Moonlight turned the stream into a flood of mercury. He waded hunchbacked through the rustling of current, hoping to pass unnoticed between the dugouts.

Pekkala was just coming level with the German positions when he heard the rustle of a rain cape being thrown back. The horses shifted nervously. Sidestepping into the weeds, Pekkala crouched down among the bristling stalks. Ten paces upstream, a man emerged from one of the dugouts. He walked to the edge of the bank. Moments later, a silver arc reached out into the dark. The soldier leaned back, gazing at the stars, then hawked and spat as he buttoned up his fly. The tiny island of saliva drifted past Pekkala's hiding place as the soldier returned to his dugout.

Pekkala moved on, deeper and deeper into the wilderness, through storms which thrashed his face with sheets of rain while lightning, like a vast electric spider, stalked the earth. When the rain stopped, he could smell wild grapes on the breeze, the scent so sweet and heavy that it hummed like music in his brain.

Now there were no more horse tracks, or tracks of any kind except those only wild animals could have made.

One warm autumn afternoon, Pekkala passed through a forest of tall red maples. Coppery beams of sunlight splashed through the trees, refracting among the branches until the air itself appeared to be on fire. High above the forest canopy, vultures circled lazily on rising waves of heat. In this place, he came across strange, shallow depressions in the earth. He had seen structures just like this, employed by Ostyak hunters in Siberia. These primitive beds, lined with moss and lichen, had been recently constructed by war parties or groups of hunters moving quickly across the landscape, without time to build proper shelters. This was the work of savages.

Pekkala knew that he was in more danger now than he had ever been before. Although he had escaped the horsemen sent to kill him, there was no hiding from these people, for whom this wilderness was home.

Then he knew it was time to stop running.

After removing the bolt from his rifle, Pekkala buried it, along with the ammunition from the black leather pouches at his waist. Then he set the useless gun against a tree and left it there. Next, he took off the ragged German uniform that he had been wearing as part of his cover for the mission and which by now was little more than rags. Knowing that he would likely be butchered at first sight of the field grey wool, he heaped them in a pile, to which he added the scrolled bark of birch trees, twigs snapped from dead pine trees not yet toppled to the ground and fistfuls of dry, crumbling lichen. With one match, the head of which he had preserved in candle wax, he soon had a fire going.

Pekkala sat naked in front of the blaze, warming his filthy skin.

They came for him soon after dark, just as he had known they would.

Pekkala heard people moving towards him through the darkness. Six he guessed. Maybe seven. No more.

He let them come.

The shadows hauled him roughly to his feet.

'Where is the bolt for that gun?' asked a man, pointing at the rifle which Pekkala had dismantled.

'Take me to whoever is in charge and I will tell you.'

'I am in charge!'

'No,' said Pekkala. 'You're just the person he sent.'

The man hit Pekkala in the face.

Pekkala staggered back and then righted himself. He touched his fingers to his lips. The skin was split. He tasted blood.

'I should kill you where you stand,' growled the man.

'Then you would have to explain why you don't have the bolt for this gun, or the ammunition you will need to use it.'

'You have ammunition?'

Pekkala nodded. 'Enough to have killed you if I'd wanted to.'

'I'll do as you ask,' said the man, 'but you may well regret what you wish for.'

The shadows closed in around Pekkala, but they were hesitant, as if his nakedness defied the rusted edges of their handmade weaponry.

'Now!' screamed the man.

Fumbling, they put a sack over Pekkala's head and dragged him away through the trees.

For several hours, they steered him through the darkness.

Branches clawed against his shoulders and the soles of his feet were cut by roots and stones. When at last the partisans lifted the sack from Pekkala's head, they did so gingerly, as if unhooding a falcon.

Pekkala found himself in the middle of a small encampment deep in the forest. His gaze fixed upon two old women, their ankle-length dresses plastered with ashes and mud, huddled around a fire and roasting a dog on a spit. Beside the fire lay a small heap of dented pans and pots, like the emptied shells of river clams. The metal spike squeaked as the dog twisted slowly above the embers, teeth bared in a blackened snarl as if to rage at its misfortune.

Clothing, more filthy and ruined than the rags he had burned in the fire, was dumped at his feet. Shivering at the clammy touch of the cloth, Pekkala struggled into a rough linen shirt with wooden buttons and a pair of wool trousers patched across the seat. The garments reeked of old *machorka*, its smell like damp leaves in the rain.

'Give him some food,' ordered a voice.

Oblivious to the heat, one of the women took hold of the dog's right rear leg. With a twisting cracking sound, she wrenched it off. Then she walked over to Pekkala, holding out the leg by its charred paw, steam rising from the splayed meat and the shiny white ball of the hip bone at the end.

Pekkala ripped away a mouthful of the scalding flesh. He had forgotten how hungry he was.

The woman stared at him while he ate, eyes glinting in her puckered face. Then she turned around and walked back to the fire.

A man appeared from the darkness. For a long time, he studied Pekkala, keeping to the edge of the light, his face masked in the shadows. 'I don't know who you are,' he said, 'but the Germans sent hundreds of men to kill you.'

'That sounds about right,' said Pekkala.

'How in the name of God did you manage to survive?'

'I'd say it was luck,' he replied.

'And I'd say it was more than that,' replied the man, as he stepped from the shadows at last. His face was surprisingly gentle. He had a rounded chin, a thin and patchy beard and thoughtful brown eyes, which he struggled to focus on his prisoner. He is an intellectual, guessed Pekkala. A man who has learned to survive by something other than brute force. Who would have kept himself clean-shaven if only he could have found a razor. A man who has lost his glasses.

As if reading Pekkala's mind, the man produced a pair of gold-rimmed spectacles, one of the temples replaced with a piece of string, looped them over his ears and continued his observation of the stranger. 'I am Barabanschikov,' he said.

'And my name is Pekkala.'

Barabanschikov's eyes widened. 'Then it is no wonder they couldn't find you. You are supposed to be dead!'

Then the darkness just beyond the firelight began to fill with whispers, swirling through the smoky air like the first gust of an approaching storm.

'You make them nervous,' observed Barabanschikov.

'That was never my intention,' replied Pekkala. 'If you let me go, I will leave you my rifle, along with the location of the place where I buried the bolt and ammunition. You won't ever see me again.'

'That would be a pity.' The man held up his hand in a gesture of conciliation, his palm glowing in the firelight. 'I was hoping you might stay here for a while. Any man who can outrun an army might have skills that we'd find useful in the forest.'

A few snowflakes made their way down through the trees.

'Winter is coming,' warned Barabanschikov. 'For a man to take his chances, out there alone in the snow, is the difference between brave and suicidal.'

Pekkala glanced about him at the ragged assembly of men and women. They had the look of death upon them, as if they knew how little time they had left. Although they did not speak, their eyes pleaded with him to stay. 'I will remain with you until the ice has melted in the spring,' he said, 'but then I must be moving on.'

'Until the ice has melted,' agreed Barabanschikov.

He stepped forward and the two men shook hands.

'I might need that rifle, after all,' remarked Pekkala.

Barabanschikov reached into his coat, withdrew a sawn-off shotgun and handed it to Pekkala. 'Take this instead. It strikes me that you are a man who does his killing at close range. A rifle is more suitable to those –' he jerked his chin towards the men who had brought Pekkala into the camp – 'who find safety in numbers and distance.'

Humiliated, the men lowered their heads and scowled at the ground.

That was in the early days, when Barabanschikov's Atrad was

not a fighting force, but just a group of terrified and haphazardly armed people who had fled into the forest and were simply trying to stay alive. It was only later that they managed to acquire enough weapons to defend themselves.

Before the war began, the Red Army had not prepared for any kind of partisan activity. Those who had proposed training soldiers in guerrilla tactics on Russian soil, in the event of an invasion, were condemned as being defeatist. Teaching Russian soldiers to fight behind enemy lines assumed that Russia could be successfully attacked, and Red Army generals had assured Stalin that this was impossible. Any officers expressing doubts were shot, with the result that, when German troops poured across the border in the summer of 1941, the Soviet High Command had no idea how to combat the enemy in territory which had been overrun.

That was left to men like Barabanschikov and the hundreds, later thousands, of Red Army stragglers, known as *okruzhentsy*, who fled into the dense forests of Ukraine. Filling the ranks of these partisan bands were escaped Red Army prisoners of war, and other soldiers who were lucky enough to have avoided the vast encirclements which trapped and then annihilated entire Soviet army groups. Many were civilians, with no military training at all. Barabanschikov himself had been a school teacher in Rovno, before his school was converted into the headquarters of the German Secret Field Police. Together, this assortment of men, women and children began to organise themselves into bands united either by race or politics or simply the need to seek vengeance.

Few of them lasted for long.

In August of 1941, an SS Cavalry Brigade infiltrated the Pripet marshes and killed more than 13,000 partisans at the cost of only two men dead.

In the winter of that year, which was one of the harshest in living memory, most of those who had escaped the massacre either froze or starved to death, because the Red Army had scorched the earth as they retreated, burning homes and crops, killing livestock and poisoning wells. Their aim had been to leave nothing but a waste-land for the enemy, but it also left nothing for those who were just trying to survive. Nor was the landscape the only thing the Red Army devastated in the path of their flight. Mass executions took place in almost every city that would fall into enemy hands. On the orders of Lavrenti Beria, head of NKVD, over 100,000 Soviet civilians were shot as the Red Army decamped from Lvov.

By the time the Germans arrived, only those who had retreated deep into the hinterland even stood a chance. But those who did soon learned how to stay alive, and to fight back.

By the spring of 1942, stories had begun to spread of a solitary beast, which roamed through the Red Forest lacquered with the blood of its prey. Some said that the stories were just that – legends fabricated by Barabanschikov himself to strike terror into those who strayed into his territory. But there were others who, with fear-softened voices, uttered the name of Pekkala, as if to even to pronounce it might call forth the monster which they said lurked inside him. They said that Pekkala was dead, killed somewhere far to the north, and that Barabanschikov himself had conjured his spirit back to life out of the black earth and twisted vines and all of the assembled horrors lurking in that wilderness.

And there were men who heard these stories, having returned home from Siberia after years of captivity in the Gulag known as Borodok, who spoke of a similar creature, known to them as the Man with Bloody Hands, which had ranged across the forest in the valley of Krasnagolyana.

Dear Mrs Vasko,

I am pleased to report that Mr Stalin himself has ordered an enquiry into your husband's arrest. It is a mark of Mr Stalin's affection and respect for the close bond between our nations that he has assigned Inspector Pekkala of the Bureau of Special Operations, the most capable detective in the entire Soviet Union, to personally undertake the investigation.

I can only imagine the distress you and your family must have been feeling recently, and I hope that this news brings some relief. I can say with virtual certainty that if Inspector Pekkala is working on this case, we will soon get to the bottom of it.

I will immediately forward to you whatever news I receive and hope that you will, in the meantime, take comfort in this excellent news.

With kind regards,

Samuel Hayes, US Embassy, Moscow

*

Dear Mr Hayes,

What great news this is! I cannot thank you enough for your help and your encouragement during this dark time. I have heard of the great Inspector Pekkala and share your confidence that my husband will soon be back with his family where he belongs, his innocence proven beyond a shadow of a doubt and this chapter of our life in Russia closed for good.

My faith in you, as well as in Comrade Stalin, has been wholly restored and I am frankly ashamed that my confidence was ever shaken to the point where doubts crept in. I join my children in expressing to you our most profound gratitude.

Yours sincerely,

Betty Jean Vasko

Making their way through the streets of Rovno, Kirov and Pekkala located the bunker without difficulty. The burlap curtain still hung in front of the door, speckled with burn holes made by embers coughed up from the blazing ruins. But when they reached the bottom of the stairs, following the beam of Pekkala's torch, they found both rooms were empty. The desks, ammunition crates and stacks of firearms had all been spirited away.

'It's all gone,' muttered Kirov. 'Everything.'

'Not everything,' replied Pekkala, shining the torch on the gore-splashed walls and ceiling.

As they inspected the room, Kirov described what had taken place.

Their search produced several empty cartridges, trampled into the dirt floor by whoever had cleaned out the room, as well as a torn and bloody bandage, which appeared to be the same one the assassin had been wearing to cover his face.

Pekkala examined the cartridges carefully. 'From a Tokarev.'

'That's right,' said Kirov. 'The missing man was carrying one in a holster.'

Pekkala held out the cartridges on the flat of his palm. 'But these are not ordinary Tokarev casings.'

'How can you tell?'

'They have been reloaded,' explained Pekkala, pointing to the base of the cartridge, which was ridged with several tiny nicks, as if some minute creature had sunk its teeth into the brass. 'You can see extractor marks. There are also crimps along the side of the cartridge, where it has been held in a vice. But the strange thing is that the primer cap doesn't appear to be a replacement. It hasn't been fired before.'

'Then why would someone bother to reload it?'

Pekkala shook his head in bewilderment. 'It's as if the bullet has been rebuilt for some reason, but as to why . . .'

'Maybe this will help to explain,' said Kirov, retrieving the fragment of lead and copper which the doctor had given him as a souvenir. 'The surgeon pulled it out of me.' He dropped the flattened round into Pekkala's open palm.

With his face only a hand's breadth away, Pekkala pushed the bullet around with his finger, like a cat toying with an insect. He raised his head suddenly. 'You are lucky to be alive, Kirov.'

'That's what the doctor said.'

'Trust me, you are even luckier than he knows. This was no squabble among the partisans. Whoever shot you and those other men was a professional assassin.'

'But how can you tell?'

'This is a specialised bullet, Kirov. It's known as a soft point. The rounds in your gun are standard issue 7.62 mm Tokarev ammunition, in which the lead portion of the bullet is completely encased in copper. Check your own weapon and you'll see.'

Obediently, Kirov removed his Tokarev, slid out the magazine and, using his thumb, pushed out a copper-jacketed round. 'You're right, Inspector. These are different.'

Now Pekkala held up the fired bullet, pinched between his thumb and index finger. 'This bullet, however, is only half sleeved in copper. The front part is left open, exposing the lead core. Once it leaves the gun, the soft point collapses into the centre, causing the bullet to expand. It shortens the range, but produces greater impact strength than a regular bullet.'

'The doctor said it was a ricochet,' said Kirov. 'I thought it looked this way because it was damaged by whatever it hit before it struck me. But now that you mention it, I can see the line where the copper jacket ends. So that's why he rebuilt the cartridges, replacing regular bullets with these soft points. But if they are so effective, then why aren't they standard issue for all Tokarev pistols?'

'The exposed lead leaves a residue in the barrel which, if the gun is not constantly cleaned, can lead to jamming and misfires. The fully jacketed bullets are more practical for use in the field. Whoever this man is, he came prepared to do his killing at close range, and he worked hard to make sure that his identity could not be traced. Even the markings on the base of the cartridge have been filed off.'

'Very thorough,' agreed Kirov, 'which makes me wonder what he had to gain by allowing me to live.'

'And you say he wore the uniform of a captain?'

'An army captain. Yes.'

'Was he wearing any service medals?'

'None that I saw.'

'Did he say anything at all?'

'When I mentioned your name, he asked if I was referring to the Emerald Eye.' Kirov shrugged. 'That was the only time he spoke, and his voice was muffled by the bandages.'

Although they continued to hunt for any trace which the killer might have left behind, the bunker yielded no more clues.

'It's time we left this butcher's shop,' said Pekkala.

'We should make our way to the Red Army garrison,' added Kirov.

'The only Red Army garrison in Rovno is Yakushkin's Counter-Intelligence brigade. They are quartered at the old Hotel Novostav, which the Germans used as the headquarters for their Secret Field Police until they pulled out last week.'

'That will be the safest place.'

'Not necessarily,' Pekkala cautioned him. 'Other than the partisans themselves, the only people who knew where and when that meeting was taking place were members of Yakushkin's brigade. Until we have established the identity of this assassin, there is no one we can trust.'

They climbed up to the street.

A bank of clouds was closing in, as if a stone were being dragged across the entrance to a tomb, extinguishing the stars which lay like chips of broken glass upon the rooftops of abandoned houses.

Kirov raised his hands and let them fall again. 'Then where are we to go, Inspector? There's a storm coming in and I'd rather not sleep in the street.'

'Luckily for us,' replied Pekkala, 'I know the finest place in town.'

*

Two hours after Kirov had checked himself out of his room at the hospital, a stranger appeared at the top of the stairs, dressed in the uniform of a Red Army officer.

Except for the splashing of sleet against the windowpanes, it was quiet in the hallway. The patients had been ordered off to sleep or drugged into unconsciousness. The night orderly lay dozing in his chair, cocooned within a pool of light from the candle which burned upon his desk. The young man's name was Anatoli Tutko and he had been released from military service on account of blindness in one eye and a haze of cataract across the other.

Reaching down, the stranger slowly placed his hand upon Tutko's forehead, the way a parent checks for fever in a child. So gently did he raise Tutko's head that the orderly was only half awake when the stranger whispered in his ear, 'Where is the commissar?'

Tutko's eyes fluttered open. 'What?' he asked. 'What's going on?' Then he felt the pinch of a knife held to his throat.

'Where,' the stranger asked again, 'is the commissar you brought in here last night?'

'Major Kirov?' whispered Tutko, so conditioned not to wake the patients after dark that even now he did not raise his voice.

'Kirov. Yes. Which room is he in?'

Tutko tried to swallow. The knife blade dragged against his Adam's apple. 'At the end of the hall on the left,' he whispered.

'Good,' said the man. 'Now you can go back to sleep,' said the man.

Tutko felt the stranger's grip loosen. A sigh of relief escaped his lungs.

In that same moment, the stranger slipped the knife blade into Tutko's neck, then twisted it and, with one stroke, cut through the windpipe, almost severing the young man's head. He laid the body face down on the desk as a wave of blood swept out across the wooden surface.

The man replaced the knife in its metal scabbard, which was clipped to the inside of his knee-length boots. Treading softly, as if the floor beneath his hobnailed soles was no more than a sheet of glass, he moved on down the hallway until he came to Kirov's room.

But it was empty.

A whispered curse cracked like a spark in the still air.

'You're too late,' said a voice.

The stranger whirled about.

Dombrowsky, unable to sleep as usual, had just wheeled himself into the hallway.

'Where is he?' asked the man.

'Gone,' Dombrowsky rolled his chair forward, the heel of his palm dragging on the wheel until it brought him to a stop before the man. 'Earlier tonight, a visitor appeared and spoke to him.'

'What kind of visitor?'

'A man. More like a ghost, the way he moved.'

'Yes,' muttered the stranger. 'That sounds like him.'

'They spoke,' said Dombrowsky, 'and then they left.'

'Do you know where they were going?'

'I don't, but nurse Antonina might. The major talked to her. He must have told her something.'

'Where is this nurse?'

'Gone home, but she lives at the end of this street, in a house with yellow shutters. I can see it from the window in my room. But you shouldn't go there, Captain. Not if you value your life.'

'And why is that?'

'She's a friend of Commander Yakushkin. His "campaign wife". That's what they call them, you know. He showed up here about a week ago, along with a battalion of Internal Security troops. Yakushkin came in here to get medicine for a stomach ulcer and she's the nurse who treated him. Since then, from what I hear,

Yakushkin has practically been living at her house. She's a good cook, you see, and Yakushkin likes his food. But even if you were foolish enough to go there at this time of night, you wouldn't get past Yakushkin's bodyguard, who is with him wherever he goes.'

'Thank you,' said the man. 'You have been very helpful. Now let's get you back where you belong.' Taking hold of the wheel-chair's handles, he turned the chair around and began to wheel him down the hall.

'My room is the other way,' said Dombrowsky.

'Yes,' said the man. 'Yes, it is.'

They moved by the night orderly's desk.

In the rippling light of the candle, Dombrowsky saw what had become of Anatoli Tutko. The thin wheels of his chair rolled through the blood which had cascaded from the desk and pooled across the floor. 'Why are you doing this?' he whispered frantic-ally, his hand skidding uselessly upon the rubber wheels as he tried to slow them down. 'I won't say a word. No one believes me, anyway.'

'I believe you,' said the man and, with one sudden, vicious shove, he pushed Dombrowsky's chair over the edge of the stairs and sent him tumbling to his death.

*

'And what is the finest place in this town?' asked Kirov, as he followed Pekkala through the bombed-out streets. 'From what I've seen, that isn't saying much.'

'I am taking you to a safe house which was used during the oc-cupation,' answered Pekkala.

'But I thought the Barabanschikovs lived in the forest.'

'They did, and they still do, but Barabanschikov made sure that he still had access to Rovno. It was important to keep an eye on those who came and went from the headquarters of the Secret Field Police. Several of the merchants in this town – tailors, cobblers, watchmakers – were actually members of the Barabanschikovs, and the Field Police officers became their best customers. Some of them liked to talk while their watches were being repaired or the hems taken up on their trousers and any piece of information they let slip would find its way to Barabanschikov. Many important meetings were held here between the various partisan leaders, right under the noses of the police, which was the last place they ever thought to look. Barabanschikov himself chose this house, and when we get there, you'll see why.'

By now, the sleet had turned to hail, stinging their faces and rattling like grains of uncooked rice upon the frozen ground.

The cold leached its way through Kirov's tunic and up through the soles of his boots. He hoped the house was comfortable, with soft beds and blankets and a fire. Perhaps there might even be food, he thought. Fresh bread might not be too much to ask.

Pekkala ducked into a narrow alleyway, which was flanked on either side by tumbledown wooden fences, some of them held up only by the weeds and brambles which had grown between the slats.

By following this maze of paths, Pekkala was able to stay clear of the streets, where people gathered around oil-drum fires and dogs fought in the dirty snow for scraps of rotten meat.

Opening an iron gate, Pekkala stepped into an overgrown garden and beckoned for Kirov to follow.

Through tall, dishevelled grass, each strand bowed with its minute coating of ice, the two men crept towards the house.

The back door had been boarded up and the shutters on the windows fastened closed with planks of wood

'How do we get inside?' asked Kirov.

At that moment, Pekkala seemed to vanish, as if the earth had swallowed him completely.

Rushing forward, Kirov found himself at the edge of a deep but narrow trench which had been dug against the outer wall of the house.

'Come on,' Pekkala called out of the darkness of the trench, 'unless you want to stay out there all night.'

Before he jumped, Kirov turned and looked back in the direction from which they had come. He could make out little more than the silhouettes of houses and the tumbledown fences which separated their gardens. Wind slithered through the grass, whose brittle strands crackled like electricity. Just then, Kirov caught sight of a dog, loping along the alleyway. As the animal drew close, Kirov realised that it was, in fact, a wolf. It stopped at the end of the garden, then turned and looked at him, its mean, thin face spliced by the iron railings of the gate. They watched each other, man and beast, breath rising like smoke from their nostrils. There was something about its stare which snatched the last faint trace of warmth from Kirov's blood and he felt colder than he'd ever been before, as if a layer of frost had formed around his heart. The wolf moved on and Kirov scrambled to catch up with Pekkala.

Report on Arrest of William Vasko
Pekkala, Special Operations
Dated December 10th, 1937
REPORT CENSORED

In accordance with the instructions of Comrade Stalin, I have
conducted an interview with William Vasko at Lubyanka, where he
has been held in solitary confinement since his arrest and transfer
from the Ford Motor Car plant in Nizhni-Novgorod. The
circumstances of his arrest involved allegations that he was
attempting to flee the country illegally, along with his wife and
children. Although I have found no documentary evidence of this,
Vasko readily admitted that he had planned to return his wife and
children to the United States, which is their country of citizenship.
However, Vasko denied that he himself intended to flee and further
questioned whether such a departure would have been illegal,
even if he had chosen to do so. Vasko initially refused to divulge the
reasons why he was choosing to send his family away. However,
when I travelled to Nizhni-Novgorod and began interviewing some
of his fellow American workers, it soon became apparent that they
believed Vasko to be behind the arrests of numerous other workers
at the plant. In fact, by the time I arrived, over half the workforce
had been taken into custody on charges ranging from sabotage to
subversion to threats made against the leadership of the Soviet
Union. His former comrades at the factory firmly believed that
Vasko's reports to Soviet security services had caused a large
number of them to be arrested. These workers readily admitted
that they had threatened Vasko with bodily harm if he did not
immediately resign from the plant's workforce.

On my return to Moscow, I interviewed Vasko for a second time. When confronted with these accusations, Vasko admitted that he had denounced a number of them to the authorities. However, he went on to explain that [the following section of the report is blacked out] xxxxxxxxxxxxxxxxxxxxxxxxxxxxxxxxxxxxxxxxxxxxxxxxxx. Vasko's journey to the Soviet Union was xxxxxxxxxxxxxxxxxxxxxxxxxxxxx. Vasko asserted that his wife and children were not aware of xxxxxxxxxxxxxxxxxxxxxx. When he realised that his workmates had stumbled upon the truth, or part of it, at least, fearing that his life was in danger, he did indeed attempt to resign from the plant. His request was denied, however, and he was forced to continue his work. Over the next few weeks, Vasko's situation at the plant continued to deteriorate. He received threats on an almost daily basis and he was otherwise shunned by his colleagues. He began to believe that his family were also in danger. After one final appeal to quit the plant was denied, he took the first steps towards repatriating his wife and children to America. This, he believes, is what led to his arrest. He expressed concern that his wife might be forced to leave the housing provided for her at the plant and that she had no means of income. He had not heard from her, nor had he been allowed to make contact since his arrest, and he no longer knew whether she was still receiving his salary. He implored me to look into the matter personally and also to make his situation known to xxxxxxxxxxxx of xxxxxxxxxxxxxxx, who, he believed, could secure his immediate release.

My subsequent enquiry to the Ford Motor Car plant revealed that Mrs Vasko left her housing in Novgorod and that she is currently staying at a homeless shelter in Moscow.

My enquiry to xxxxxxxxxxxxxxxx of xxxxxxxxxxxxxx has not yet received a response.

My recommendation is for Vasko's immediate release and for the swift location of his family, with whom he should be united. Given the innocence of his wife and children, I recommend that their return to the United States be granted if that is the family's wish. As for Vasko I recommend that

XXXXXXXXXXXXXXXXXXXXXXXXXXXXXX.

Signed – Pekkala, Special Operations.

Handwritten note in margin: Complete report suppressed. Authorise immediate transfer of document to Archive 17. Signed - JS.

Having reached the safe house, Pekkala stopped next to an opening in the wall which had been camouflaged with the tattered
remains of a German army blanket. He pushed aside the frozen
wool and ducked inside, followed by Kirov a moment later.

They found themselves in what had once been a root cellar.
The air was still and damp.

After climbing a ladder, they emerged on to the ground floor
of the house. It was dark until Pekkala lit a match and then a
soft glow spread around the room, revealing a table in the centre,
surrounded by an assortment of dilapidated chairs. Against the
walls, Kirov saw a crumpled heap of discarded clothes which the
former occupants had used for bedding. Some were made from
the dull field grey of German army cloth, others from the strange
pinkish brown of Russian uniforms and one, which had either
been riddled with bullets or else chewed by rats, Kirov couldn't
tell which, bore buttons crested with the double-headed eagle of
the Tsar. He could almost hear the lice scuttling along the seams.
The place smelled of sweat and tobacco, and the exhausted air felt
heavy in their lungs.

Pekkala found an oil lamp resting on the windowsill. He lit the
wick and carried the lamp over to the table.

Kirov looked around the dingy room. 'You call this the best
place in town?'

'You're welcome to find someplace else.'

There was no arguing with that. 'And you think we will be safe here?' he asked.

'We used this as a hideout during the entire occupation. Every building on this street was searched at one time or another, but this one they left alone.'

'But why?'

'The owners died of typhus.'

'Typhus!' exclaimed Kirov. 'We should get out of here immediately!'

'Relax,' Pekkala told him. 'This house has saved more lives than it has taken.' He picked a coat off the pile and spread it on the floor. Then lay down on it and pulled another coat on top of him. 'Now get some sleep. Tomorrow you will meet the Barabanschikovs.'

Reluctantly, Kirov sat down with his back against the wall. In spite of the cold, he set his heel against the pile of dirty clothes and pushed them all away.

For a while, he sat there, hugging his ribs and listening to the storm howl down the chimney. He felt pain where the bullet had gone in, as if some small, persistent creature was gnawing its way through the scar. Leaning over to the lamp, he doused the light. Blackness crowded in around him. 'I suppose there is nothing to eat?' he asked.

He received no reply. Pekkala was already asleep.

*

Just before dawn, Pekkala awoke with a start. He sat up and looked around. The first grey slivers of dawn showed through cracks in the boarded-up windows.

On the bare floorboards beside him, Kirov lay curled in a ball and shivering in his dreams.

Rising to his feet, Pekkala picked up one of the coats and draped it over Kirov. Then he climbed down into the root cellar, pushed aside the blanket and stepped out into the ditch which had been dug along the edge of the house.

His first breath was like pepper in his lungs.

It had snowed in the night. Even the ruins looked clean.

Through eyes bloodshot with fatigue, Pekkala stared over the edge of the ditch, past the jungle of white-dusted grass to the alley where he had almost lost his life the year before.

*

Pekkala had lived among the partisans for several months before he made his first visit to Rovno, in order to rendezvous with Barabanschikov at the safe house. He had nearly made it there when he accidentally turned down the wrong side street and found himself in an alleyway which was blocked off by a pile of broken furniture. As Pekkala paused, trying to get his bearings, a man appeared from behind the makeshift barricade. From his black uniform with its silver buttons and a soft cap with shiny patent leather brim, Pekkala knew he was a member of the Ukrainian Nationalist Police. This paramilitary group consisted of Russian collaborators, tasked by their German masters with rounding up anyone who posed a threat to the German occupation. They had a reputation for summary brutality, particularly against those suspected of being partisans.

'Stop!' shouted the man. He wore round glasses, balanced on a long, thin nose. Beard stubble made a blue haze under his pasty skin. To Pekkala, he looked a like a big, pink rat. 'Papers!' he barked as he advanced upon Pekkala, one empty hand held out and the other one gripping a revolver.

Pekkala thought about running, but he knew he'd never make it to the end of the alleyway before the rat man gunned him down. On the orders of Barabanschikov, Pekkala did not carry a gun of his own. There was no possibility of shooting his way out of police custody and the mere possession of a gun was grounds for immediate execution. The only thing Pekkala carried was an old switchblade, its dull iron blade stamped with the maker's mark of Geck in Brussels, and the stag-horn grips worn almost smooth from years of use. It had been old even when Pekkala spotted it one Sunday afternoon laid out on a table in the market across from his office in Moscow, along with a leather cigar case, a wallet made from crocodile and a pair of gold-rimmed glasses; the mute companions of some traveller's life now finished with his journey. Tucked deep in his pocket, with the policeman's revolver only inches from Pekkala's forehead, the knife was useless to him now.

With no choice but to play the role which Barabanschikov had taught him as a cover, Pekkala pulled a crumpled identity book from the top right pocket of his shirt. The paper was soggy from the rain. The book was real, but it had been altered to fit Pekkala's physical description. Knowing that the alterations wouldn't pass close scrutiny, Pekkala struggled to keep his hands from shaking as he held out the book to the policeman.

The man plucked the book from Pekkala's hand and opened it. 'Name?'

'Franko,' replied Pekkala. 'Oleksandr Franko.'

'It says here you are a leather tanner.'

'That's right.'

'Show me your hands.'

Pekkala held them out, palms up.

The rat man tilted his head back, peering out from under the brim of his hat. 'My uncle was a tanner and his hands were always stained.'

'The tannery is closed.'

'And you're from Rovno?'

'No. From Zoborol.'

'Well, as it happens, so am I.' The policeman brought his gun closer, until the barrel nudged against Pekkala's cheek. 'I know everyone in that village, but I don't know you, Oleksandr Franko.'

Slowly, Pekkala raised his hands, suddenly conscious of his appearance – the hand-carved toggles on his coat and the dirty, twisted strings which fastened them, the wooden-soled shoes fixed to their leather tops with carpeting nails, the knees of his trousers patched with sacking cloth. Dishevelled though Pekkala was, he looked no different from most people in this town, for whom the war had cut off all vestiges of the life which they had once taken for granted.

The man nodded towards the barricade. 'Go on.'

Pekkala squeezed past a broken chest of drawers and, a few minutes later, found himself in the front hall of a small municipal station which had been taken over by the Nationalist Police.

Sitting at a desk was an officer, his grizzled, unwashed hair piled up like ashes on his head. He demanded Pekkala's identity book, glanced at it and slapped it shut. 'Put him in the cell.'

'But there's no room,' the rat man protested.

'Then cut parts off until he fits,' growled the officer, 'and when you get back, I want you to take this identity book over to the German garrison and have Krug check it over.'

'It isn't right, I can tell you,' said the rat man. 'I mean, it's real but . . .'

A withering stare from the officer choked the words off in his throat. 'Just do what I tell you to do.'

The rat man grabbed Pekkala by the collar of his coat and, without searching him, led his prisoner down a corridor to a cell already so crowded that those in the middle had to stand. Fear clawed up his spine as he recalled the convict train on which he had travelled to the gulag of Borodok. He thought of the convicts who had died on their feet, their eyes cataracted with frost. The walls seemed to ripple with the faces of the dead and he heard again the sound of wheels clacking over the tracks.

A woman crouched against the concrete wall made a space for Pekkala. In the glare of a naked bulb hanging from the ceiling, Pekkala saw lice, tiny and translucent, scuttling across her scalp.

An hour later, footsteps sounded in the corridor and the rat-faced man appeared, swinging a wooden truncheon by its leather cord. He swung open the barred metal door.

Instinctively, the people in the room lowered their eyes. But one man, standing near the front, was not fast enough.

The rat man raised his truncheon and brought it down on the top of the prisoner's skull.

The prisoner's legs buckled as if a trap door had opened beneath his feet. He fell face down and blood began to spread across the floor, reflecting the light of a single bulb, which blazed in its wire cage on the ceiling. The occupants of the cell shuffled back from the creeping red tide, the heels of their shoes clicking dryly over the concrete.

The policeman stepped over to Pekkala. Ignoring the puddle of blood, he tracked red footprints across the floor. 'Krug doesn't like the look of your pass book. He said it had been altered, which I could have explained to him myself. Instead of that, I had to go all the way down the street to the German garrison and show them my own damned identity book so that I could get inside the building and be told what I already know!'

'Rusak!' shouted a voice from down at the end of the corridor. 'Bring him here!'

Now Rusak took Pekkala by the arm and hauled him out into the corridor. He marched Pekkala past an empty cell where two policemen, stripped down to their shirts and with black braces stretched over their shoulders, sat cleaning their revolvers using handkerchiefs dipped in an ashtray filled with gun oil.

In the front hallway, the ash-haired officer was standing in the doorway, hands in his pockets, looking up at the rain which had just begun to fall. 'Who are you?' he asked Pekkala, without bothering to turn around.

Pekkala did not reply.

'That's what I thought,' whispered the officer, as he stepped aside to let them pass.

Rusak pushed Pekkala ahead of him.

Pekkala gasped in a lungful of clean air as he staggered into the street. 'Where are you taking me?' he asked.

'To a bigger cell,' Rusak answered. 'That other place is too crowded. That's all. It's nothing to worry about.'

It was those last few words which made Pekkala realise that everything he had just heard was lies. Now his heart pulsed in his throat. His breathing came shallow and fast.

Rusak walked him across the street and down an alley between two rows of buildings. The alleyway was bordered by high brick walls on either side. Coal dust lined the path, glittering in the damp air.

Rusak walked behind him, splashing through puddles in the alley.

Shivering as if he were cold, Pekkala put his hands in his trouser pockets. In his right hand, he took hold of the switchblade.

'Chilly today, isn't it?' asked Rusak. 'Well, don't you worry, pal. You'll soon be warm again.'

As Rusak spoke, Pekkala heard the unmistakable rustle of a pistol being drawn from its holster. In that moment, Pekkala stopped thinking. He pulled the knife out of his pocket, pressed the round metal button on the side, releasing the blade, and swung his arm around.

Rusak had no time to react. The knife struck him on the side of the head and the blade vanished into his temple. The rat man's face showed only mild astonishment. His right eye filled with blood. He dropped the revolver, took one step forward and then fell into Pekkala's arms.

Pekkala laid him down. Then he set his boot on Rusak's neck, pulled out the blade and wiped it on the dead man's coat. For a moment, Pekkala waited, watching and listening. Satisfied that they were alone, he folded the blade shut and returned the knife to his pocket.

He took hold of Rusak by the collar of his tunic and dragged him down the alley. Rusak's boots laid a trail though the glittering black coal dust. Ten paces further on, Pekkala came to a place where the brick wall was recessed, forming a space like a room with three sides and no roof. Judging from stains on the brick, the space had once been used to store garbage ready for collection. Now it was filled with half a dozen bodies, some soldiers and some civilians. They had all been shot in the back of the head and piled on top of each other. Their faces were shattered, the corpses wet from the rain.

Pekkala dumped Rusak on the pile. Then he took a few steps backwards, as if expecting Rusak to rise from the dead, before he turned and ran.

At the safe house, he met up with Barabanschikov. It turned out that the partisan leader had also been stopped at a police roadblock on the other side of town, but had managed to talk his way out of it.

'You ran into the wrong people, that's all,' said Barabanschikov. 'It was just bad luck that you were arrested.'

'Maybe so,' replied Pekkala, 'but I'll need more than luck to survive.' From that day on, he carried the shotgun in his coat.

Memo: Joseph Stalin to Henrik Panasuk, Lubyanka.
December 11th, 1937

Liquidation of prisoner E-15-K to be carried out immediately.

*

Memo: Henrik Panasuk, Director, Lubyanka, to
Comrade Stalin. December 11th, 1937

In accordance with your instructions, prisoner E-15-K has been
liquidated.

'The Rasputitsa will come early this year,' said a voice behind Pekkala.

Pekkala was startled at first, but then he sighed and smiled. 'There is only one person who can sneak up on me like that.'

'Luckily for you, that person is your friend.'

'Good morning, Barabanschikov.'

Almost hidden among the skeleton-fingered branches of a Russian olive tree, Barabanschikov sat on an upturned bucket. He wore fingerless wool gloves and a cap pulled down over his ears. Lying across his lap was a Russian PPSh sub-machine gun fitted with a 50-round drum magazine. Such weapons, once almost impossible to obtain, were now commonplace among the partisans. Barabanschikov had been sitting there long enough that a fine layer of snow had settled upon his shoulders. The former school teacher had long ago given up shaving and a dark beard covered his face. His eyes, once patient and curious as he gazed across the rows of desks each morning while his students pulled notebooks from their satchels, had taken on a burning intensity brought on by malnourishment, insomnia and prolonged fear. Those children he once taught might not have recognised him at all, but for the gold-rimmed glasses he still wore.

Cupping his gloved hands to his mouth, Barabanschikov puffed warm breath on to his frozen fingers. 'Have you found out yet who did the killings in the bunker?'

'Not yet,' replied Pekkala, 'but I am working on it.'

Barabanschikov reached down and gently patted Pekkala's face, the rough wool of his glove snagging against Pekkala's three-day growth of stubble. 'You had better work fast, my old friend. There has already been a gunfight between a Red Army patrol and a group of partisans searching for whoever killed their leader. Two partisans are dead. Three soldiers are wounded. We are fast approaching the moment when nothing can prevent an all-out war between us and the Red Army. In the war we have fought until now, all we had to do was survive until the Red Army pushed back the invaders. But the storm that is coming is not like any other they have seen. You know Stalin. You know what he is capable of doing. And unless you do something to stop this, he will annihilate us all.'

'That's why I have brought in some help,' said Pekkala. 'Come inside, Barabanschikov. It's time you met the commissar.'

*

Kirov looked around him blearily. It was dark in the room. Only a few chinks of daylight worked their way in through gaps in the boards which had been nailed over the shutters. For a moment, he stared in confusion at the greatcoat which had been draped across him. Then he pushed it away, stood up and began slapping at his clothes, hoping to dislodge the lice which he felt sure had taken up residence in his uniform.

Having finished this frantic ritual, Kirov fished out a box of matches and lit the lantern. It was only then that he realised there were two men sitting at the table, both watching him intently.

One of them was Pekkala.

The other, Kirov had never seen before. With rags for clothes offset by an oddly dignified pair of gold-rimmed spectacles, he looked like a shipwrecked millionaire.

'This is Major Kirov,' said Pekkala.

'And I,' said the stranger, 'am Andrei Barabanschikov. So, Commissar, you are here to help us catch a killer.'

'That's right,' replied Kirov.

'It seems to me that you need look no further than the ranks of your own people.'

Kirov bristled at the remark. 'Why would you say that?'

'From what I hear, the man who killed Andrich and those partisans was wearing a Red Army uniform.'

'It was probably stolen.'

'Perhaps,' admitted Barabanschikov, 'but then there is the matter of your survival,' said Barabanschikov. 'Doesn't it strike you as unusual? The only person I can think of who might hesitate to kill a Russian commissar,' he paused, 'is another commissar.'

'I did not come here to solve your murders, Comrade Barabanschikov, or to become one of your victims, either,' Kirov pointed at the tear in his tunic where the bullet had gone in. 'As far as I'm concerned, if Stalin has given the order to lay down your weapons, then that is exactly what you should do. This is simply a choice between life and death.'

'Enough!' shouted Pekkala. 'If even you two can't see eye to eye, then what hope is there of peace?'

'But we do agree,' insisted Barabanschikov. 'About one thing, at least. The major is correct that this is indeed a choice between life and death. But what he does not seem to understand is that the choice is ours to make, not theirs.'

Their conversation was interrupted by the sound of a heavy

diesel engine and a squeak of brakes in the alleyway behind the house.

'They're here,' announced Barabanschikov.

'Major Kirov,' said Pekkala as he rose from his chair, 'I would like for you to meet some friends of mine.'

Parked in the alley was a German military Hanomag truck, with SS number plates and a black and white Maltese cross painted upon each door of the driver's cab. Its windscreen had been cracked into a spray of the silver lightning bolts, still tinted with the blood of the driver whose head had collided with the glass when an ambush ran it off the road the week before.

Crowded into the back were the truck's new owners: an assortment of heavily armed men, most of them bearded, their hair long and unkempt. They were armed with weapons of all types – German Mausers, Russian Mosin-Nagants and Austrian Steyr-Mannlichers. Others had no guns at all, but carried butcher's knives, sledgehammers and hatchets. Their clothing was equally varied. One had crammed himself into the silver-buttoned tunic of a Ukrainian Nationalist policeman, the black cloth gashed across the back where its former occupant had been hewn down with the same axe carried by the man who wore it now. Others were swathed in the dappled camouflage smocks of Waffen SS soldiers, or the deer-brown wool of greatcoats scavenged from the graves of Polish soldiers. They wore bullet-punctured helmets, cloth caps snatched from the heads of men as they begged for their lives or braided garlands of twigs which they carried on their heads like crowns of thorns. One was barely in his teens, a *gymnastiorka* tunic hanging scarecrow-like from narrow shoulders and a sub-machine gun monstrous-looking in his arms. Beside him stood an older man, his face pockmarked and ears so whittled down by frostbite they looked as if they had been chewed by a dog. This man carried no weapon at all, but only a stick carved from white birch. There was no glint of kindness in their eyes, nor of any emotion that could have brought about a moment's hesitation in the furtherance of butchery.

Like miners emerging from a tunnel deep beneath the ground, Pekkala and Barabanschikov blinked in the glare of sunlight.

Catching sight of Pekkala and their leader, the partisans raised their grizzled paws at them and bared their teeth in smiles, but they regarded Kirov, and the red stars on his sleeves, with undisguised contempt.

The bullet-riddled door opened on the driver's side. A man in a black leather coat got out and approached Barabanschikov. The driver was short and barrel-chested, his broad face scalpeled with pale creases in the smoke-stained skin.

After exchanging a few words, Barabanschikov turned to Kirov and Pekkala. His face was grim. 'There's been another killing,' he said.

'Who is it?' asked Pekkala.

'Yakushkin, Commander of the Red Army garrison. My men have just found his body. You'd better come quickly.'

Without another word, they all climbed into the back of the truck. Crammed among the partisans, they sped away down the street, careening around piles of bricks, the husks of burnt-out vehicles and the carcasses of horses, still fastened to the traces of wagons they'd been pulling when they died.

Memo: Office of Comrade Stalin, Kremlin, to
Third Western Division of Foreign Affairs.
December 12th, 1937

You are instructed to prepare documents of voluntary transfer of
citizenship from the United States of America to citizenship of the
Soviet Union for William H. Vasko. You are authorised to backdate
documents to September 1st, 1936. Work is to be carried out
immediately by order of Comrade Stalin.

Signed – Poskrebychev, secretary to Comrade Stalin

*

From the office of Joseph Stalin, Kremlin
To Ambassador Joseph Davies, US Embassy,
Mokhovaya Street. December 16th, 1937

Ambassador –

On behalf of Comrade Stalin, I am replying to your request for
information on the arrest of American citizen William H. Vasko. We
regret to inform you that no such American citizen has been
arrested. However, the Central Records Office of the 3rd Western
Division of Soviet Foreign Affairs indicates that, on September 1st,
1936, a William Vasko voluntarily transferred citizenship from the
United States to the Soviet Union. This transfer is a matter of public
record and can be accessed through the Central Records Office at
any time. As such, if the arrest of Comrade Vasko had, in fact, taken
place, it would be a matter for Soviet Internal Security and not for
the United States Embassy. However, I have been authorised to
inform you that Comrade Vasko is not currently under arrest or in

detention at any Soviet facility.

Comrade Stalin expresses his hope that your inquiry into this matter has been resolved and hopes that, in future, your embassy staff will conduct a more thorough investigation into such matters before referring them to the Kremlin.

Signed – Poskrebychev, secretary to Comrade Stalin

The night before, while Kirov and Pekkala made their way towards the safe house, Fyodor Yakushkin, commander of the SMERSH Brigade, had been waiting for his dinner in a dilapidated apartment near the hospital.

A smell of cooking filled the room.

Perched on a chair which was too small for him, Yakushkin rested his fists upon a table set for two. He was a heavy-set man with a bald head and fleshy lips set into a thick, square jaw. Since his belly was too large for him to wear his gun belt comfortably while sitting, he had taken it off and hung it over the back of his chair. Out of habit, he removed his pistol from its holster and laid it within reach on the table. Then he sighed impatiently as he looked around at the blue sponge-printed flower pattern dabbed on to the butter-yellow wall, the delicate curtains and the framed pictures of a squinting, shifty-looking old man and an equally pugnacious old woman in a head scarf. Their stares made him uneasy. Adding to his discomfort was the fact everything around him looked breakable, as if all he had to do was touch the pictures or the curtains and they would come crashing to the floor. This impression of flimsiness included the chair on which he sat. He was afraid even to lean back, in case it collapsed underneath him.

Yakushkin's mood had been soured even before he arrived by news of Colonel Andrich's murder. Yakushkin had met with Colonel Andrich on several occasions. He had warned the colonel that a truce with the partisans could never be achieved, but Andrich was determined to succeed. Yakushkin could not help admiring the colonel's tenacity, even though he was, himself, convinced of the inevitable failure of the mission. As a gesture of goodwill, Yakushkin had even loaned the colonel his own chauffeur, Sergeant Zolkin, along with his beloved American Lend-Lease Willys Jeep.

Now Zolkin was missing, probably lying dead somewhere among the ruins. His jeep had been found, still parked outside the bunker, although so riddled with shrapnel that the motor pool mechanics weren't sure it would ever run again.

The driver and the Willys Jeep could be replaced, but Andrich could not. As far as Yakushkin was concerned, the blame for these killings lay entirely with the partisans. They had been given a chance for peace, and they had squandered it. From now on, he thought to himself, the partisans will have to deal with us, and we do not negotiate.

Yakushkin was proud of his brigade's bloody reputation, so much so that when its former commander, Grigori Danek, began to show a change of heart, Yakushkin was forced to take action.

In the old days, Danek had ordered his troops to open fire at the first sign of trouble, and the resulting massacres combined into a tally of butchery unmatched by any other branch of NKVD.

'The only thing that impresses me,' Danek had once growled to Yakushkin in one of his vodka-fuelled tirades, 'is the efficiency with which we dispatch our enemies into the afterlife.'

But with the end of the war now in sight, Danek had begun to see things differently. He believed that the role of SMERSH had to change, and change quickly, before they found themselves scapegoats in the post-war world for all manner of atrocities, even those which they had not actually committed. In a conflict already brimming with horrors, what made SMERSH different was that the blood on their hands came mostly from their own countrymen.

This detail had never bothered Yakushkin, who saw his brigade as an instrument of vengeance for all who opposed Stalin's will, no matter where they came from.

Danek spoke incessantly of a day of reckoning which he felt must surely come for those who had dispensed this vengeance.

Finally, Yakushkin had heard enough. When he encountered Danek, alone and too drunk to stand in an alley in the city of Minsk, he strangled the commander with his bare hands, employing an efficiency of technique which even Danek might have found impressive if he had not been on the receiving end of it.

In the days that followed, Yakushkin himself was put in charge of leading a thorough investigation into Danek's murder, which naturally produced no results. The lack of reaction from Moscow was Yakushkin's first real sign that Danek's change of heart had come under unfavourable scrutiny from someone other than himself.

As the natural choice to succeed Danek, Yakushkin proved so successful that he had recently been informed of his transfer to headquarters in Moscow, to take effect as soon as this current task had been completed. For Yakushkin, this was a chance of a lifetime. Nothing could be allowed to prevent it, even if that meant the death of every partisan in Ukraine.

Such lofty goals do not come cheap to those who set them, and Yakushkin's nerves were strained almost to breaking point.

The one thing which gave him comfort was the smell of food coming from the kitchen around the corner. Nurse Antonina was making *tsapkhulis tsveni*, a stew made with *myslyvska* sausages, apples, canned beans, eggplant and dried chilli peppers – all of which he had brought her as a gift the day before, with the understanding that they would be used to prepare a meal of which she would be allowed to eat a small portion. Yakushkin's mouth flooded with saliva as he smelled the cardamom and pepper with which the sausages had been seasoned.

Since Yakushkin had begun paying visits to Antonina, the nurse had prepared several memorable meals: partridge in sour cream, venison with cranberries and *khachapuri* cheese bread. Of course, he had been obliged to supply the ingredients for these as well. A nurse at a field hospital could hardly be expected to find enough butter, eggs and meat to feed herself, let alone a man with such an appetite. But for someone of Yakushkin's rank, these things were not hard to come by. It was finding someone to prepare them which provided the greater challenge.

Yakushkin listened to Antonina's footsteps as she moved around the kitchen, the soft knocking of a wooden spoon against the sides of the stew pot as she stirred the meal and her humming of a tune he had not heard since childhood and whose name he'd never known.

It was past Yakushkin's normal dinner time, but it had taken much longer than expected to oversee the clearing-out of munitions from the bunker where Andrich had been killed. By the time he arrived on Antonina's doorstep, she had already gone to bed, but since Yakushkin had no intention of leaving without supper, he cajoled her into preparing a meal.

Yakushkin would have settled for a bowl of *kasha*, but instead Antonina had insisted on making a stew, which was taking forever to prepare, using all the ingredients he had given her.

Now Yakushkin wished he hadn't come at all. In the hour he'd spent waiting, his stomach had become an empty chasm. When he got hungry like this, he became irrationally bad-tempered. His bodyguard, Molodin, knew to carry food on him at all times for just such occasions. The careers and even lives of men had been saved by Molodin's quick thinking, as he pressed into the commander's hand an apple, or a scrap of sweet *churchkhela*, made from rendered grape juice, flour and chopped walnuts, or a two-day-old *vareniki* dumpling stuffed with pickled cabbage, carefully saved in Molodin's handkerchief.

Too irritated to sit still, Yakushkin got out of his chair and strode to the top of the stairs. The staircase descended to a narrow hallway, at the end of which was a door leading out to the street. Antonina's apartment had no rooms on the ground floor, which was taken up by another apartment. 'Molodin!' he boomed.

The front door opened and, a moment later, Molodin himself appeared at the bottom of the stairs. He was a slight but agile man, with a pale, angular face, neatly shaved head and eyes the milky green colour of opals. Draped across his shoulders was a rain cape, in whose folds the sleet clustered like frog spawn. Slung across his chest beneath the cape, Molodin carried a PPSh sub-machine gun. 'Is everything all right, Commander?' he asked, and, as he spoke, his hand appeared from beneath his dripping rain cape. Pinched between his fingers was a piece of cheese, which he had been saving for his own breakfast. 'Something to eat, perhaps?'

'Keep it!' Yakushkin smiled down at him. 'I can't steal another man's meal!' The truth was, Yakushkin would gladly have eaten Molodin's last crumb of food, but he did not like the look of that cheese, cracked and yellowed like an old toenail, or the unwashed hand which held it out to him.

Molodin nodded, relieved not to be parting with his rations.

'Don't worry,' said Yakushkin. 'There'll be plenty to eat when we get to Moscow.'

Molodin smiled gratefully although, in truth, he detested city life, and would never have set foot in Moscow unless ordered to do so.

'Go on!' Yakushkin waved him away cheerfully. 'Back to work!'

'Yes, Commander,' replied Molodin, as he returned to his post outside the front door.

With his mood somewhat restored, Yakushkin returned to the little dining room. Easing himself back into the flimsy chair, Yakushkin picked up the knife, and examined the cutting edge, turning it in the light of an oil lamp in the middle of the table. Then he wiped the blade on his trouser leg and returned it to its place. After that, he repositioned his gun beside the knife, as if it were a piece of cutlery essential to the meal.

'It's almost ready,' Antonina called to him from the next room. 'It took a little longer than I expected.'

'I will miss your cooking when I'm transferred to Moscow.'

'You don't have to miss it. You don't have to miss anything at all.'

Yakushkin gave a nervous laugh. Antonina had made no secret of the fact that she wanted to accompany him to Moscow. He was her ticket out of this godforsaken place, for which her skill in the kitchen was not the only talent she seemed willing to provide. And now she spoke of Moscow as if he had already agreed to take her there, which he most definitely had not.

It was common practice for women to accompany high-ranking officers in the field, although spouses left at home were kept as ignorant as possible of the existence of these campaign wives. But Yakushkin didn't have a wife at home and he didn't want one out here either, especially one sporting a black eye; the result, she had told him, of trying to restrain a delirious patient at the hospital. What Yakushkin wanted was a decent cook, who would place his meal upon the table and then leave him to eat it in peace, rather than engage in banter whose horizontal outcome was never in serious doubt.

Antonina's smiling face appeared around the corner, her forehead glistening with sweat from working over the stove. 'Won't it be nice to have a family to come home to in Moscow?'

'A family?' he spluttered. 'Well, I don't know . . .'

'You seem so uneasy, my love,' she said. 'Do you not enjoy our time together?'

'Of course I do!' Yakushkin gazed disconsolately at the empty plate. For pity's sake, he thought, just bring out the food and stop talking.

'When will we be leaving for Moscow?'

We, he thought. There is no we. The moment was fast approaching when Yakushkin would need to explain this to Antonina, but he had delayed this conversation for as long as possible, because he was in little doubt as to how disappointed she would be. And disappointed women were rarely good cooks. 'It all depends upon those blasted partisans,' he told her. 'If things go the way they seem to be headed, my soldiers will soon be killing them in the hundreds.'

'How could that be, after everything we have endured together in this war against the Fascists?'

'I have asked myself that same question many times, darling. But as with everything in war, the answer is seldom what it should be. I believe these partisans, living behind the lines, have become infected with ideas that do not correspond to those of Comrade Stalin and the Central Committee. The simplest thing would be for them all to lay down their guns, come out of their forest lairs and place their collective fate in the hands of the Soviet Union, as it was before the war began. But it appears from recent events that this isn't what they want.'

'Then what do they want?'

Yakushkin shrugged. 'I'm damned if I know. I don't think they know either. And they just killed Colonel Andrich, the only man who might have had a clue.'

'You really think the partisans killed him?'

'Certainly. Who else?'

'But what about the partisan leaders who died with him?'

'They were leaders, yes, but each of his own tiny kingdom. Every partisan band has its own allegiance, and its own ideas about the future of their country. The only dream they have in common is to live in some fantasy of a world that never existed and never will. Hiding out in the woods for all those years has given them an illusion that such fantasies are possible. Whoever murdered the colonel and the others must have been convinced that this future did not include cooperating with the Soviets. The colonel was their best, perhaps their only hope. If Andrich had lived another month, he might have been able to win over enough of the Atrads that all the others would have followed. Instead, he was butchered by the very people he was trying to help. And now,' Yakushkin clenched his fists and held them out, 'the partisans and the Red Army are like two trains, racing towards each other on the same track. And I tell you, Antonina,' He drew his fists together, cogging the knuckle bones, 'those trains are about to collide.'

Just then, Yakushkin heard a noise somewhere behind him. It was a faint scuffling sound, but unmistakable. Turning suddenly, his hand reached out for the gun. But there was only the wall and a chest of drawers. He blinked in confusion. 'Is someone else here?' he asked.

'Somebody else? Besides your bodyguard, you mean?'

Yakushkin pointed at the chest of drawers. 'What is behind that wall?'

'The next door neighbour's apartment, but I think it's empty now. Why?'

Yakushkin shook his head. 'I thought I heard someone.'

'This old house is full of noises,' she told him. 'It's probably just the storm outside.'

More likely a rat, Yakushkin thought to himself.

At that moment, the door opened downstairs as Molodin stepped in out of the rain, closing the door behind him.

Yakushkin didn't mind Molodin coming into the house without permission, but he felt a twinge of embarrassment that his bodyguard would now be able to overhear the silly things he was forced to say to Antonina. 'Don't worry, Molodin!' he called out. 'I promise to save you some food.'

'Here it is!' said Antonina, as she came around the corner with the glazed earthenware pot containing the stew.

Yakushkin clapped his hands together. 'At last!' Just then, he heard the stairs creak as Molodin began making his way up to the apartment. 'Not yet, Molodin!' he called out. 'I have not even begun the meal!'

Antonina placed the pot before Yakushkin, handed him a serving ladle, then took her seat at the opposite side of the table.

Yakushkin rose to his feet, like a man about to give a speech.

'Beautiful,' he said, as he gazed into the stew, breathing the fragrant steam which dampened his red face. 'Truly a wonder of the world!' In that moment, Yakushkin's heart softened and he felt ashamed. What a fool I'd be, he thought, if I let this woman go. Of course I will take her to Moscow and we will be that happy family she spoke about.

Lifting his eyes, Yakushkin cast an adoring glance at Antonina, but was surprised to see she wasn't looking back at him. Instead, she was staring at the doorway with a startled expression on her face.

He turned to follow her gaze.

In the doorway stood a captain of the Red Army, his tunic darkened by the freezing rain which had soaked him to the bone. His hands were tucked behind his back, as if standing at ease on a parade ground. Water dripped from his elbows on to the scuffed floorboards.

'Who are you?' Yakushkin demanded angrily. 'Has something happened at the garrison? Speak up, Captain! State your business and be gone.'

But the man said nothing, and he made no move to leave. Instead, he turned and stared at Antonina.

They know each other, thought Yakushkin. And suddenly he felt the burn of jealousy for a woman he had never wanted until now. He rounded upon Antonina. 'Who is this man to you?' he asked.

'I've never seen him before!' replied Antonina, her voice quavering as she spoke. 'I swear.'

Yakushkin didn't believe her. 'I trusted you,' he snapped, 'but I promise that is over now!'

'Yes,' said the officer. 'It's over now.' From behind his back he drew a gun.

A wave of helpless dread passed through Yakushkin's mind. He glanced down at his Tokarev, which lay beside the empty dinner plate. The captain had already drawn his gun. Yakushkin knew it was too late to save himself. He looked across at Antonina. 'I could have loved you,' he said, and then he snatched up the pistol and shot her in the chest.

At that same instant, a bullet crashed through the back of Yakushkin's skull. He fell forward on to the table, which collapsed beneath his weight. The contents of the earthenware pot spilled across the floor and cutlery crashed to the ground.

Antonina was still alive, but barely. The force of the bullet had knocked her out of her chair. Now she lay on her back, her legs askew like those of a dropped marionette. She tried to speak, but her words were lost in the blood which spilled from the corners of her mouth.

The man stepped carefully across the room, avoiding the steaming pieces of sliced apple, boiled sausage and shattered crockery. Curiously, he looked at the woman. From the look on his face, it would have been clear to Yakushkin that these two had never met before. He bent down and gently put his hand upon her forehead. 'Where is the major you treated at the hospital?' he asked quietly. 'The one named Kirov. Where is he now?'

'Still there,' she whispered.

'No,' the man told her. 'He's gone. Where did he go?'

She stared at him blankly.

'You don't know, do you?' asked the man.

Her lips moved feebly, but she made no sound.

Slowly he moved his hand down from her forehead, until he was covering her eyes. Then he set the pistol against her left temple and pulled the trigger. The gun bucked and, in the flash of burning powder, some of her hair caught fire. He brushed it away from her face. Reeking metallically, the burned strands crumbled into ash.

The man stood and made his way back down the stairs. Before he vanished out into the storm, he paused to glance at Molodin, who lay in the hallway, tongue protruding from between his purple lips, and eyes bulging grotesquely from the garrotting wire sunk into his neck.

Memo from Joseph Davies, US Ambassador to
Moscow, Yacht 'Sea Cloud', Stavanger, Norway to
Counsellor Richard Sparks, Acting Supervisor of
US Embassy, Moscow. December 21st, 1937

I order you to terminate the employment of Samuel Hayes,
secretary at the Embassy, effective immediately. His gross
negligence with regard to a recent inquiry into the arrest of a
Soviet citizen has caused grave and unnecessary friction
between this office and the office of the Kremlin,
notwithstanding the considerable efforts made by me
personally into resolving the case. Had I been aware of the
facts, now provided to me by the Soviets, I would never have
taken such steps. Mr Hayes' obligation to pursue the facts
before risking an international incident was entirely
neglected. His conduct, which is entirely out of keeping with
the highest standards of the US Diplomatic Corps, merits
nothing less than his dismissal and return to the United States
on the next available transport.

Signed – Joseph Davies, Ambassador

PS See to it that the cases of champagne ordered for the
upcoming reception of Soviet dignitaries are kept at a
suitable temperature until ready for use.

Minutes after leaving the safe house, the Hanomag truck pulled up beside the building where Yakushkin and the nurse had been killed. Outside its front door, a partisan stood guard. He was tall and bony, with sunken cheeks, narrowed eyes almost hidden under a floppy, short-brimmed cap, and armed with a German MP40 sub-machine gun. He wore a mixture of military and civilian gear: grey wool riding breeches, worn through at both knees and with leather panels along the inside of each thigh, had been tucked into knee-length lace-up boots. His jacket was a lumpy woollen thing, oddly tight about the shoulders but with arms so long the man had been forced to roll them up, revealing the black and white striped lining. The garment had been cinched around his waist with a German leather belt. The aluminium buckle, once emblazoned with an eagle, a swastika and the words 'Gott Mit Uns', had been ground down and polished smooth, and the shape of a red star cut out of the centre, a common modification among the partisans.

'Good morning, Malashenko.' Pekkala nodded to the partisan as he and Barabanschikov climbed down from the truck.

'Good morning, Inspector,' replied the man. He stood aside to let Pekkala by, but when Kirov tried to pass, the partisan blocked his way. 'Not you, Commissar.'

'The commissar is helping us,' said Barabanschikov.

Malashenko shot a questioning glance at his commander, and

for a moment seemed ready to defy him. 'First time for every-thing,' he muttered, as he grudgingly moved out of the way.

Barabanschikov rested his hand upon Pekkala's shoulder. 'I must leave now, but Malashenko will remain with you for protec-tion.'

'I don't need a bodyguard,' said Pekkala.

'Consider it as insurance against your ending up as the next man on this assassin's list of victims. Use the safe house for as long as you need it. Our patrols will keep an eye on the place.' With those words, Barabanschikov climbed into the truck and the Hanomag disappeared down the road in a blue cloud of diesel exhaust.

'Why haven't the police been informed about this?' Kirov asked Malashenko.

'There are no police,' he answered. 'Not any more.'

'Then what about the Red Army? Why aren't they guarding the crime scene?'

'Because they haven't found it yet.'

'So who reported the incident?'

'The locals did. To us. We are the only ones they trust, Com-missar, and there is good reason for that.'

Now Pekkala turned to Malashenko. 'Does anyone at the gar-rison know that Yakushkin is even missing?'

'They knew he was gone from the barracks last night,' replied the partisan, 'but no one looked for him until this morning. They are aware that he had been spending time with Antonina Baran-ova, the woman who lived in this house. It won't be long before they find out he was here.'

'And where is this woman?'

'Upstairs with a bullet in her brain,' Malashenko told him, 'the same as Commander Yakushkin.'

'How long have we got to examine the crime scene?' asked Pekkala.

'Five minutes, maybe less. But we need to be gone before then. Once those soldiers realise their commander is dead, they'll arrest every partisan they can lay their hands on.'

'We'll be as quick as we can,' Pekkala assured him.

In the front hallway, Kirov almost tripped over the body of Yakushkin's bodyguard, Molodin. No one had touched him. He straddled the narrow space of the hallway, neck bent against the lower part of the wall so that his head was upright. Molodin's left arm had been dislocated in the struggle and now his hand hung poised above his face, fingers strangely clawed, as if to cast a spell upon himself. The dead man's lips had turned a livid purple, as had the tips of his fingers and his skin was grey and patched with blooms of yellowish-blue.

At the top of the stairs, Kirov and Pekkala entered the little dining room where the two murders had taken place. The air smelled of the stew which Antonina had prepared. Congealed fat merged with the blood of the victims, staining the bare wooden floor. Lying in among the broken plates, the knives and forks and the remains of the uneaten dinner, lay the bodies of Yakushkin and the woman.

Kirov gasped as he realised she was the nurse who had treated him at the hospital.

Antonina lay on her back, eyes half open and the side of her skull shot away. Her teeth had been stained red with her own blood.

Pekkala crouched over Yakushkin's body, which lay rigor-mortised like a statue tumbled from its pedestal. The commander lay on his right side, his right arm tucked under him and his left stretched out in front of him, as if reaching towards the gun he had been carrying. The point-blank shot which killed him had done so much damage that if it were not for the insignia on his uniform, he might have been unrecognisable.

'That appears to be the general's gun.' Kirov pointed at the Tokarev lying on the floor. 'He must have drawn his weapon, but by then it was too late to use it.'

'Possibly.' Pekkala lapsed into silence as he stared at the corpse of the woman.

'Why "possibly"?' asked Kirov. 'You think he might have wounded the assassin?'

Pekkala nodded towards the dead woman. 'Look at the placement of the shots.'

'One to the head and one to the chest.'

'Which tells you what, Kirov?'

'That the woman wasn't killed by the first bullet that struck her.'

'Not killed, perhaps,' agreed Pekkala, 'but mortally wounded for certain.'

'I don't see what you're getting at, Inspector.'

'The first bullet struck her dead centre in the chest, as if she was a target at a shooting range. After sustaining that injury, she had, at best, a few minutes left to live. Nothing could have saved her. The assassin would have realised that.'

'And you're wondering why he bothered to administer a coup de grace when he knew she would be dead before he even reached the street?'

Just then, Pekkala spotted something. He bent down over the

shellac of congealed blood which had seeped out around the corpses.

Kirov clenched his teeth as he watched Pekkala's fingers reach into the gore.

When Pekkala straightened up, he held in his hand three empty pistol cartridges.

'Are they the same kind we found in the bunker?' asked Kirov.

Pekkala examined them closely. 'Two of them show signs of having been reloaded,' he replied, 'but the third one does not.'

Kirov picked up the commander's gun and removed the magazine. 'There is one bullet missing from the magazine. The rest are standard ammunition.'

'Which means that the assassin fired twice,' Pekkala pointed at the two bodies, 'and that Yakushkin's final act was to murder the woman with whom he was just sitting down to dinner.'

'Why would he fire at her and not at the man who was trying to kill him?' Kirov wondered aloud. 'Could she have been the murderer's accomplice?'

'The general must have thought so,' said Pekkala, 'but what I don't understand is why the gunman would take the time to finish her off when every second spent at the crime scene increased his chances of being caught as he tried to escape?'

'He must have chosen not to let her suffer any longer than was absolutely necessary.'

'Because she was a woman?' suggested Pekkala.

'That can't be it,' replied Kirov. 'He didn't hesitate when he killed those two secretaries in the bunker.'

Pekkala waved his hand over the bodies. 'Then something else happened here. Whatever the answer, it points towards a weakness in his character.'

'If you call compassion a weakness.'

'In his line of work,' replied Pekkala, 'that's exactly what it is.'

Just then, they heard a sound, a scuffling which seemed to be coming from inside a chest of drawers set against the wall.

Both men lunged for their weapons. In an instant, Pekkala's Webley and Kirov's Tokarev were aimed at the bulky wooden structure.

Without a word, Kirov stepped over to the chest of drawers. He knelt down, knees cracking, and set his ear against the side panel. For a moment, he remained there, motionless and listening.

Then both men heard a strange and high-pitched sound, like that of a trapped bird, coming from the same location.

Caught off guard by the noise, Kirov tipped backwards, landing heavily upon the floor. He scrambled backwards, then jumped once again to his feet. 'What was that?' he whispered to Pekkala.

'I think it was the sound of someone crying,' replied Pekkala. Stepping over to the chest of drawers, he gently tapped the barrel of the Webley against the wood. 'Come out,' he said gently. 'No one is here to hurt you.'

'I can't,' replied a voice, so faint that they could barely make it out.

'Why not?' asked Pekkala.

'You have to move the chest,' replied the voice.

'It's a child!' gasped Kirov. Setting his weight against the chest of drawers, he moved the structure aside, revealing a hole in the wall behind. It had been crudely excavated, the sides hacked from the plaster. The stumps of wooden laths protruded like the ends of broken ribs. The hole itself was narrow, far too small for anyone to stand inside and too short to lie down in. Curled in a foetal position, with her knees drawn up to her chin, was a young girl, no more than ten years old. She wore a tattered blue coat and worn-out shoes, fastened by a strap with flower-shaped buckles, which must once have been saved only for special occasions.

Immediately, Pekkala put away his gun and knelt down beside the hole. 'What is your name?' he asked gently.

'Shura.'

'It's safe to come out now, Shura.' He beckoned to her with his blood-stained fingers.

The girl stared at him, her eyes reddened from hours of weeping.

'What happened?' she asked. 'Why was there shooting? Why is the table tipped over? Who is that lying on the floor? Is that the general?'

'We are trying to answer those questions,' Pekkala shifted his stance to block the girl's view of the carnage, while Kirov removed his tunic and laid it over the dead woman's face. Then he gathered up the once-cheerful white and yellow table cloth and heaped it on the shattered ruination of the general's skull. Pekkala kept talking to the girl. 'And I think you might be able to help us, but first tell me, Shura, who put you in this place?'

'My mother.'

'And your mother's name is Antonina?'

'Yes,' she told them. 'When the general comes to visit, my mother takes me to my grandmother's house. But if there isn't time, she makes me hide in here.'

'Why? Did she think that the general would hurt you?'

'No, that's not it,' she replied. 'She said that if the general knew about me, he might not come at all. She didn't want him to know that she had a child. He brought food with him, you see. My mother always saved some for me. But then, last night, someone came up the stairs.'

'How many of them were there?'

'Only one.'

Pekkala narrowed his eyes. 'Are you certain, Shura? Only one?'

'I heard his footsteps. If there were more, I would have heard them, too. I thought it was the general's helper, Molodin. He knows I live here, but he promised not to tell. Sometimes he would come by with gifts for me.'

'How do you know it wasn't him?' said Pekkala.

'I heard a voice and I knew it wasn't Molodin. And I heard my mother's voice, too. But softly. I couldn't tell what they were saying. After that, the gun went off again.'

Pekkala nodded, trying to conceal his emotions. Just then, he noticed the blood on his fingers, tucked his hand behind him and wiped it on the back of his coat.

'Are you hurt?' asked the girl.

'No,' replied Pekkala. 'I'm fine, Shura. Won't you come out now? It's safe. No one is going to hurt you.'

The girl crawled out of the space and Pekkala swept her up in his arms.

'Is that my mother lying there?' From the flat tone of her voice, it was clear that she already knew. In the hours she'd spent huddled in the blindness of that hiding place, the girl had pieced together images from what she'd only heard.

'Look at me,' said Pekkala.

As if lost in a trance, Shura continued to stare at the hulk of the dead general, his stiffened body like an island on the blood-daubed floor, and the granite pallor of her mother's legs protruding from her skirt.

'Look at me, Shura,' he repeated.

This time, the girl obeyed.

'I want you to do something for me,' Pekkala told her. 'I want you to close your eyes and let me carry you downstairs. It is better not to see what's here. Do you understand?'

The girl's eyes slid shut like those of a doll tilted on to its back.

Pekkala carried her down, stepping over the body of the guard, and out into the street.

'My God,' said Malashenko, his gaze fastening upon the little girl. 'What is she doing here?'

Hearing a familiar voice, Shura opened her eyes and looked around, squinting in the harsh daylight.

'You know this girl?' Pekkala asked Malashenko.

'I do,' he replied.

Pekkala set her down and she walked over to Malashenko, who crouched down and placed her on his knee.

'Shura,' said the partisan, 'do you recognise me? I was a friend of your mother's.'

'I know who you are,' replied Shura.

'Do you know where her grandmother lives?' Pekkala asked Malashenko. 'Can you take her there?'

'Yes,' he replied, 'but I am supposed to be guarding you.'

'Meet us at the safe house when you're done. We'll manage until you get back.'

'Yes, Inspector. I promise to return right away.'

'Move fast, Malashenko,' said Kirov. 'Here come Yakushkin's men.'

They all heard it now, the sound of a vehicle fast approaching from the direction of the hospital.

'You had better leave with me, Inspector,' said Malashenko. He shifted the little girl off his knee and rose to his feet. 'Your friend might be safe in that uniform of his, but you won't be safe among the soldiers.'

'Don't worry,' Kirov assured him. 'I guarantee Pekkala's safety.'

'Your guarantee?' asked Malashenko. 'What use is that? The promise of a commissar is no better than the oath of a whore.'

The words were not even out of Malashenko's mouth, before Kirov's gun was levelled at his face.

The speed of Kirov's draw left Malashenko wide-eyed with astonishment. 'You see?' spluttered the partisan, not taking his eyes off the weapon. 'You see who these men really are?'

'Major,' said Pekkala, 'you will put the gun away. And you!' he turned to Malashenko. 'Go now, before that mouth of yours gets you in more trouble than I can get you out of.'

Fascinated, the little girl had watched all this. Now she reached out her arms to be carried as Malashenko slung the sub-machine gun on his back, and he lifted her up and vanished down an alley just as a Red Army truck appeared around the corner, and began speeding towards the yellow house.

'What was that just now?' demanded Pekkala. 'Have you completely lost your mind!'

'No,' Kirov said through clenched teeth, 'but that's what I'd like him to think.'

Internal Memo, Office of Immigration and
Naturalisation, US Embassy, Moscow. December
28th, 1937

Application for replacement of US passports for Mrs William
H. Vasko, aged 42, her son Peter Vasko aged 16 and daughter
Rachel Vasko, aged 9.

Filing of application delayed pending payment of $2 US
Dollars per passport. Applicant did not have required US
Dollars and will return shortly.

*

Police Report, Kremlin District, December 29th,
1937

Arrest of Betty Jean Vasko and two children, charged with illegal
possession of foreign currency pursuant to NKVD directive 3/A
1933.

*

Minutes of Central Court, Moscow, March 4th,
1938

Prisoners G-29-K Betty Jean Vasko, G-30-K Peter Vasko, and
G-31-K, Rachel Vasko convicted of currency manipulation and
illegal possession of foreign currency. Sentenced to 10, 5 and 2
years respectively. Transport to Kolyma.

One hour later, Kirov and Pekkala were standing in the office of Captain Igor Chaplinksy, a slight man with thinning hair and a sharply angled face who had, until Yakushkin's death, been second-in-command of the garrison.

Only days before, this building had been the central headquarters of the German Secret Field Police for the entire Western Ukraine. They had left in a hurry, abandoning most of their equipment – typewriters, radios and drawers full of documents, some of which had been burned in the courtyard below, while the rest had either been torn to shreds or else smashed into uselessness by the rifle butts of the departing soldiers.

Commander Yakushkin's staff had moved into the building less than twenty-four hours after the previous tenants had taken to their heels. In their rush to establish a headquarters, there had been no time to remove the broken equipment and it remained as it had been left by its owners, in tangles of ripped-out wiring, broken glass tubes and a confetti of multicoloured requisition slips. There was even a large and mysterious splash of dried blood, fanned out like the feathers of a peacock on the wall behind Chaplinsky's desk.

Chaplinsky's first thought, after the Inspector and his assistant had identified themselves, was that he would somehow be held accountable for Yakushkin's death, about which he had been notified even as Pekkala was climbing the stairs to his office. The fact that Pekkala had arrived in the company of a major of Special Operations convinced him that his fate was already decided.

'I had no idea where the commander was last night,' said Chaplinksy, clasping his hands together in front of his chest like a man wringing water from a rag. Although the gesture was intended to reinforce the sincerity of his defence, it gave instead the impression of a man begging for mercy which, as far as Chaplinsky was concerned, was not far from the truth. 'He did not tell me where he was going. And I ask you, comrades, was it even my duty to ask? Commander Yakushkin was often absent, particularly at night. Am I responsible for his private life! No! I am a simple soldier in the service of his country. That is all. I serve the Soviet people. I . . .'

Pekkala leaned forward. 'Captain Chaplinsky,' he said softly.

Chaplinsky cut short his monologue. 'Yes?' he almost sobbed.

'We are not here to charge you with his murder.'

'You aren't?' Chaplinsky settled back in his chair as if he were deflating. 'Then why are you here, gentlemen?'

'We were investigating the murder of Colonel Andrich,' explained Pekkala. 'Now, unfortunately, that investigation has expanded to include Commander Yakushkin.'

'And one more, as well, I'm afraid,' said Chaplinsky, 'although I'm not certain it is related to your case.'

'Who else has been killed?' asked Pekkala.

'A hospital orderly by the name of Anatoli Tutko. He was knifed to death last night at about the same time as Commander Yakushkin was murdered. Tutko worked on the same floor as the nurse with whom Yakushkin was involved. As I say, it may not be related, but you can be certain of one thing, Inspector.'

'And what is that?' asked Pekkala.

'That the partisans are behind all these killings.'

'They seem equally convinced that you are to blame.'

'Andrich was working for us!' Chaplinsky said indignantly. 'And no one in the Red Army would dare lift a hand against Commander Yakushkin. The partisans must have found out what was coming to them and decided to take vengeance before we had even begun.'

'What is coming?' asked Kirov. 'What are you talking about?'

Chaplinsky snatched a piece of paper off his desk. 'These are my orders to prepare for an all-out assault against the partisans. The message just came through from Moscow, and we are now on full alert until the command comes through to commence the attack.'

'Comrade Chaplinsky,' said Pekkala, 'you must do everything you can to delay taking action, at least until I can find out who is really behind the murders of Colonel Andrich and Commander Yakushkin, or the result will be a needless slaughter.'

'I am well aware of what the cost will be in blood, Inspector, but what would you have me do? An order is an order, especially one from the Kremlin.'

'A commander in the field,' said Kirov, 'is always afforded some discretion.'

'Commander?' echoed Chaplinsky.

'Of course,' Kirov told him. 'You are in charge now, after all.'

Everything had happened so suddenly that this fact had not yet dawned upon Chaplinsky. Yes, he thought to himself. I *am* the commander. And his face assumed a solemn gravity.

'So you will do what you can?'

'As commander,' said Chaplinsky, 'I assure you that I will.'

'There is one other matter,' said Kirov.

'Anything to assist the men of Special Operations,' Chaplinsky answered grandly.

'We would be grateful for some kind of transport while we carry out our investigation.'

'Of course. You may have Sergeant Zolkin for as long as you need him.'

'Zolkin?' asked Kirov, remembering the man who had met him at the airstrip upon his arrival in Rovno. 'I thought he was killed in the air raid the other night.'

'He is very much alive, I assure you,' said Chaplinsky. 'You can find him at the motor pool, down in the courtyard of this building. Sergeant Zolkin will drive you wherever you need to go. Just don't go too far. I have just received word that the Germans might be mounting an attack to retake Rovno. There is heavy fighting west of here. Our troops are holding them for now, but there is a chance, a good chance, that the Fascists might break through as early as tomorrow. If that happens, we have been ordered to defend this town, no matter what the cost.'

*

'The death of that orderly was no coincidence,' remarked Pekkala, as they made their way downstairs.

'I agree,' replied Kirov. 'The gunman went to find the nurse, hoping she could lead him to Yakushkin. It was the orderly who told him where to go.'

'There is one other possibility,' said Pekkala.

'And what is that, Inspector?'

'He might have been looking for you.'

Emerging into the courtyard, they found it crowded with vehicles in various states of disrepair. A heap of bullet-shredded tyres lay in one corner and mangled pieces of exhaust pipe clattered with a ring of metal on stone as they were tossed by grease-blackened mechanics on to the tiles of what had once been the summer dining area of the hotel.

In the centre of the courtyard, Pekkala and Kirov discovered Yakushkin's jeep. Its olive-drab paint had been gashed down to the bare metal in places where shrapnel had torn through the bonnet and cowlings. Two men in blue overalls huddled over the engine.

'Zolkin?' asked Kirov, unsure which one he should be talking to.

Both men turned and squinted at the new arrivals. Neither was the Sergeant. One man aimed a greasy spanner at the other side of the courtyard to where Zolkin was sorting through a heap of punctured radiator hoses. His unbuttoned *telogreika* revealed a sweat-stained undershirt beneath. 'I thought you were dead!' he exclaimed, when he caught sight of Kirov.

'I thought the same of you,' replied the major. 'What happened to you when the bombing started?'

'I was on the other side of the street, buying a mug of tea from some old woman when the bombs started falling. She and I ended up down in her basement. A bomb fell so close by that the house collapsed on top of us. We weren't hurt, but it took me several hours to dig our way through the rubble. By the time I got us out of there, the locals told me that a number of bodies had been removed from the bunker. They said everyone down there had been killed.'

'I was only wounded,' Kirov explained. 'It seems that we have both been lucky.'

'I thought so, too, until I heard about the death of Commander Yakushkin.'

'That news has travelled fast.'

'Everyone in the garrison knows about it,' replied Zolkin.

'You were supposed to go with him to Moscow, weren't you?'

Zolkin sighed and nodded. 'So much for the chance of a life-time.' But then he raised his head. 'Unless . . .'

'Unless what?' asked Kirov.

'You could take me with you when you return,' suggested Zolkin. 'I would gladly serve as your driver in Moscow, if you don't already have one.'

'Sergeant,' Kirov began, 'I'm afraid . . .'

'We don't have a driver,' said Pekkala.

Kirov glanced at him in confusion. 'I drive us everywhere!'

'If you want to call it driving.'

'Are you going to compare my driving with yours? Because if you are . . .'

Zolkin had been watching this exchange like a spectator at a tennis match, but now he raised his voice. 'Comrades!'

The two men turned to look at him.

'I will be the best driver you have ever had,' Zolkin assured them.

'You would be the *only* driver we have ever had,' said Pekkala, 'and I see no reason why you should not come with us to Moscow.'

'Do you have the authority to get me transferred?' Zolkin asked.

Pekkala smiled and handed Zolkin his pass book.

Zolkin opened it and read the text inside. 'You are Inspector Pekkala?' He raised his head and stared.

'Yes, he is,' Kirov answered with another sigh of annoyance, 'and, unfortunately, you will find, if you read that little yellow piece of paper in his pass book, that he most definitely has the authority required to transfer you to Moscow.'

Zolkin squinted at the Classified Operations Permit. Slowly, he read out part of what it said. 'May pass into restricted areas and may requisition equipment of all types, including weapons and vehicles . . .'

'And drivers, too,' Pekkala added cheerfully.

'Congratulations,' Kirov growled at the sergeant. 'It seems that you will soon be on your way to Moscow.'

The sergeant's mouth hung open for a moment. Then he reached out and clasped Kirov's hand in both of his. After nearly dislocating the major's wrist, Zolkin turned his attention to Pekkala and, grasping the Inspector's hand, gave him the same bone-jarring treatment. 'When do we leave?' he asked.

'As soon as we have solved these murders,' answered Pekkala.

'In the meantime,' added Kirov, 'Commander Chaplinsky has appointed you to be our driver. That is, if you have still have a vehicle which runs.'

'We are working on that now,' said Zolkin. 'The Jeep should be fixed by tomorrow, as long as you don't mind a few chips to the paint.'

'We are staying at a house not far from here,' said Pekkala. He gave Zolkin the directions. 'As soon as you are ready, come and find us.'

'Very good, Comrade Major.' Zolkin clicked his heels and set off towards the mechanics, buttoning up his jacket as he went.

Now that they were alone, Kirov turned to Pekkala. 'A chauffeur?' he asked.

'I've always wanted one,' Pekkala replied smugly.

'But you don't even sleep in a bed!' shouted Kirov.

Their conversation was interrupted by a long, low rumble in the distance.

'It's early in the year for thunder,' remarked Kirov, glancing up at the sky.

'That is not thunder,' said Pekkala. 'That's artillery.'

(Postmark: Vladivostock. May 10th, 1938)

To:

Mrs Frances Harper

Hague Rd,

Monkton, Indiana, USA

Dear Sister,

I must be brief. Last year, Bill got arrested by the Russian police. I don't know why. They just took him away and I haven't seen or heard from him since. Then, last month, I was also arrested. The Russian authorities charged me with carrying 6 American Dollars, which I did have but I needed them in order to pay for replacement passports for Peter, Rachel and me. We needed those passports because all of our papers were taken from us when we first arrived in Russia. They promised to give everything back but never did. The American Embassy would only take dollars, not Soviet money, but the Russians consider it a crime to own dollars, so they sentenced me to 10 years of hard labour. They also handed out sentences for the kids. Even little Rachel! But at least we are all together and, God willing, we will stay that way. There are hundreds of us here at this holding camp in Vladivostok on the Pacific coast. We have crossed almost half the length of Russia to get here and conditions are very bad. It is very cold and we have not had a proper meal in weeks. We are waiting to board a cargo ship, which will take us on a six-day journey across the Sea of Okhotsk to the Kolyma Peninsula, where we will begin our years of penal servitude in the city of Magadan. The stories they tell about Kolyma make me wonder how long the children and I can possibly last. One of the other prisoners told me that, at the Sturmovoi gold mine, where many of us will be put to work, the life expectancy is less than one month. Frances, I beg of you, do what you can for us. Write to the State Department in Washington. Go there yourself if you have to. But you must act quickly. We are leaving now. I have paid one of the guards to mail this letter and I pray that it will reach you soon.

Your sister, Betty Jean.

Intercepted and withheld by Censor, District Office 338 NKVD, Vladivostok

After dropping the girl off at her grandmother's house, Malashenko did not return immediately to the safe house, as he had promised Pekkala he would do.

Instead, he made his way alone into the forest east of Rovno. Following trails used only by himself and wild dogs, Malashenko arrived at an old hunter's cabin. The cabin stood at the edge of a muddy path once used by wood cutters but abandoned since the outbreak of the war. Three kilometres to the north, the path connected with the main road running out of Rovno, but it wasn't even on the maps.

Before the war, the cabin had been the home of a gamekeeper named Pitoniak. The building had been well-constructed, with an overhanging roof, earth piled up waist deep around the logs which formed the walls, as well as a floor tiled with interlocking pieces of slate. The cabin's inner walls had been insulated with old newspaper shellacked in place, and a potbellied stove kept it warm in wintertime.

Pitoniak had built the cabin with his own hands and the few people who knew of its existence, besides Pitoniak himself, had been killed off in the opening days of the German invasion. After the Germans took over in Rovno, he had simply continued with his duties, expecting at any moment to be relieved of his post by the occupying government. Instead, to Pitoniak's astonishment, he continued to receive a monthly pay cheque, as well as his fuel and salt allotment, as if nothing had ever happened. For a while, it seemed as if Pitoniak's luck might last throughout the war.

But it ran out one dreary February morning, when he encountered a small group of former Red Army soldiers who had escaped from German captivity and were now living in the forest. Their weapons had been fashioned in the manner of their ancestors, from sharpened stones and fire-hardened sticks and the gnarled fists of tree roots wrestled out of the black earth.

Pitoniak had been patrolling in a desolate valley, where he knew a pack of wild boar spent the winter. To get there and back was a full day's walk from his cabin, but he was curious to see if the boar had produced any offspring that year. Pitoniak had set out before sunrise and arrived at the edge of the valley just before noon.

It was here that he ran into the soldiers.

There were only three of them and they were lost. They had been wandering in circles for days. Pitoniak gave them what little food he had brought with him – a small loaf of dense *chumatsky* bread, made from rye and wheat flour, and a fist-sized piece of *soloyna* bacon.

He offered to lead the men back to his cabin, and to put them in touch with a partisan Atrad under the command of Andrei Barabanschikov, which had begun forming in a remote area to the south of his cabin.

The soldiers agreed at once, and Pitoniak led them from the valley where they would soon have perished without his help.

Arriving at the cabin, Pitoniak built a fire in the potbellied stove.

The men stood by, hands held out towards the heat-hazed iron, faces blotched white with the beginnings of frostbite. They spat on the stove plates, watching their saliva crack and roll around like tiny fizzing pearls before it disappeared. When their clothing warmed, the men began to scratch themselves as dozens of cold-numbed lice came back to life.

Taking pity on these men, Pitoniak fed them *sapkhulis tsveni* stew made from deer kidneys, dill pickles and potatoes, which he had made for himself before he set out for the valley.

The soldiers wept with thanks.

After they had eaten, they sat naked by the stove, running candle flames up and down the seams of their shirts and trousers. The fires spat as lice eggs exploded in the heat.

When this was done, the soldiers bathed in an old wooden barrel filled with rainwater which stood behind his cabin.

As Pitoniak watched them set aside the filthy remnants of their uniforms and step out of their boots on to pale, trench-rotted feet, Pitoniak wondered if the Barabanschikovs would even take them in – three more mouths to feed and the men half dead as they were.

He was not the only one to have these thoughts.

That night, as the men lay sleeping, one of the soldiers rose to his feet, took up Pitoniak's gun and shot the gamekeeper where he lay in his bunk. Then he turned the gun upon the other two men, killing them as well.

The name of this man was Vadim Ivanovich Malashenko.

After burying the bodies in a shallow grave, Malashenko made himself at home in the cabin. Over the next month, he steadily ate his way through Pitoniak's food supply.

When Malashenko's strength had finally returned, he set off in search of the Barabanschikov Atrad and it was not long before their paths crossed in the Red Forest.

Seeing that this former soldier had a gun and was not on his last legs, like so many others who had come to them, the Barabanschikovs accepted Malashenko into their ranks.

He had been with them ever since.

Malashenko never mentioned the cabin to the other partisans, but sometimes he went back there on his own. In the evenings, he would sit by the fire, staring at the newspapers on the walls. The shellac had aged with time, forming a yellowy glaze over the pages. The papers dated back to the 1920s and although Malashenko couldn't read, the thousands of unfamiliar words transformed into a thing of beauty separate from their hidden meanings.

By the end of 1942, Malashenko had become convinced that the days of the Barabanschikov Atrad were numbered, along with all the other partisans in the region. Hidden among the trees, he had seen the SS death squads at work – trenches dug in the sandy soil and truckload after truckload of civilians, partisans and captured Red Army prisoners arriving at the place of execution. Stripped naked, they filed into the pits, huddled and obedient, where they were dispatched by men wearing leather aprons and carrying revolvers. It was the acceptance of their fate which haunted him, even more than the killings, of which he had already seen more than one man could properly encompass in his mind.

Malashenko knew that he would have to act now if he wanted to avoid ending up in a pit like those others but, at first, he had no idea how to proceed. After several days of pondering the situation, he came upon a solution which would allow him not only to survive but to prosper in this war.

It had been staring right at him, every time he walked into town.

Among the new occupiers of Rovno were men with big ideas,

which only the privilege of rank could bring to life. He saw them in their finely tailored uniforms, gold rings winking on their fingers. He watched them sitting in the cafés, now open only to their own kind, laughing with beautiful women, whose shoulders had been draped with precious furs. As Malashenko passed by, staring with undisguised longing at their steaming cups of coffee and the fresh bread on their plates, they glanced at him and looked away again, as if he had been nothing more than a handful of leaves stirred up by a passing gust of wind. The disdain of these women only increased his admiration for the officers who owned them. For such men, Rovno was only a stepping stone, a place to be plundered of its wealth before setting off once more upon the road to greatness.

One person in particular had caught his eye; Otto Krug, director of the German Secret Field Police – the Geheime Feldpolizei – for Rovno and the surrounding district.

For a man like that, thought Malashenko, information is the source of power. And I have information.

But what to ask for in return? Cash was no good. When paying for food or clothes or tobacco, Malashenko could no more easily explain a wallet crammed with Reichsmarks than he could afford to let his partisan brothers know that he had been collaborating with the enemy. It had to be something that would not raise the suspicions of those who, like Malashenko himself, suspected the worst in everyone.

The answer came to him as he trudged through the forest one day, gathering mushrooms for the partisans' communal cooking pot. It was a warm afternoon and perspiration trickled down his forehead, stinging his eyes and wetting his dusty lips. And suddenly Malashenko realised what he would ask for in payment.

'Genius,' he muttered, licking the sweat from his fingertips.

The answer was salt. He would trade information for salt. Throughout history, people had substituted salt for money. Even the Roman soldiers, whose isolated garrisons had once clung like limpets to this landscape, received salt as part of their salaries.

Salt had always been expensive, even before the war, but once the fighting began all available reserves had been snatched up by the military. Only those crafty enough to have hidden away their supplies could get their hands on it now. Malashenko might not have been rich. He might not have been the kind of man for whom salt was always within easy reach. But Malashenko was exactly the kind of individual who might have hidden his supply from the claws of government. That was a story even the most suspicious of his neighbours would believe.

These days, a person could buy anything with salt. From now on, that was exactly what he intended to do.

On his next visit to Rovno, Malashenko walked into the headquarters of the Secret Field Police, located in the former Hotel Novostav. With cap in hand and gaze lowered humbly to the floor, he stood before the desk of Otto Krug.

Krug was a giant of a man, with a boiled red face, wispy white hair and huge fists tucked into pale green doeskin gloves, like bunches of unripe bananas. He wore these gloves, even inside his office, due to a bad case of eczema that split his fingertips and left his knuckles raw. The condition had appeared shortly after his arrival in Rovno, and he blamed it entirely on the stresses of his new job.

As a result, Krug despised Rovno. He hated everything about it. Even before he arrived to take up his post, Krug had already begun scheming for promotion to one of the larger, more important cities of this soon-to-be conquered nation. Minsk perhaps. Or Kiev. Odessa. Stalingrad. In the wide scope of Krug's ambition, even Moscow was not out of the question, provided he first took advantage of all the opportunities available to him here in Rovno.

When Malashenko explained that he was a trusted member of the elusive Barabanschikov Atrad, Krug pulled out a Luger pistol and laid it on the desk in front of him. 'Why should I let you walk out of here alive?' he asked.

With his eyes fixed on the gun, Malashenko explained what he was prepared to do.

Without moving the Luger from the desk, Krug brought out a bottle of apricot brandy, poured a measure into a glass and slid it across the table to the dishevelled little man. Then he sat back, gloved fist gripped around the neck of the bottle.

Malashenko poured it down his throat and the soft sweetness of the fruit was so perfectly contained within the glassy liquid that he could almost feel the downy softness of the apricot's skin against his lips.

'Assuming I can use this information,' said Krug, 'what do you want in return?'

When Malashenko named the manner of his payment, Krug had to stop himself from laughing out loud at his good fortune. Whole warehouses of salt were no more than a requisition slip away.

Krug slid the bottle across to Malashenko. 'Help yourself,' he said.

The men shook hands before they parted company, the Chief of Secret Field Police towering over the diminutive Malashenko.

Soon afterwards, the salt began to flow.

In brown, moisture-proof half-kilo bags, Malashenko marked

his own path to prosperity. He hid this newfound wealth in a secret underground chamber, dry and lined with stones, which he had constructed in the woods behind Pitoniak's cabin.

Whenever Malashenko learned of anything which he thought might be of interest to Krug, he found some excuse to visit Rovno and then paid a visit to the Geheime Feldpolizei.

In order to be able to leave the Atrad's hiding place in the forest and visit Rovno on a regular basis, Malashenko established himself as a courier to the hospital in town. Although wounded partisans could not be brought to the hospital, which was constantly being watched by the German authorities, sympathetic Russians who worked there could still smuggle out medicine to the Atrads. Occasionally, doctors or nurses could be persuaded to make visits to the Atrads. Malashenko acted as a courier for both the medicine and the doctors, who would be blindfolded and led down as many winding trails as possible on their way to the hiding place, so as not to be able to repeat the journey on their own. Once they arrived at the Atrad, the doctors would perform surgeries in the most primitive conditions imaginable. But it was better than nothing at all.

Part of Malashenko's agreement with Krug was that he would continue to carry out his duties as a courier, even though the German authorities were well aware of what he was doing. Krug considered the stolen medical supplies and the occasional doctor visit a small price to pay, compared to the information Malashenko supplied about partisans in the region.

As a result of Malashenko's information, numerous Atrads were wiped out.

The Barabanschikovs, however, remained untouched. Malashenko credited this to his value as an informant, but that was only partly true.

The local anti-partisan troops had found the Barabanschikovs so elusive that Krug decided it would be easier just to leave them alone for now, and to focus on easier targets. Krug had long since realised that the war against the partisans could only be won in stages, and not in one all-out attack. The day would come when Krug would focus all of his resources on destroying the Barabanschikovs. For now, however, Krug had good reason to leave them in peace.

Malashenko always delivered his information in person to Krug, not trusting any intermediary or other form of communication, since he could neither read nor write. He entered the Feldpolizei headquarters through a tunnel which ran from a bakery across the road directly into the basement of the old hotel. Krug had ordered the tunnel to be built, not as a means of conveying informants into the building, but as a means of his own escape if the headquarters ever came under attack.

The amount of salt Krug paid out varied, depending on the value of the information, but Malashenko never had cause to complain. No matter how trivial the news, Krug never turned him away. He even handed over an extra bag of salt at Christmas.

But the next year brought changes. First came the defeat of the German Sixth Army at Stalingrad. Then the mighty clash of armour at Kursk, from which the Red Army emerged victorious. By the autumn of 1943, the German army was in full retreat. Even the most fanatical among them began to realise that their fate was sealed. Soon, Malashenko knew, the Soviets would be his masters once again.

This conclusion came without a trace of joy or gratitude that the hour of Russian liberation was at hand. Instead, all that

Malashenko felt was a shudder of dread, clattering like a knife blade down the ladder of his spine. He harboured no illusions that the defeat of Germany would bring peace to his world. The terror meted out by Nazi gauleiters would simply be replaced by the heavy-handed justice of the commissars, as it had been before the war began.

Anticipating the imminent arrival of the Soviets, partisan activity in the forests around Rovno had increased. Some of their attacks, on railway lines, German patrols and even on Rovno itself had turned into full-scale battles. Successive air raids, first by the Red Air Force and then by the Luftwaffe, had reduced the lives of those few surviving inhabitants of the town to something out of the Stone Age.

Although he continued to supply information to Krug, and Krug continued to pay for it as generously as ever, Malashenko knew the day was fast approaching when this arrangement would come to an end.

The last piece of intelligence he sold to Krug was a rumour he had picked up about a former partisan, Viktor Andrich, who would soon be arriving from Moscow with a mission to negotiate an end to all partisan activity in the region. At this time, the Red Army was only 20 kilometres from Rovno and Malashenko knew that this might be his final chance to profit from his arrangement with Krug.

Arriving at Feldpolizei headquarters, Malashenko found the place in a shambles. In the hotel courtyard, clerks were pitching armfuls of documents into a huge fire. Stray pages wafted away from the blaze, flecking the ground with rectangles of white so that the courtyard resembled a jigsaw puzzle with half its pieces missing.

Malashenko discovered the garrison commander at his desk,

still wearing his doeskin gloves and cradling a litre of Napoleon brandy, not the cheap apricot schnapps with which he plied his informants. With this brandy, Krug had once hoped to celebrate the unconditional surrender of Russia. He had entertained great notions of his role in the future of this country. In these moments of supreme confidence, he had whispered to himself the titles and awards he believed would soon garnish his name. But now Krug's career lay in tatters, and he glimpsed the future – of a Berlin consumed in flames and Red Army soldiers fighting house to house among the ruins. By the time Malashenko entered the room, Krug had drunk most of the brandy and his vision was so blurred that at first he barely recognised the partisan.

'I have information for you,' said Malashenko, eyes fixed on Krug's Luger, which lay upon the desk, just as it had done at their first meeting.

'And I have some for you,' replied Krug. 'We're leaving!'

'So I see.'

'Which means,' Krug paused to swig from the bottle, 'that your information is no longer of any use to me.'

'Very well,' said Malashenko, turning to leave. He didn't put it past Krug to finish him off with that Luger, now that their dealings were done, and he made up his mind to get out of the building as quickly as possible.

'On the other hand,' said Krug.

Malashenko turned. 'Yes?' He expected to find Krug's Luger aimed in his direction, but was relieved to see the weapon still lying on the desk.

'You may as well tell me what it is.'

Malashenko explained what he had heard about Colonel Andrich.

'That's it?' asked Krug. 'That's all you've got?'

'It ought to be worth something,' answered Malashenko.

Krug breathed in deeply, the air whistling in through his long, thin nose. 'That's what you all say,' he muttered.

'All who?' demanded Malashenko. 'It's just me standing here.'

Krug laughed. 'You think you are the only partisan who works for me?'

'Maybe not,' admitted Malashenko, 'but after all I've done for you, are you really going to send me away empty-handed?'

Krug sighed. 'I suppose you haven't been completely useless.' He reached down beside his chair, lifted up a bag of salt and tossed it on to the desk. 'My last one,' he whispered. 'Take it. Take it and get out of here.'

Malashenko did as he was told.

After the partisan had gone, Krug raised himself uncertainly to his feet, crossed the room to an Enigma coding machine and relayed a message to Berlin, stating that Rovno was in imminent danger of being overrun by the Red Army. The message went on to say that a Soviet colonel named Andrich had been dispatched by Moscow to negotiate a ceasefire between the various partisan groups after the German army had pulled out of the region. From other sources, Krug had learned that a force of Soviet Counter Intelligence troops was also on its way to Rovno, to deal with the situation by force if Andrich's negotiations proved unsuccessful.

As the message transmitted, Krug thought about the plans he had made for himself, tracing the arc of his ambition higher and higher through the ranks until, at last, he would find himself sitting side by side with the great and living gods of the thousand-year empire to which he had sworn his allegiance. His musings were interrupted by a rustling at his windowpane. He turned to see a piece of paper, smouldering at its edges, blown by a gust of wind against the glass. Walking over to the window, he squinted at the document. It was a copy of a recommendation, made out to Krug himself, for an Iron Cross First Class. In exchange for a month's leave, Krug had persuaded his second-in-command to fill out and sign the necessary paperwork. The recommendation had been sent to Berlin several weeks previously but there had been no acknowledgement of its receipt. Another gust of wind snatched away the paper, giving Krug a view down into the court-yard below, where men from his staff were still burning heaps of documents. Caught in the rising smoke, more pieces of paper fluttered up into the air beyond Krug's window and, for a while, he watched them with the fascination of a child as they side-slipped into the milky sky. Then Krug sat down at his desk, put the barrel of the Luger in his mouth and blew his brains out.

Japanese Coast Guard Officer Hiroo Nishikaichi,
Wakkanai Station, Hokkaido. June 21st, 1938

A Russian cargo vessel, the 'Yenisei', has run aground on the
Tetsumu shoals, north of the island of Reshiri. It was spotted by
Japanese fishing vessels drifting without power one week ago in
the sea of Okhotsk. It appears to be one of the many prison ships
travelling between Vladivostok and Kolyma. We approached the
'Yenisei' and signalled our willingness to assist, but were waved
away by men with guns. We continue to monitor the situation.

*

Report of Imperial Japanese Coast Guard Officer
Hiroo Nishikaichi, Wakkanai Station, Hokkaido.
June 23rd, 1938

A small vessel of Russian origin arrived at the stranded cargo vessel
'Yenisei' early this morning and removed the crew. The ship was
evidently on its journey back to Vladivostok from Kolyma after
delivering a cargo of prisoners when it lost power. The ship appears
to be in very bad repair. These vessels, we have learned, are often
sold by the Americans to the Russians when the Americans have
determined that the ships are no longer seaworthy. The ships are
sold for scrap, but the Russians then immediately return them to
service. It is no wonder that a ship such as the 'Yenisei' should have
suffered a breakdown.

*

Report - June 28th, 1938

The 'Yenisei' now appears to have been abandoned by the Russians. High winds from the recent storm have caused the vessel's hull to shift. It is now listing hard to starboard and appears to be taking on water. Commander Sakai is in agreement with me that the ship is now in danger of floating free of the shoals. Commander Sakai has approved the measure of boarding the ship and cutting holes in its hull to ensure that the vessel will not drift into the shipping lanes before it sinks.

*

Report - June 29th, 1938

At approximately noon today, my crew and I boarded the 'Yenisei' with the intention of cutting holes in the hull in order to ensure that the wreck did not become a hazard to shipping in the event that it drifted free of the shoals. Using axes and acetylene torches, we cut through the hull on the port side aft. Even before we had completely removed the section, my crew and I observed that the cargo area below was filled with bodies. We realised that the 'Yenisei' had been on its outward voyage and not bound for home empty, as we had believed when the crew was evacuated. The crew of the 'Yenisei' had abandoned the convicts to their fate. The compartment had flooded almost to its entire depth and we saw no signs of life among the dead, which numbered in the hundreds. Moving to the forward section, we cut another section from the hull and discovered yet another compartment filled with bodies. This compartment was partially flooded and we found several of the prisoners still alive. They had crawled upon the dead to stay clear of the water, the temperature of which would otherwise have ensured their deaths. We were able to rescue fifteen people. At that point, the 'Yenisei' began to shift again and we were forced to abandon our search for more survivors. As we had feared, the ship had begun to float free from the shoal. No sooner had we returned to the ship with the survivors than the 'Yenisei' slid off the shoal and sank. Of the fifteen people we rescued, three died before we returned to Wakkanai Station. The remaining passengers, eight men and four women, were immediately transported to the Sapporo Naval Hospital and quarantined. While most of the prisoners are Russian, one of them, a young man about seventeen years old, claims to be an American. All are now being treated for starvation and hypothermia and some are not expected to survive.

*

Coded Message. Enigma Cipher. Rotor
Configuration 573
German Embassy, Tokyo
To: Abwehr Headquarters, 72-76 Tirpitzufer,
Berlin

Have been approached by American male, approx 18 yrs old, claiming to be survivor of shipwreck involving soviet prisoners bound for Kolyma. Says family emigrated to Russia 1933. Reports whole family murdered by Soviets. Mother and sister died on ship.

Coded Message. Enigma Cipher. Rotor
Configuration 870
Abwehr HQ
To: German Embassy, Tokyo

Why did he not go to American Embassy?

Coded Message. Enigma Cipher. Rotor
Configuration 224
German Embassy, Tokyo
To: Abwehr Headquarters, 72-76 Tirpitzufer,
Berlin

Claims he does not trust them. Says they will hand him back to
Soviets.

Coded Message. Enigma Cipher. Rotor
Configuration 190
Abwehr HQ
To: German Embassy, Tokyo

Does he speak Russian?

Coded Message. Enigma Cipher. Rotor
Configuration 513
German Embassy, Tokyo
To: Abwehr Headquarters, 72-76 Tirpitzufer,
Berlin

Fluently.

Coded Message. Enigma Cipher. Rotor
Configuration 745

Abwehr HQ

To: German Embassy, Tokyo

Is US Embassy aware of his location?

Coded Message. Enigma Cipher. Rotor
Configuration 513

German Embassy, Tokyo

To: Abwehr Headquarters, 72-76 Tirpitzufer,
Berlin

Negative.

Coded Message. Enigma Cipher. Rotor
Configuration 298

Abwehr HQ

To: German Embassy, Tokyo

Bring him in.

One week after the death of Commander Krug, and with Red Army troops now in full control of Rovno, Malashenko was contacted by another person who had been collaborating with the Germans during their occupation of the town.

Malashenko was astonished to discover that this person was nurse Antonina from the Rovno hospital, who had regularly supplied him with stolen medications and who had, more recently, been seen in the company of Commander Yakushkin. The meeting took place when Malashenko arrived at the hospital, ostensibly to receive treatment for scabies. In fact, he was there to collect penicillin, bandages and suture thread for the partisan medical officer, a former butcher named Leiferkus, who had turned his old trade of disassembling the carcasses of animals into reassembling his fellow men as best he could when no actual doctors could be found.

Even though the Germans had pulled out of Rovno, most of the Atrads, the Barabanschikovs included, had no intention yet of simply laying down their arms before the Soviets. This meant that, for Malashenko, his missions into Rovno continued just as they had done before.

In the dozens of times Malashenko had met with Antonina over the years, he never once considered that she might also be collaborating with the enemy. But this, Malashenko realised, was the genius of the disguise which Krug had fashioned for her. Krug had said there were others, and Malashenko wondered how many, whose paths he crossed each day, were hiding the same lie as his own.

Antonina, for her part, was equally amazed to learn the truth about Malashenko. She had received a message from Berlin on a radio provided by Krug, to be used only if Krug himself was captured or killed by the enemy. 'In two days, you will receive a visitor,' she told Malashenko.

'What visitor?' he asked nervously.

'I don't know who,' replied Antonina, 'but they have ordered you to rendezvous with him three days from now.'

'Ordered?'

'Did you think you were finished with these people?' Antonina laughed. 'You will only be finished when you, or they, or both of you are dead.'

'All right,' grumbled Malashenko, 'but I expect to get paid.'

'That is between you and them,' she said. 'Where shall I say you'll be meeting this visitor?'

Malashenko thought for a moment and then gave her directions to Pitoniak's cabin. 'Tell them I'll be there at dusk. I'd feel better if I knew what this was about.'

'So would I,' replied Antonina, 'but neither of us do so there's no point in worrying about it.' She put several vials of penicillin in front of him, along with a stack of bandages, medical tape and suture thread. 'You'd better carry those out of here, in case your people wonder what you're doing.'

Malashenko rolled up his trouser leg and used the medical tape to strap the vials to his calves. Bald patches on his skin showed where previously applied strips of tape had been pulled away, leaving freckles of dried blood in the flesh.

'How are you planning to get out of here,' asked Antonina, 'now that the Red Army has arrived?'

'Out?' replied Malashenko. 'Where would I go?'

'Any place at all, as long as it is far from here.'

'I hadn't thought about it.'

'Well, you'd better start,' Antonina told him. 'If they find out you've been collaborating with the Germans . . .'

Malashenko stopped wrapping the tape around his leg. 'Why would they find out,' he asked menacingly, 'unless somebody told them?'

'You should worry less about somebody giving you up and a little bit more about how things will change for us now that the Red Army is here. Better to leave and find some place where you can start again.'

'Is that what you're going to do?' asked Malashenko, suddenly nervous that he did not have a plan of his own.

'I've got an idea,' she answered cryptically, 'and if all goes well, I'll be riding out of here in the arms of Commander Yakushkin.'

You're a cold-hearted bitch, thought Malashenko, but he just nodded and smiled and hurried on his way.

*

The operation to assassinate Colonel Andrich had begun within hours of Krug's message arriving at Abwehr Headquarters. Admiral Canaris, head of German Intelligence, had immediately grasped the vulnerability of the Kremlin's plan. If Andrich could be liquidated, the Red Army would become bogged down in a war with their own people, diverting valuable troops from the front line and weakening the strength of the Soviet advance. All this, and significantly more if the full extent of the Admiral's plan could be achieved, would be accomplished with the death of a single man, provided he was found in time.

Realising that the only way to achieve their objective would be to send an assassin, Admiral Canaris summoned SS Sturmbann-führer Otto Skorzeny of the Brandenburg Kommando to a private meeting.

Skorzeny had carried out numerous commando operations during the course of the war including, in September of 1943, the rescue of Benito Mussolini from the castle of Gran Sasso, where the Duce was being held in captivity by Italian Communist partisans.

At his office on the Bendlerstrasse in Berlin, Canaris explained the situation to the six-foot-four-inch Skorzeny, who stood uncomfortably in Canaris's drawing room, boots creaking as he tilted slowly between his heels and the balls of his feet, while the Admiral's two dachshunds sniffed at his legs.

'It could be done,' said Skorzeny, when he had listened to the Admiral's plan, 'but doesn't Abwehr have agents of its own to carry out the task?'

'We do,' replied Canaris. He was a tall man, with a gaunt face and deep-set eyes. His once blond hair had turned almost completely white and his lips twitched nervously whenever he listened to other people speak, as if forcing himself not to interrupt.

'So why do you need me?' asked Skorzeny.

'Because what we don't have is someone I can count on to deliver that agent to Rovno. That is why I've called on you, Skorzeny, because I know you can get the job done.'

'As I understand it, Admiral, Rovno is now under Red Army control.'

'And does that represent an insurmountable obstacle for you, Skorzeny?'

Skorzeny paused for a moment. 'Not at all, Admiral, provided I am given the necessary resources.'

'You may have whatever you need.'

'And who is this agent, Admiral?'

'His name is Peter Vasko.'

'That sounds vaguely familiar.'

'He came to us through the Embassy in Tokyo, back in '38.'

'Yes,' said Skorzeny, 'now I remember. The American.'

'I would not call him that, if I were you. But yes, that is the man in question. Provided you can get him across the lines, Vasko will have no difficulty infiltrating Rovno as a Russian. He speaks the language and, thanks to his training with us, he is also an expert in firearms and explosives.'

At that moment, the phone rang, loud and jarring in the cramped space of the office.

Canaris picked up the phone. 'Yes?' As he spoke, he turned in his chair, until he was facing away from Skorzeny, and lowered his voice to a murmur.

Skorzeny took advantage of the disruption to kick one of the dachshunds and send it yelping under the Admiral's desk.

Canaris turned to see what had caused the commotion, but by then Skorzeny appeared to be engrossed in studying the books which lined one wall of Canaris's study.

Canaris hung up the phone. 'You leave tonight, Skorzeny. Vasko will be ready. Any questions?'

'I do have one.'

Canaris held out a hand, palm up, in a conciliatory gesture. 'By all means.'

'Are you certain it is wise to involve the SS in an Abwehr operation? Our two departments have been in conflict ever since the war began, and especially after Himmler took over the Intelligence Branch of the SS following the death of Reinhardt Heydrich.'

Skorzeny was telling the truth, and the source of this rancour between the two departments had largely been the result of a dispute between the SS and the Abwehr in the very area where Vasko would be carrying out his mission. Soon after the German invasion of Russia in 1941, Abwehr agents had begun working with local Ukrainian leaders to consolidate anti-Communist militias. Abwehr's Eastern Group I, which was given responsibility for this large-scale operation, operated out of Sulejowek, across the border in occupied Poland. They succeeded not only in winning the support of the influential partisan leader Melnyk, who worked for the Germans under the code name 'Konsul I', but they were also able to recruit several companies of Ukrainian troops, who became known as the Gruppe Nachtigall.

How far-reaching this operation might have been would never be known, because it was derailed by the arrival of SS execution squads, known as Einsatzgruppen, which began a series of mass executions in the same region where Abwehr had been working to win over the local population.

Disillusioned Ukrainians, who had initially welcomed the arrival of German troops, now turned upon those they had seen as liberators and began a struggle against both the Fascists and the Communists.

Canaris had never forgiven the SS for their role in the failure of the Abwehr's operations in the East. He had made no secret of that fact, which was why Skorzeny had good reason to wonder why the leader of the Abwehr would seek the assistance of an SS Sturmbannführer.

'I chose you,' explained Canaris, 'because you are the best we've got, and also because this operation is too important to be waylaid by departmental politics.'

'I understand, Admiral, and I am grateful for your confidence in me.'

'And with that confidence in mind, I order you to maintain absolute secrecy with regard to this operation. No activity report is to be filed. No communication is to be made once the operation is under way. There will be no debriefing afterwards. No one may know. Absolutely no one. Not even Himmler!'

Skorzeny's eyebrows rose almost imperceptibly.

'Is that clear?' asked Canaris.

'Yes, Admiral. It is.'

'You have your orders.' Canaris waved him away. 'Make them so.'

Immediately after Skorzeny's departure, Canaris picked up the phone. 'Get me Vasko,' he ordered.

Two hours later, Vasko was standing in the room. He was of middle height, with a small mouth and large, staring blue eyes, which seemed to take in everything around him without looking at anything in particular. His hair, which he combed straight back on his head, was thin and the same dull shade of brown as the fur on the back of a mouse. He had an unremarkable face that appealed neither to women nor to men, and which allowed him to vanish in a crowd, ignored even by those who had stood in his presence, some of whom he had sent to their graves on the orders of Admiral Canaris.

'Sit,' Canaris gestured towards a chair. 'Are you hungry? Thirsty?'

'No, Admiral. Thank you.'

'Skorzeny has agreed to transport you across the lines. You

leave tonight. The mission is going ahead.'

'But why bring in Skorzeny?' demanded Vasko. 'Surely the Abwehr have people who can get me through the lines.'

'None who are as capable as Skorzeny,' replied Canaris, 'and if this mission goes wrong, I will need someone to take responsibility. Who better than the SS?'

'And if it succeeds?'

'Then Hitler's flagging confidence in the Abwehr will be restored, and that slack-jawed chicken farmer Himmler will have no choice except to sing our praises to the heavens.' Canaris lifted a sealed envelope from his desk and held it out.

Vasko leaned forward and slipped it from the Admiral's grasp.

'Once Skorzeny has brought you through the lines,' Canaris continued, 'you will be guided to your target by a partisan named Malashenko. He is a member of the Barabanschikov Atrad, and has served as an informant to the Secret Field Police in Rovno. The rendezvous point is an old hunter's cabin in the forest south of Rovno. You'll find the map coordinates inside that envelope.'

Vasko tucked it into the inside chest pocket of his coat. 'How much did you tell Skorzeny about the operation?'

'As much as he needs to know, but no more. Skorzeny is aware that you are going in to liquidate Colonel Andrich but, like you, he knows nothing at all about the full extent of the mission, or the agent who will be carrying out the secondary phase.'

'Forgive me, Admiral, but are you sure it's right to separate the two phases of the mission so completely? If I knew who this second agent was . . .'

'Then you would be in a position to give up the name of the agent if, God forbid, you were ever captured. Or vice versa. He does not know you and you do not know him. That is how I want it and, believe me, so do you.'

'Yes, Admiral.' Vasko stood up to leave.

'There is one more thing.' Opening a drawer in his desk, Canaris removed a bar of gold as long as his outstretched hand and as wide as his first three fingers. The finish of the gold was not shiny but rather a dusty brass colour. The surface bore several stamps, indicating its weight, purity and Reichsbank inventory number. Carefully, he set it down in front of Vasko. 'Your guide is expecting to be paid.'

'As much as that?' remarked Vasko.

'If everything goes according to plan, Colonel Andrich will soon be dead, and Stalin himself will not be far behind. For that,' said Canaris, 'one bar of gold is a small asking price.'

*

Malashenko stood in the doorway to his cabin, smoking a cigarette as he watched a man approaching down the centre of the path.

He wore the uniform of a Red Army officer, and all he carried with him was a leather satchel of the type used by blacksmiths for holding horse shoes. 'You must be Malashenko,' he said.

'I am. And who are you?'

'A stranger bearing gifts. That's all you need to know.'

Malashenko flicked away his cigarette and stood aside to let him pass.

Inside the cabin, Vasko removed his gun belt, from which hung a holstered Tokarev and a Russian army canteen. He laid them on the table, then sat down and waited while Malashenko brewed coffee made from chicory in an old pan on the stove.

'What is it you want from me?' asked the partisan, as he poured the dark and bitter-smelling drink into a chipped enamel cup.

Vasko took the mug and turned it so that the handle was facing away from him but he did not lift it from the table. 'You recently passed on information about a man named Colonel Andrich.'

'That's right. He arrived in Rovno two days ago.'

'I need you to tell me where I can find him.'

'That's a nice pistol,' said Malashenko, eyeing the gun belt on the table. Slowly, he reached out towards it.

'If you want to keep those fingers,' said Vasko, 'don't touch anything that doesn't belong to you.'

Grumbling, Malashenko withdrew his hand.

'Just do as you're told and you will be well rewarded,' Vasko told him.

'How well?'

Vasko opened the satchel and pulled out something which had been placed inside an old grey sock. He set it on the table and pushed it across to Malashenko.

Malashenko picked up the sock and tipped the bar of gold on to the table. The spit dried up in his mouth. 'Why are you paying me so much?' he asked warily.

'If it were up to me, I wouldn't, but this is what the Admiral thinks you're worth.'

Malashenko thought about Antonina's advice, to leave Rovno and never come back. Better to travel with one bar of gold, he told himself, than with a hundred bags of salt.

Vasko slid the bar back into the sock and returned it to his farrier's satchel. 'Are we agreed?'

Malashenko nodded slowly. 'Stay here tonight,' he said. 'You will be safe. I'll be back in the morning, after I have found your Colonel Andrich.'

That first night in the cabin, as Vasko lay in the bunk, surrounded by the distantly familiar smells of Russian black bread, Russian tobacco and the fishy reek of Russian boot grease distilled from the rotted husks of Lake Baikal shrimp, he listened to the steady thudding of artillery in the distance.

He put his hands against his ears, hoping to block out the sound. But it didn't work. The relentless pounding of the guns seemed to rise up from the earth beneath the cabin, until even the air he breathed appeared to tremble.

Vasko moaned and rocked from side to side, plagued by memories of the days he had spent in the hold of that prison ship bound for Kolyma after it had run aground on the shoals of Re-shiri Island. Each wave that struck that crippled vessel sounded like a cannon ball against the iron hull. As the freezing water rose higher and higher in the cargo bays where he and the others had been left to die, Vasko had focused on the sound of the waves in order to drown out first the screams, then the pleas, then prayers and at last only the whimpering of those who had abandoned any hope of rescue. By the time the Japanese Coastguard peeled away a section of the hull to let them out, the sound of those waves had fixed forever in Vasko's mind, until it had become like the beating of a second heart, driving him so close to madness that he could no longer recall how it felt to be sane.

*

It did not take long for Malashenko to learn both where and when Andrich's meeting with the partisan leaders would take place. For a man of his particular abilities, few secrets could stay hidden in the rubble of that town.

First thing the following morning, he delivered the information to Vasko.

Within six hours, Andrich and the partisans who'd been with him were dead. Not long afterwards came the news that Commander Yakushkin had also been murdered.

As soon as Malashenko had dropped off the little girl at her grandmother's house, ignoring the old woman's questions about her daughter, he made his way back to the cabin where Vasko had been hiding in order to collect his bar of gold.

But Vasko wasn't there.

Assuming that he had been tricked, Malashenko turned around and headed back to Rovno, roaring curses at the treetops on his way.

*

Admiral Canaris was sleeping in his chair, as he often did after a lunch at Horchner's, his favourite restaurant in Berlin. With his hands folded across his stomach and a pair of slippers on his feet, these brief moments of oblivion had lately become his only respite from the unending stream of bad news which occupied his waking hours.

There was a gentle knocking on the door and Canaris's adjutant, Lieutenant Wolke, entered the room. He was a young man, with a straight back, rosy cheeks and honest-looking eyes. He carried a print-out of a message just received from an informant behind the Russian lines.

The Admiral's dachshunds, which had also been taking a nap,

looked up from their cushioned chair and, recognising Wolke's familiar face, lowered their heads and went back to sleep.

Moving almost silently across the room, Wolke placed the message upon the Admiral's desk.

The Admiral breathed in deeply, then exhaled in a long, snuffling breath, but did not wake.

Wolke gritted his teeth. The Admiral did not like to be woken, but the message had been classified A3, which meant it was of the highest importance and required immediate attention. Which meant waking Canaris, whether he liked it or not.

Wolke cleared his throat.

Canaris's eyes slid open. He blinked uncomprehendingly at Wolke, as if he had never seen the man before.

'Admiral,' said Wolke, his voice barely above a whisper. 'An A3 has just come in.'

Slowly, Canaris sat forward, rubbing the sleep from his face, and picked up the piece of paper with one hand. At the same time, he reached out with his other hand, fetched his glasses and perched them upon his long and dignified nose.

The message contained an intercepted Soviet radio transmission indicating that Colonel Andrich had been killed in a shoot-out with Soviet partisans.

'Good,' muttered Canaris. 'They have taken the bait.' It was exactly what he had been hoping for.

But the second half of the message was not.

It went on to say that Commander Yakushkin, of the NKVD's motorised rifle battalion, currently stationed in Rovno, had also been found dead. It gave no details about where Yakushkin died or who had killed him or what the circumstances had been. Canaris cursed under his breath.

'Is everything all right, Admiral?' asked Wolke.

'No,' replied Canaris. 'No, it is not.' But he did not explain further, and Wolke knew better than to ask. 'Has there been any word from Vasko?'

'No news yet, Admiral.'

Canaris let the telegram slip from his fingers. 'As soon as he returns to Berlin, have him sent straight to my office.'

'Yes, Admiral.'

'And Wolke . . .'

'Yes, Admiral?'

'In the event that Vasko does not appear, type up a report placing the blame upon Otto Skorzeny.'

Wolke nodded. '*Zu Befehl*, Herr Admiral.'

*

Having carried out the liquidation of Colonel Andrich, Vasko spent the rest of that day, as well as the following day, lying low in the ruins of an abandoned house not far from the hospital where Major Kirov was being treated for his gunshot wound.

By doing so, he was directly disobeying the orders of Admiral Canaris to immediately transmit the message that his task had been carried out, after which Skorzeny would dispatch a guide to escort him back across the lines.

He guessed that, by now, word of the colonel's murder might already have reached Berlin. If so, Skorzeny would be waiting for the signal.

But the news that Pekkala was alive had thrown Vasko's mind into confusion. When that gawky Commissar had stumbled down into the bunker, calling out Pekkala's name like some fragment of an ancient spell, Vasko heard again his mother's voice, assuring him and his sister that their father would soon be back where he belonged, thanks to the work of the incorruptible Inspector. 'Our prayers have been answered,' she assured them and, for a while, at least, the young Vasko had believed this fairy tale.

It wasn't until his mother's arrest on the charge of possessing foreign currency that Vasko realised Pekkala had betrayed them. But only when the judge at the People's Tribunal read out the length of their sentences, to be served in the Gulag at Kolyma, did Vasko understand the magnitude of this treachery.

Weeks later, when their ship ran aground on the shoals of Tetsumu, and Vasko had remained alive in the freezing darkness of that flooded compartment by clinging to the grotesque heap of drowned bodies, he swore that if he ever made it out of there he would consecrate his life to avenging the deaths of his family.

By 1941, under the personal guidance of Admiral Canaris, Vasko had become an agent of the Abwehr. Late that same year, news reached him that Pekkala had been killed not far from the Tsar's summer estate at Tsarskoye Selo. At the time, Vasko did not know whether to feel satisfaction that the Emerald Eye was dead or disappointment that he had not been responsible for it.

But when he learned that Pekkala had somehow cheated death, Vasko knew at once what he must do, even if it meant disobeying Canaris.

This was the reason why Vasko had not executed Commissar Kirov that night in the bunker. He reasoned that, once Pekkala learned of Major Kirov's injuries, the Inspector would visit him at the hospital. All that Vasko had to do was wait until Pekkala made contact with the major, then finish them both off together.

That first night, from his hiding place among the ruins, Vasko kept watch on the front door of the hospital, waiting for the moment when Pekkala would arrive. But after waiting for almost two days, and with no sign of the Inspector, Vasko knew he had to act or risk losing his chance to kill Pekkala. He waited until the middle of the night, then made his way into the hospital, determined either to extract the Inspector's whereabouts from the major or, if Kirov didn't know, to kidnap the wounded man and thereby, he hoped, to draw Pekkala out into the open.

When Vasko learned from Captain Dombrowsky that the major had already gone, he pursued the only lead he had left, which brought him to the nurse's house. There, Vasko stumbled across Commander Yakushkin and his bodyguard. The killing of Yakushkin, although it must have seemed a calculated attack to those who found his body, was no more than a collateral necessity. Vasko's real target that night had been the nurse, from whom he hoped to learn the major's location, but Yakushkin, mistaking Vasko's presence for that of a rival, had foiled his plan with a bullet through the woman's heart.

After leaving the apartment, Vasko had returned to the ruined house where he had hidden for the past two days. Knowing that even in the uniform of a Red Army officer, his solitary presence at that time of night would attract unwanted attention, Vasko decided to wait until first light before returning to the cabin, which was some distance outside the town. Once there, he would enlist Malashenko's help in tracking down Pekkala.

Shortly before dawn, a group of partisans arrived in a battered truck and entered the house where Yakushkin and the nurse had been killed. When Vasko recognised Malashenko among them, he knew that this must be the famous Barabanschikov Atrad. They departed soon afterwards, leaving Malashenko behind to guard the place.

While Vasko was debating whether to leave cover and approach Malashenko, to see if the partisan knew anything of Kirov's whereabouts, the Barabanschikovs returned.

Vasko was astonished to see Major Kirov climb down from the truck, along with a tall man in civilian clothes. The moment Vasko realised he was looking at Pekkala, he felt his whole body go numb. His first thought was to open fire immediately and keep shooting until he ran out of bullets, in the hopes that a lucky shot might bring down the Inspector. It took all his self-control not to squander the only chance he knew he was likely to get. With a truckload of partisans between him and the Inspector, and only a pistol for a weapon, especially one loaded with bullets which were only accurate at close range, Vasko knew that he would never make the shot before the partisans gunned him down.

At the same time, Vasko realised that since Pekkala was now investigating the murder of Commander Yakushkin, it was only a matter of time before the Inspector tracked him down.

Vasko knew his best, perhaps his only, hope, was to let Pekkala do precisely that. Only in this way, thought Vasko, can I lure him to a place of my own choosing, where his death will not come at the cost of my own life.

For now, though, his primary concern was to leave this hiding place where, if discovered, it was clear he wouldn't stand a chance. Vasko decided to make for the cabin in the woods; the only place he could think of where he might be safe.

No sooner had the Barabanschikovs left, however, than Red Army soldiers arrived and began patrolling the streets, obviously looking for whoever had murdered their commander.

The Red Army continued its patrols until just after sunset, by which time Vasko was cold, exhausted and hungry.

Just as he was preparing to move out, gangs of partisans appeared and began going door to door, intent on capturing whoever had murdered their leaders in the bunker the night before.

Vasko was trapped in the ruins, as a routine quickly established itself whereby the Red Army controlled the streets by day and the partisans took over after dark. By the morning of the second day, he had eaten his way through the small tin of emergency rations he always carried with him on missions. The rations came in a small, oval tin and consisted of chocolate heavily laced with caffeine, which offered him little more than an upset stomach and a case of jangling nerves.

Vasko knew that time was running out. Pekkala was still out there somewhere, and Skorzeny would not wait forever.

Vasko decided that, if the situation had not changed by the following morning, he would walk out in the daylight, hoping that the green metal lozenges on his collar tabs, denoting the rank of captain, might buy him at least a moment's hesitation from any Red Army patrol which crossed his path. A moment would be all that he needed. As for trying to slip past the partisans, Vasko did not think much of his chances.

That night, wild dogs howled among the ruins. Vasko heard their snarling as they feasted on the dead. With frozen fingers locked around the gun, Vasko curled up in a ball beneath a sheet of corrugated iron. Sleet and rain pelted down upon him, the sound of it amplified against the rusted metal. That night, over the muttering of the wind, Vasko picked up fragments of voices and the noise of babies crying. Once, he caught the sound of balalaika music.

At last, when the dawn began to glimmer in the sky, Vasko was preparing to leave cover when a gunfight erupted between a crew of partisans returning to their base and a Red Army squad just heading out on patrol. From his hiding place, Vasko witnessed the battle. Some of the stray shots even slammed into the woodwork above his head. The Red Army soldiers pulled back, bringing their wounded with them as they headed for the safety of their headquarters, which had been fortified with barbed wire and sandbags. The partisans carried away two of their men who had been killed in the skirmish, and faded back into the darkness. In a matter of minutes, the streets were empty and quiet. But Vasko knew it might not stay that way for long. Both sides would almost certainly return with reinforcements. Taking advantage of the lull, he slipped away and was soon beyond the outskirts of the town.

*

'I've searched the whole place,' said Kirov, as he trampled down the rickety stairs of the safe house. 'There's no sign of Malashenko anywhere.'

'He should have been here by now,' muttered Pekkala, as he walked over to a window and peered out through a crack in the shutters.

'So much for our bodyguard,' grunted Kirov as he sat down in one of several mismatched chairs, tilted back and set his heels up on the table. 'I'd gladly trade him for a plate of blinis.'

'Blinis,' Pekkala echoed thoughtfully.

'With sour cream and caviar,' continued Kirov, locking his hands behind his head, 'and chopped red onion and a glass of cold vodka.'

Pekkala stared at the ceiling with a distant look in his eyes. 'I can't even recall the last time I had a good meal.'

'We'll soon put that right,' Kirov assured him. 'Once we get back to Moscow, we can return to our ritual of Friday afternoon meals, at which, with your permission, Elizaveta will become a permanent guest.' The major smiled happily, his thoughts returning to their cosy little office, with its temperamental stove and wheezy samovar and the comfortable chair which they had salvaged off the street. 'What do you say to that, Inspector?'

But there was no reply. Pekkala remained by the window, staring out into the street. Snow had begun to fall again. Fat, wet flakes slid down the weathered old shutters.

There was something about the way he stood; sombre and alone, which made Kirov realise that the fears he had secretly been harbouring ever since he'd found Pekkala might come true after all. 'You're not coming back to Moscow, are you?' he asked.

*

'Skorzeny, you idiot!' Seated at his desk, in a high-ceilinged office on Prinz Albrechtstrasse in Berlin, Heinrich Himmler, lord of the SS, roared out his disapproval. 'Why didn't you inform me about this mission?'

'I received a direct order from the Admiral not to share details of the mission with anyone. Anyone at all.' Skorzeny shifted uneasily, knowing that his excuse was unlikely to appease the Reichsführer.

'I am not "anyone"!' barked Himmler, fixing Skorzeny with his grey-blue eyes, which appeared strangely calm, in spite of his obvious rage. 'I am commander of the SS of which, as of today, at least, you're still a member!'

'And Canaris is an admiral,' replied Skorzeny, 'and his orders were perfectly clear.'

'If your orders were to tell no one,' Himmler leaned forward, placing his hands flat upon the desk, the thumbs side by side, in a way that reminded Skorzeny of the Sphinx, 'then why are you telling me now?'

'I believe that something may have gone wrong. Vasko was parachuted over the abandoned village of Misovichi, not far from the rendezvous point. There he was due to meet with a partisan named Malashenko, who has been working with the Abwehr's Secret Field Police. Vasko made a low-level jump over the target and his chute was seen to open properly. Twenty-four hours ago, a reconnaissance aircraft reported seeing smoke rising from the chimney of a cabin where the meeting was due to take place.'

'So far,' said Himmler, 'it sounds as if everything has gone according to plan.'

'Yes, Reichsführer,' replied Skorzeny. 'Up to that point, I had no reason for concern, but Vasko was supposed to have contacted us immediately upon completion of his mission, at which time we would dispatch another agent to guide him back through the lines.'

'Perhaps the answer is simply that he has not yet carried out his task.'

'That's just it, Reichsführer. He has.'

'How do you know?'

'We received confirmation from one of our informants in Rovno. The target, Colonel Andrich, has been eliminated. Vasko should have contacted us by now. I am afraid that his radio might have been damaged, leaving him unable to communicate, or even that he might have been captured.'

'And it has suddenly occurred to you,' said Himmler, 'that it might not reflect well upon on the SS if Canaris chose to blame us for Vasko's disappearance.'

Skorzeny nodded grimly.

Himmler removed his pince-nez glasses, the silver frames glittering in the light of his desk lamp. 'This agent who has been assigned to guide Vasko back to our lines? Is he one of theirs or one of ours?'

'He's ours,' Skorzeny assured him. 'It's Luther Benjamin.'

'A capable man.' Himmler nodded with approval. 'And where is Benjamin now?'

'He is currently travelling with soldiers who are engaged in an attempt to recapture Rovno from the enemy. As soon as we receive word from Vasko that his mission has been completed, we will relay a message to Vasko and . . .'

'There is to be no more waiting!' As Himmler spoke, he polished his glasses vigorously with a black silk handkerchief, even though they were already clean. 'Inform Benjamin that he is to proceed immediately to the rendezvous point. If Vasko is there, Benjamin will proceed with the original evacuation plan.'

'Yes, Reichsführer.' Then Skorzeny paused. 'And if Vasko isn't there?'

'Then Benjamin is to return immediately on his own, and Vasko will be abandoned to his fate, just like the pompous admiral who sent him on this suicidal errand.'

*

'I knew it!' shouted Kirov, swiping his heels off the table and jumping to his feet.

Pekkala turned away from the window and glanced at the major. 'Knew what?' he asked.

'That you're not coming back to Moscow! But why, Inspector? You have a life waiting for you there, as well as people who rely on you, not to mention friends, one of whom came all this way to find you!'

'You don't understand,' began Pekkala.

But Kirov hadn't finished yet. 'Why would you choose to remain among the partisans? Where are they, now that we need them? Where is Malashenko? Where is Barabanschikov? I'll tell you where they are! They've disappeared, because that's what they do best. And who knows where they've gone? Search for them now and all you'll find are their abandoned forest hideaways. Is that where you're going? Is that where you plan to spend your life, in the company of ghosts?'

'Kirov!' shouted Pekkala.

Startled, the major fell silent.

'Be still,' Pekkala told him, 'and I will explain everything.'

Bewildered, Kirov slumped back into his chair. 'Very well,' he said. 'I owe you that much, I suppose.'

As Pekkala began to speak, he felt a part of himself pull free from the heavy shackling of his bones and vanish into the past, like smoke coiled by the wind into the sky.

*

Deep in the Red Forest, not far from the Barabanschikov camp, was a lake called the Wolf's Crossing. At first, the name made no sense to Pekkala. Only with the arrival of winter did he finally grasp its meaning, as packs of yellow-eyed wolves would lope across its frozen surface, bound on journeys whose purpose seemed a mystery even to the beasts who had embarked upon it.

Sometimes, Pekkala went out there alone to fish. The water in the lake was brown like tea from all the tannins in the pines which grew down to its banks, and contained perch and trout and even some landlocked salmon. Using an axe, Pekkala chopped several holes into the ice, then fed a line into each one. Straddling the holes was a cross-shaped contraption made from twigs bound together with dried grass. When a fish pulled on the line, the cross would tilt upwards and Pekkala would know he had a bite.

But he had to be patient. Hour after hour, he would stand bent-backed like an old hag, wrapped in the shreds of an old army blanket, shuffling his feet to stay warm, his only company the whirlwinds of glittering snow dust, spiralling like dancers across this frozen desert.

Sometimes the reward was hardly worth the effort, but on rare occasions when the lake yielded more fish than the partisans could eat, the extras would be dried over a smouldering birch-wood fire, the two halves of their bodies split like wings, and packed away in a storehouse he had built, raised above the ground on stilts to keep away the mice in wintertime.

Stray leaves, dry and curled, blew out into the lake. There, warmed by the sun, they melted their perfect forms into the ice, as if to remind him that spring would come again, in those times when it seemed as if winter would never end.

It was out of this wilderness, on the coldest day he'd ever known, with sunlight blinding off the snow and a fierce blue sky, the colour of a Bunsen burner flame, that a man appeared who would change Pekkala's life forever.

He had been gathering the fish he'd caught that day – one speckle-backed trout and three perch – when he glimpsed a figure in the distance, heading directly towards him.

Pekkala did not run, or reach for the gun in his coat. There was something about the forlornness of this creature which made him more curious than afraid.

Silhouetted against the blinding snow, the figure seemed to change its shape, separating from itself and merging together again, like a drop of dirty oil in water.

Only when the man was almost upon him could Pekkala clearly distinguish the tall, dishevelled man, clothed in a tattered coat, whose torn hem dragged through the snow. Rags bound his feet instead of shoes. He carried no weapon, or any equipment at all. Covering his face was a sheet of white birch bark which had slits cut into it – a primitive but effective measure against the glare of snow which would otherwise have blinded him. With the scarf about his face and eyes hidden behind this paper scroll, his human shape seemed almost accidental.

For a moment, the man stood in front of Pekkala. Then he tore away his mask, revealing a face so creased with dirt and worry that it seemed no more alive than the bark which had concealed it. He dropped to his knees, snatched up a perch and, ignoring dorsal spines which punctured his fingertips like a fan of hypodermic needles, he tore into the meat.

When nothing remained in his hands but a fragment of the tail, the man finally looked up at Pekkala. 'The last man I expected to find out here,' he said, 'was the Emerald Eye himself.'

'How do you know me?' asked Pekkala.

The man offered no words of explanation. Instead, he simply removed his cap, grasping it from behind and tilting it forward off his head in the manner of the old Tsarist soldiers, and it was in this movement that Pekkala finally recognised the man, whom he had last seen in a clearing on the Polish border, just weeks before the outbreak of the war. His name was Maximov. A cavalry officer before the Revolution, Maximov had become the driver and bodyguard of Colonel Nagorski, the secretive designer of the Red Army's T34 tank. Known to those who operated the 20-ton machine as the Red Coffin, this tank had been one of the few weapons in the Soviet arsenal which outgunned its German counterparts. While other Russian tanks proved to be no match for German armour, the T34 had held its own against all but the largest enemy weapons. In the winter of 1941, with the German army within sight of Moscow, the T34 had kept running when the temperature dipped below minus-60, thanks to the low-viscosity oil used in its engine, while the cold transformed the German panzers into useless hulks of iron.

Nagorski did not live long enough to see his great invention put to use. He was found shot to death in the muddy swamp which served as a testing ground for his machines.

It was during the investigation of Nagorski's murder that Pekkala first came in contact with Maximov. For a while, it had seemed as if Maximov himself might be the killer, but Pekkala's investigation eventually disclosed that Nagorski's own son had fired the shot that ended his father's life. Maximov had gone on to assist Pekkala and Kirov in tracking down a missing T34 prototype. Their search led them to the German-Polish border, where Alexander Kropotkin, an old acquaintance of Pekkala's and a bitter enemy of Stalin, was attempting to stage an attack on German troops stationed nearby. With this suicidal move, Kropotkin was less interested in killing the enemy than in providing Hitler with an excuse to invade the Soviet Union. In those days, he was by no means alone in thinking that only with the destruction of the Red Army could Stalin be removed from power and that even Nazi occupation was better than continuing to live under the boot of the Communist Party.

Having located the missing tank, Kirov had disabled the machine using an anti-tank rifle equipped with experimental titanium bullets. The T34 was destroyed, and Kropotkin died in a blaze which engulfed the crew compartment. But when the fire had died down enough for Pekkala and Kirov to approach the wreck, they discovered that Maximov had disappeared. Upon their return to Moscow, Kirov wrote in his report that Maximov had been killed in the shoot-out and his body consumed in the inferno of the burning tank. Although Pekkala said nothing to contradict this, privately he had always suspected that Maximov might have survived after all.

The reason Pekkala kept these thoughts to himself was that, although Maximov had so far been able to conceal his former career as a Tsarist officer, the truth would undoubtedly have surfaced now that Maximov had been drawn into the spotlight of this investigation. Far from being the recipient of a medal for his heroism, it was more likely that Maximov would be arrested for his past deeds in the service of the Tsar. For Maximov, the future would have led only to the Gulag, which was why Pekkala turned a blind eye to a missing motorcycle that he had spotted near the tanks before the battle, and the faint but unmistakable impression of tyre tracks leading away through the forest.

Pekkala had never known where Maximov disappeared to that day, nor had he expected to set eyes on him again, since both men knew that to be seen back in Russia was a virtual guarantee of death.

And yet here he was: filthy, starving and alone.

'You had better come with me,' said Pekkala.

Together, the two men set out across the ice towards the dark wall of the forest.

A short time later, they had entered the outskirts of the camp. Small fires burned outside the primitive shelters, known as *zemly-ankas*, where the partisans lived. The cold air smelled of pine-wood smoke and roasting meat.

Pekkala brought Maximov to the fire in the centre of the camp, where he knew Barabanschikov would be.

'Where did you find him?' asked Barabanschikov.

'Out on the ice,' replied Pekkala, and he went on to tell the story of his acquaintance with Maximov, from Nagorski's murder right up until the day he disappeared.

By the time Pekkala had finished, most of the camp had gathered by the fire to listen.

Barabanschikov listened intently, sitting on a tree stump, arms folded and leaning forward so as to catch every word. 'Well, Maximov,' he said when Pekkala had finished, 'I think it's time you told us where you've been since you and the Inspector parted company.'

Maximov explained how he had travelled all the way to the French coast before selling his motorcycle and using the proceeds to purchase a ticket to America. Three weeks later, he had arrived at Ellis Island and from there made his way to New York City.

He had worked in several jobs – as doorman at the Algonquin Hotel, as a longshoreman in Hoboken and as a croupier in an Atlantic City casino before settling down as a chauffeur for the mayor of that town, a profession not unlike the one in which he had been working when circumstances forced him out of Russia.

'What happened?' demanded Barabanschikov. 'Did you commit a crime and have to leave?'

Maximov shook his head. 'There was no crime.'

'Problems with a woman, perhaps? A broken heart can send a man to the other end of the earth.'

Maximov smiled. 'No broken heart.'

Barabanschikov shook his head in confusion. 'Yet here you are. But why?'

'I couldn't just stand by and watch this country get destroyed,' answered Maximov, staring at the faces which peered back at him from the shadows, their dark eyes wide with curiosity.

A murmur of approval rose from the gathered listeners.

'Then, for as long as you wish, Maximov, you are welcome here with us,' announced the partisan leader. 'But first you must do what every stranger does when they come into my camp.'

'And what is that?'

'Empty your pockets!'

Maximov did as he was told, laying out his meagre possessions on the trampled ground.

Only one thing caught Barabanschikov's attention. It was a little clockwork mouse, with a dented metal shell, a key sticking out of its side and three tiny wheels underneath.

Barabanschikov snapped his fingers at the toy. 'Give me that.'

Maximov handed him the mouse.

'You brought this from America?'

'I did.'

'Think of all the things you could have carried with you from America,' Barabanschikov remarked incredulously. 'A Colt revolver perhaps, or a Bowie knife, or a Hamilton pocket watch. But no. You have brought a clockwork mouse. What is it? A present for somebody?'

'It is,' admitted Maximov.

With a grunt of curiosity, Barabanschikov tried to wind it up, listening to the click of the cogs as if he were a safe cracker gauging the tumblers of the lock. But, having done this, he found that the wheels wouldn't turn. 'It's broken! What kind of present is that?' With a growl of disgust, Barabanschikov tossed the mouse over his shoulder into the dark.

'Will that be all?' asked Maximov.

'Yes,' Barabanschikov replied gruffly. 'Now go and get some food and then we'll find you a place where you can sleep.'

'You are a soft touch,' said Pekkala, after Maximov had been led away to eat.

In spite of Barabanschikov's bluster, Pekkala had never known him to turn anyone away.

Barabanschikov's reply to this was a long and wordless growl.

'Perhaps this will cheer you up,' said Pekkala as he handed over the trout he had caught that afternoon.

'Ah!' Barabanschikov took the fish in his outstretched hands. 'Is there anything finer in the world?'

On the way back to his hut, which was a circular lean-to fashioned out of branches interwoven with vines, which the partisans referred to as a *tchoom*, Pekkala retrieved the broken clockwork mouse and put it in his pocket. The next morning, he returned the toy to Maximov.

By then, Maximov had bathed. His face was clean and he wore a different set of clothes. He took the mouse in his hand as if it was a living thing and slipped it into his pocket.

For several weeks, Maximov remained at the camp and it was during this time that Pekkala explained how he had come to be living among the Barabanschikovs. He found it easy to speak with Maximov. Even though the two men did not know each other well, the experiences they had shared in their days of service to the Tsar gave them a common outlook on the world. This strange communion with the past brought to their conversations a familiarity which would otherwise have taken years to cultivate.

'I am only passing through,' Pekkala explained to Maximov. 'There is someone I must search for.'

'Who?' asked Maximov.

'A woman to whom I was engaged,' replied Pekkala. 'She left for Paris, just before the Revolution. I was supposed to meet her there. It had all been arranged. But by the time the Tsar gave me permission to leave, the borders were already closing. I was arrested by Revolutionary Guards as I attempted to pass through into Finland. From there, they sent me to prison. And after that, the Gulag at Borodok.'

'Does she even know you are alive?' asked Maximov.

'That is only one of many questions I must answer,' replied Pekkala, 'which is why, as soon as the snow melts, I will turn my back on Russia once and for all.'

'Then you and I are bound in opposite directions, Inspector.'

'It seems that way,' agreed Pekkala.

Winter was ending. The snow began to melt. Often they were startled by the gunshot echo of ice cracking out on the lake. The time of the Rasputitsa was coming. Soon everything would turn to mud.

One morning, the camp awoke to find that Maximov had gone. There had been no warning. No goodbyes. He had simply disappeared.

Troubled by the man's sudden departure, Pekkala tracked his

movements through the half-melted snow to the edge of the lake, where Maximov's footprints set out across the ice. There Pekkala stopped, knowing it was suicide to continue.

The surface was rotten and unstable. No one who knew anything about the conditions at this time of year would ever have set foot upon it, for fear of falling through into the freezing water beneath. And once beneath the ice, it was almost impossible to find your way back to the surface. Even if you could, it was extremely difficult to climb from the water and make your way from there to firmer ground.

Pekkala scanned the horizon, hoping for a glimpse of Maximov, but there was nothing. He knew that, even if this former soldier of the Tsar survived the crossing of the lake, the chances of him living through this war, with enemies on either side, were slim to none.

But maybe, thought Pekkala, those odds mean nothing to him.

In Siberia, Pekkala had seen men fall into a dream that blinded them to their true limitations, until both the wilderness and the freedom that lay beyond it became more symbol than reality. Out on those ragged edges of the planet, the false promise of how far a person could go upon the power of his dreams alone inevitably proved to be fatal.

Standing at the edge of that lake, Pekkala wondered whether Maximov's dreams had led him to his death. He doubted if he'd ever know.

Returning to his cabin, Pekkala discovered Maximov's clockwork mouse resting on a log which jutted from the wall of the hut. It had been left there as a gift.

Pekkala brought the little toy inside the hut, determined to restore it to working condition if he could. By the light of a lamp made from deer fat floating in an old tin can, with a scrap of old shoelace for a wick, he carefully removed the outer shell. It was only then that he realised why the mechanism had been jammed. Placed inside the humped back of the mouse was a diamond as large as a pea, beautifully cut into an octagon. As soon as he removed it from the toy, the tiny wheels began to buzz and spin and the key in the side of the mouse revolved, moving slower and slower, until it finally clattered to a stop. Pekkala held the diamond in his palm, tilting his hand one way and then another, studying the way each facet caught the lamplight. Then he wrapped it up in a dirty handkerchief and tucked it in his pocket.

'The beast has come to keep me company!' cried Barabanschikov, when he caught sight of Pekkala later that morning. The partisan leader was sitting on a tree stump beside the smouldering remains of the previous night's fire.

Pekkala sat down beside his friend.

Barabanschikov picked up a stick and stirred it in the grey dust, turfing up embers still glowing like fragments of amber. 'He's gone, hasn't he?'

'Yes,' replied Pekkala.

'And soon you, too, will be leaving on your journey to the west,' said Barabanschikov. 'I have not forgotten our agreement.'

'I might not be leaving, after all,' said Pekkala.

The stick froze in Barabanschikov's hand. Slivers of smoke rose from the blackened wood. 'I thought that your mind was made up.'

'It was until Maximov appeared.'

'What did he say to talk you out of it?'

'It's not what he said,' answered Pekkala. 'It's what he is doing that convinced me. He left behind everything that was safe to come back here, even though the only thanks he is likely to get is to be killed by the very people he has come to help.'

'You've been on that same journey all your life,' said Baraban-schikov.

'There were times,' admitted Pekkala, 'when I thought that journey would end here in these woods.'

Barabanschikov slapped him gently on the back. 'We have managed to survive so far, haven't we? I am no longer afraid of death, Pekkala, only of squandering the memory of every good thing I have achieved in this life by burying it beneath terrible deeds that I have done to stay alive.'

'You have saved more lives than just your own,' Pekkala told him.

'And will it be enough?' asked Barabanschikov.

'There is no judgement that an honest man should fear,' Pekkala told him.

'That is an easy thing to say, Inspector, but how can an honest man live in a country whose leaders are not?'

'The answer,' replied Pekkala, 'is to tread softly, to stay alive and to do whatever good you can along the way.'

'No matter what happens from now on,' said Barabanschikov, 'let us promise to live by those words.'

*

'I made that promise to him,' said Pekkala, as the memory of that day faded back into the darkness of his mind.

'So you *are* coming back to Moscow?' stammered Kirov.

'Yes,' replied Pekkala, 'and I would have told you so earlier if you'd given me the chance.'

'But that is excellent news!' In a moment, Kirov was back on his feet. He slapped Pekkala on the back, raising a haze of dust from the soot-powdered wool of the Inspector's coat.

Their conversation was interrupted by the tearing sound of heavy machine guns followed, soon afterwards, by the roar and clank of armoured vehicles.

'Could those be ours?' asked Kirov.

Pekkala shook his head. 'There is no Soviet armour in Rovno.'

'So the enemy has broken through.'

'Yes,' agreed Pekkala, 'which means we need to find a place to hide, if it isn't already too late.'

*

Luther Benjamin moved cautiously through the woods, passing through the deserted town of Misovichi on his way to the rendezvous site. He had set out before sunrise that morning, hiking south to clear the combat zone before turning east and crossing into enemy territory. Although he had met with no difficulties so far, Benjamin had been warned by Skorzeny that the cabin was difficult to spot and he was worried that he might miss it altogether in this wilderness. If it had been anyone other than Vasko, Benjamin might have considered turning back before travelling any further.

But Vasko was a friend.

He and Benjamin had gone through training together at the School of Special Weapons and Tactics, located in the Berlin suburb of Zossen, before Benjamin was transferred to the SS, while Vasko was chosen for service in the Abwehr. Of the fourteen men and women in that class, he and Vasko were the only ones still living.

In the case of Luther Benjamin, that was due to nothing more than luck. He had just returned from three months' recuperation after being injured in a gunfight after his cover was blown in Zagreb and he barely escaped with his life. Although Benjamin had made a full physical recovery, according to the medical report, his mental state was such that the doctor recommended he not be sent on any further missions.

Recalled to duty in Berlin, Benjamin had expected that his tasks would, from then on, be no more arduous than filing reports, but when Skorzeny came to him and explained the mission, Benjamin knew that he couldn't refuse.

Skorzeny had his doubts as to whether Benjamin was fit for active duty, but he had orders from Canaris to act immediately. Given that Benjamin was the only agent available at the time, it was only a matter of hours before Vasko's old friend was on his way.

Since then, Benjamin had been travelling with advance units of the 27th SS Grenadier Division 'Langemarck', which had been tasked with recapturing Rovno. The Division was made up mostly of Flemish volunteers, whose language, unintelligible to Benjamin, sounded to him like men trying to speak with pebbles in their mouths.

Benjamin did not know how long it would take Vasko to carry out his mission, so he was not unduly alarmed as the days passed with still no message from Skorzeny.

When the signal eventually came through, ordering him to proceed, the Flemish Grenadiers were still heavily engaged west of Rovno and it was unclear whether the hoped-for breakthrough would come about. At the time Benjamin set out, the Langemarck Division was at a standstill outside the village of Yaseneviche, still some distance from its intended destination.

When Benjamin read that he was to return alone if Vasko was not at the meeting place, he suspected that something must have gone wrong, but he had no choice except to go through with the mission.

In spite of the dangerous situation, Benjamin succeeded in making his way through the lines, carefully noting the territory as he moved along, in preparation for his return journey.

Benjamin had been on the point of giving up when he finally spotted the cabin, almost hidden among the trees. Pausing a short distance from the structure, he unbuckled his rucksack, which contained ammunition, a radio and medical supplies in the event that Vasko might be wounded. Benjamin hid the rucksack in a hollow in the ground, where a tree had been uprooted long ago, then drew his sidearm, a Walther P38, and advanced towards the cabin.

Cautiously, he peered in at the window. In the gloomy light of the interior, he could see a table in the centre of the room and a bunk in the corner. A blanket crumpled on the bunk was the only sign he could detect that the cabin might be occupied.

Benjamin crept around to the back and tried the door. It was unlocked and swung open with a creak. He could smell the smoke of a recently extinguished fire. Standing to one side, he whispered Vasko's name into the gloom.

There was no reply.

Benjamin could feel the stillness of the place, as much as he could see it with his eyes. Slowly, he stepped into the cabin, his gun held out. A single glance told him that the place was no longer occupied, although it was clear that someone had been here recently. Lying on the table were a few dried pieces of black Russian army bread, as well as a Soviet military canteen in its primitive cloth cover.

As Benjamin inspected the contents of the room, he discovered a small radio of the type issued to German field agents, hidden under a tarpaulin. Then he knew he had found the right place. Although his orders were to return immediately if Vasko was not at the rendezvous point, the presence of the radio was a clear indication that Vasko had been there. Faced with the thought of abandoning his friend, Benjamin decided to wait a while and see if Vasko showed up.

Benjamin sat down at the table, picked up a piece of the Russian bread and gnawed off a mouthful. After chewing for a couple of seconds, he spat it out on to the floor, wondering how humans could subsist on food like that. Then he reached for the canteen, intending to wash out his mouth. He was just about to unscrew the cap when he felt something underneath the canteen cover which made him pause. It might just have been a twig that had worked its way between the metal and the cloth, but something about it made Benjamin uneasy. Gently he shook the canteen. Water splashed about inside. Then he undid the single metal button which held the cloth cover in place and removed the canteen. As he held up the metal flask, he spotted what he had originally mistaken for a twig. It was a thin copper wire, soldered to the base of the canteen and running all the way up to the cap. The wire had been taped to the metal with black electric tape.

Benjamin held his breath. With acid slithering in his guts, he carefully replaced the canteen on the table.

He recalled the moment in his training when he and the other agents had been shown various items of sabotage which they might one day be required to use. There were pieces of plastic explosives, shaped and painted to look like coal, which could be thrown into the tenders of trains and would detonate when shovelled into the engine. There were hollowed-out books with spring triggers fitted into the covers which, when opened, would detonate enough explosives to blow the roof off a house. There was even a slab of explosives designed to look like a chocolate bar. The explosives had been covered in real chocolate and wrapped in paper with the brand name 'Peters' on the outside. If a piece of the chocolate was snapped off, it would trip a detonator located inside the bar. And there were canteens, just like the one before him. Explosives were packed into the lower section, with a thin metal panel fitted into the upper section to allow it to hold water. The two pieces were then soldered back together and a copper wire strung between the cap and a detonator lodged inside the lower portion. The suspicions of any soldier would be set aside when he heard the water in the canteen, but unscrewing the cap would trigger the bomb in his hands.

Benjamin sat back and stared at the canteen which, he now realised, Vasko must have brought with him from Berlin when he first set out on the mission. 'You bastard,' he whispered, closing his fists to stop his fingers from trembling.

Outside, it began to rain. Benjamin listened to the rustle of droplets coming down through the trees. A moment later, it was pouring.

Steering his mind back on course, he remembered that his first task once he reached the rendezvous point was to establish contact with Abwehr in Berlin. Rather than get soaked retrieving his backpack, Benjamin picked Vasko's radio set off the floor and brought it to the table, where he set it down and checked that the battery was charged. He set the small Morse code pad in front of him and turned on the radio, which came to life with a faint hum.

Then he plugged the earpiece into the machine. After entering his identification code as a prefix to the message, he typed out: *Expect contact shortly. Will advise.*

Benjamin finished the transmission with a secondary authentication code. Then he picked up the earpiece. As he had learned in his training, he did not press it directly against his ear but rather against his temple. The signal, when it came in, was often marred by interference so that the individual key strokes sometimes appeared to merge together unintelligibly. Pressing the earpiece against his temple allowed him to isolate the message from the interference.

Benjamin did not have long to wait. Through the veil of static, he picked up the shrill notes of the Morse code reply. It was only one word: *Understood.*

Benjamin wondered if it was Skorzeny himself on the other end. He imagined the giant, safe in the radio room on the second floor of SS Headquarters in Berlin. He wished he was there now. It won't be long, Benjamin thought to himself. If those Flemish soldiers break through to Rovno, Vasko and I can ride back to Berlin in comfort, instead of slogging our way out through the forest. And then maybe they will give us both a desk job for the rest of this damned war.

The thought of that cheered him up. Smiling, Benjamin leaned forward and turned off the radio. Curious, he thought, as he heard not one click but two.

*

Just before sunrise that morning, a wild dog had picked up the scent of a man moving through the woods east of the village of

Misovichi. Most wild animals would have steered clear of a human, but this dog had not always been wild.

It had once belonged to a farmer named Wolsky, who raised goats and sheep and some pigs, whose wool and meat his family had sold at the market square in Tynno for generations.

Wolsky had named the dog Choma, after a local man who once cheated him in a business deal. He would bring the dog to the market place and make the dog catch scraps of meat and bone for the amusement of his customers, and all the while the farmer would call out the name of Choma, scratching his ears and slapping the dog's shaggy fur.

One day back in the summer of 1941, not long after the invasion had taken place, a truck filled with Ukrainian Nationalist partisans rolled into Wolsky's farmyard. Among the partisans was Choma, the man who had once cheated Wolsky, and who had heard about the naming of the dog.

When Wolsky came out of his house to see what was going on, Choma shot him in the chest and left him lying face-down in the mud. Then he went looking for the dog, intent on killing it as well.

Choma found the dog asleep beside the barn. His first shot missed, gouging a fist-sized chunk of wood from the wooden boards above the dog's head. By the time Choma had steadied his hand to take a second shot, the dog had already vanished.

It had been living in the woods ever since. In that time, the dog had forgotten its name, and almost everything about its former life, until the day it picked up the man's scent. More out of curiosity than hunger, it followed the stranger, keeping always at a safe distance, until they arrived at the cabin.

The man went inside the building.

The dog hung back among the trees, sniffing the air for some clue as to what might be happening.

A short while later, the dog heard the muffled thump of an explosion inside the cabin. In a flash of light, the glass window sprayed out of its frame as if it had transformed into water. This was followed by a wave of concussion which sent the dog skittering away, but it soon doubled back, sniffing at the shards of glass which littered the ground, until it came upon the arm of a man, smouldering and severed at the elbow. It remembered the way the old farmer used to throw it pieces of food and how the other people used to clap and cheer when it leaped into the air to catch the scrap of meat. For a second, he remembered his name.

Then the dog picked up the arm and carried it away, deep into the perpetual twilight of the forest.

*

Outside the safe house, the sound of armoured vehicles was growing louder.

'We must get back to the garrison,' said Kirov. 'It's the only fortified location in town. If we run flat out, we can be there in five minutes.'

Pekkala paused to check that his Webley revolver was loaded. He had forgotten to test-fire the weapon and now it was too late. He would just have to hope that Lazarev had worked one of the miracles for which he was already famous, or else this weapon might blow up in his hands the second he pulled the trigger.

Suddenly, the sound of an approaching vehicle filled the air. The floorboards shuddered beneath their feet. Seconds later, a German half-track rumbled past.

The half-track was followed by a squad of infantry. Some were members of the Flemish SS, identifiable by the three-branched swastika 'trifos' on their collar tabs, a yellow shield emblazoned with a black lion on their left forearms and, just beneath it, a black and white cuff title with the word 'Langemarck' etched out in silver thread. These were the troops which had been given the task of breaking through to Rovno, although by the time the skeletal rooftops of the town at last came into view so few were left that they had now been reinforced by other soldiers pulled from decimated units in the area, turfed out of their beds at field hospitals or hauled off trains by members of the German Military Police, the Feldgendarmerie, as they made their way home on the only leave some of them had seen in more than three years. Among these Belgians walked men from Croatia, from Spain, from Norway and from Hungary, all of them communicating in some bastard Esperanto, cobbled from their native tongues and the snippets of German they had picked up in their service to the Reich.

With bayonets fixed upon their Mauser rifles, they moved at a slow trot to keep up with the machine. Their clothing was a threadbare collage of the battles they had seen. Some still wore the bottle-green collared tunics in which they had marched into Poland in the autumn of 1939. There were jackboots that had marched down the Champs-Elysées in the summer of 1940, and ankle boots looted from Dutch army warehouses, with laces made from scraps of radio wire and loose heel irons that jangled like spurs as they grazed over stones in the road. Slung from belts, some carried canvas bread bags bleached by the African sun out in the Sand Sea of Calanscio. Their sharply angled helmets hid beneath tattered strips of camouflage cut from old shelter capes, or covers fashioned out of rusty chicken wire, on which could still be seen the traces of white paint daubed upon them when their owners huddled freezing in the ruins of Borodino in the winter of '41.The faces of these men appeared primordial, their smoke-clogged pores and blistered lips like scraps of leather thrown out by a tanning yard. Their bodies were those of young men, but shrunk to bony scaffolding beneath the patched and filthy grey of Wehrmacht uniforms. Although the shape of them was human, in the hollow darkness of their eyes, and with frost-bitten ears worn down like chips of sea glass, they were no longer recognisable as men. They bore no resemblance to the postered images which had propelled them on this journey, whose only outcome, they now realised, would be annihilation. They were all that remained of their generation; restless husks of who they'd been before they went away, unknowable now to those they left behind and in the ice-filmed puddles where they glimpsed their sad reflections, unfamiliar even to themselves.

Somewhere up the street, just beyond Pekkala's field of view, the half-track came to a squeaking halt.

'There are more of them out back,' whispered Kirov. 'They're moving through the alleyways.'

At that moment, Pekkala spotted two soldiers walking directly towards the house. 'Go!' he whispered to Kirov.

The two men dashed across the room, slid down the ladder into the root cellar and closed the trap door on top of them, just as the front door blew open, splintered by a rifle butt.

The soldiers searched the house, floorboards groaning under the cautious tread of their hobnailed boots.

Huddled in the darkness, only a hand's breadth below, Kirov and Pekkala knew that it was only a matter of time before the soldiers discovered the narrow trench which led directly to the root cellar. And when they did, there would be no way out.

*

The first thing Vasko saw when he came in sight of the cabin was sunlight glinting off the shards of broken window. The door to the cabin was wide open, with one of its hinges torn off. Vasko realised immediately that one of the explosive devices with which he had booby trapped the cabin must have detonated.

Probably that fool Malashenko, he thought, nosing around to see what he could steal. I warned him not to touch things that didn't belong to him. But, to be certain, Vasko drew his gun and circled around through the trees, searching for any sign of movement as he approached the cabin door.

Picking a stone from the ground, he rolled it into the dark, knowing that anyone still alive inside would mistake it for a grenade. Then he waited, ready to shoot whoever came running out.

But there was no cry of surprise. No sound of footsteps or the chambering of weapons. Only the dull clatter of the rock as it skipped across the wooden floor.

Cautiously, Vasko stepped into the cabin, his gun held out and finger on the trigger.

The breath caught in his throat when he saw the carnage.

By the table, still sitting in the chair, which had tipped back against the wall, was a man without a head and missing one of his arms. The table itself had been broken almost in half, its surface cratered by a large scorch mark.

Vasko's first guess was that Malashenko had triggered the booby trap in the canteen, but then he saw the canteen lying on the other side of the room. It was dented and the metal blackened by smoke but it had definitely not exploded.

Then, looking up, Vasko spotted pieces of what he realised was his radio embedded in the ceiling. Immediately, he guessed that Malashenko had instead set off the explosive device installed in the radio. Vasko had done the rewiring himself, using the on switch as both on and off depending on which way he turned it and using the separate off switch as a trigger for the dynamite. To lose a radio when in the field was serious, but to have one fall into the hands of the enemy was a capital offence. Vasko was glad that he had taken precautions against losing the device, but it left him without a guide who knew his way around Rovno, as well as any means of communicating with Skorzeny. At least, he thought, I now have a reason for delaying my return to Berlin.

Knowing that this place might be his home for several days to come, Vasko set about cleaning up the mess. Underneath the bunk, he found the man's head, scorched and disfigured by the blast. He lifted it by the hair, so much heavier than he would have thought, and stared into its sightless eyes.

'Mother of God,' whispered Vasko, as he realised that it wasn't Malashenko after all.

The head fell from his grasp and landed with a heavy thud upon the cabin floor.

'It can't be,' he said to himself.

Praying that he might somehow be mistaken, Vasko stumbled over to the body in the chair. Fumbling with the shirt buttons, he reached under the blood-stiffened cloth and pulled out a flat oval disc made of dull grey zinc, still attached to the remains of a braided black and red cord which had once held the disc around the wearer's neck. It was a standard German military dog tag, which all personnel were required to carry in the field, no matter what uniforms they wore while undertaking operations. One side of the tag was marked SS–SD. The other side bore a cryptic combination of letters and numbers: 2/4 Hauptamt. Bln. The dog tag had been perforated down the middle and the markings repeated on both sides. In the event that the soldier was killed, one half of the oval would be snapped off for graves registration, the second half remaining with the body. The information stamped into the metal ensured that agents could identify themselves to regular German troops when they crossed back over the lines. He studied the inscription. The word 'Hauptamt' stood for 'headquarters' and 'Bln' was the abbreviation for Berlin. This was the department of the SS to which all field agents were officially assigned. No regular soldier attached to SS Headquarters in Berlin would have found himself out here, behind the lines and wearing civilian clothes. Now Vasko knew that there could be no doubt. The dead man was Luther Benjamin.

Before he left on the mission, Vasko had been informed by Skorzeny that Benjamin had been assigned to rendezvous with him as soon as the mission was completed. But no such signal had been sent. Vasko couldn't fathom why Benjamin would have set out anyway. That decision had cost the agent his life.

Vasko sat down on the bunk. He felt dizzy and sick, knowing what he had to do next. Abwehr protocol demanded that, in the event of an agent's death in the field, all evidence of him, his identity and his mission must be destroyed.

Vasko stood, his head still spinning, and reached for a lantern behind the bunk. It had escaped the blast and was still filled with paraffin. Vasko grasped the lamp and raised it above his head, ready to smash it on the floor and then, with a single match, burn the cabin to the ground. But in that moment an idea came to him which focused all the chaos in his mind. Gently, so as not to spill a drop of fuel, he replaced the lantern on the ground.

'Let him come,' he whispered to himself. 'Let Pekkala see what's left of Peter Vasko.'

*

Down in the musty-smelling cellar, Pekkala was wondering how many soldiers he could take with him before the rest of them riddled the place with bullets.

Then he heard a strange sound, somewhere in the distance, like a big door being slammed shut.

Above them, one of the soldiers swore.

A few seconds later, there was a rumble, like a train passing through the air above them, and the house shook with a nearby explosion.

Two more thuds were followed by detonations.

'What was that?' whispered Kirov, as the dirt floor trembled beneath their feet.

'Mortars,' answered Pekkala.

'Ours or theirs?'

'Either one will kill us if we don't get out of here,' replied Pekkala.

Upstairs, the soldiers had reached the same conclusion. They sprinted from the building as more explosions shook the house, followed by a thump of stones and bricks and clods of earth as they rained down over the garden.

A second later, there was a shriek, like metal claws upon a blackboard. Smoke and dust rolled beneath the canvas tarp that separated the basement from the trench outside.

The explosions came so quickly now, one after the other, that they merged into a constant roar. To Pekkala, it felt as if a herd of cattle was stampeding through his brain.

Then, just when it seemed that nothing could survive under this terrible rain, the mortar barrage ceased.

At first, Kirov could barely hear anything above the ringing in his ears but, a short while later, he picked up the sound of the half-track as it rolled back towards the west. Before long, it had faded into the distance. And then there was only the sound of wounded men, baying like dogs beside the smoking craters which would soon become their graves.

'What should we do now?' asked Kirov, his own voice reaching him as if muffled beneath layers of cotton wool.

'I think it might be best to run like hell,' replied Pekkala.

They climbed out through the trench and sprinted across the snow-clogged grass, heading for the safety of the garrison.

The two men had not gone far when they heard the sound of another engine, this one much smaller than the half-track, but headed straight towards them. Cautiously, Kirov peered around the corner of a building. 'It's Sergeant Zolkin!' Stepping out into the road, Kirov was almost run over by the newly repaired Jeep, which skidded to a stop in front of him.

'Quickly!' shouted Zolkin. 'We're expecting a counter-attack any minute.'

They piled in and Zolkin wheeled the Jeep around. Crashing through the gears as he raced back towards the garrison, the vehicle slalomed around the shattered bodies of soldiers, some of them blown out of their clothes by the force of the explosions. Outside the old hotel, two soldiers dragged aside a barbed wire barricade just in time to let them pass and the Jeep roared into the courtyard.

As Pekkala clambered out, he stared up at the shattered windows and the bullet-pocked walls. Here and there, he could see a rifle pointing from a room. Through an open doorway, he watched as wounded men, trailing the bloody pennants of hastily applied field bandages, were being carried down into the basement of the building.

'They've hit us twice already,' said Zolkin. 'If it hadn't been for the mortars, they would have made it past the barricade.'

'Where did the mortars come from?' asked Kirov. 'I don't see any in position here.'

Zolkin shook his head. 'They weren't ours. Those rounds came in from somewhere on the other side of town. We think it might be a Red Army relief column approaching on the road from Kolodenka. Commander Chaplinsky has been trying to make radio contact with them, but so far without success. With luck, they might get here before the next attack.'

He had barely finished speaking when they heard the clatter of enemy machine guns and the monstrous squeaking of tracked vehicles, somewhere out beyond the barricades. The Langemarck Division had returned.

'So much for the relief column,' muttered Zolkin. 'It looks as if we're on our own.'

Commander Chaplinsky met them in the doorway of the garrison. His face was blackened with gun smoke, making his teeth seem unnaturally white. Behind him, in what had once been a grand foyer, three exhausted soldiers sprawled on an ornately upholstered couch which had been dragged out into the open. Others lay around them on the floor, oblivious to the jigsaw puzzles of broken window glass beneath them. The worn-down hobnails on their boots gleamed as if pearls and not steel had been set into the dirty leather soles.

'Find yourself a gun.' Chaplinsky gestured towards a heap of rifles belonging to those who were now being treated in an improvised dressing station in the old luggage room of the hotel. 'We're going to need everyone who can pull a trigger.' As he spoke, some of the more lightly wounded soldiers emerged from the dressing station, took up their weapons and returned to their posts.

Kirov and Pekkala each picked up an abandoned rifle and made their way along the hall until they found an empty room. The windows had been smashed out and furniture lay piled into the corner. Spent rifle cartridges and the grey cloth covers of Russian army field dressings littered the floor where a man had been wounded in the last assault.

'From the look of things here,' said Kirov, 'this might not be the best place to make a stand.'

'If you know of a better one, go to it,' answered Pekkala.

With a grunt of resignation, Kirov sat down on the floor with his back against the wall.

Pekkala stared through the empty window frame, eyes fixed upon the horizon, where dust churned up by the fighting dirtied the pale blue sky. 'He's out there,' Pekkala said quietly.

'Who?' asked Kirov as he checked his rifle's magazine to see if it was loaded.

'The assassin,' replied Pekkala.

'And so is half the German army, Inspector. Are you trying to tell me you're still fixated on arresting a single man?'

Pekkala turned and studied him. 'That is exactly what I'm telling you.'

'You're going to get us both killed,' said Kirov. 'Do you realise that, Inspector?'

'If we worried about the risks every time we set out to find a criminal, we would never arrest anyone.'

Kirov laughed bitterly. 'Elizaveta was telling the truth.'

'The truth about what?' asked Pekkala.

'About you! About this!' He kicked out with his heel, sending spent cartridges jangling across the floor. 'Wherever you go, death follows in your path.'

'She said that?'

'Yes,' answered Kirov.

'And you believed her?'

'I just told you I did.'

'Then why the devil did you come out here to find me?' demanded Pekkala. 'To prove that she was right?'

'I didn't come here because of what she said!' shouted Kirov. 'I came here in spite of it.'

There was no time for Pekkala to reply. He ducked for cover as a stream of tracer fire arced towards them from a gap in a stone wall across the street. Bullets spattered against the walls, raising a cloud of plaster dust.

'Here they come,' muttered Kirov.

*

Malashenko approached his cabin in the woods. After finding the cabin deserted, Malashenko had returned to Rovno, intending to meet Pekkala at the safe house, as he had promised to do. But no sooner had he reached the outskirts of the town when an attack began from the west. With machine gunfire whip-cracking in the air above him and mortars falling in the nearby streets, Malashenko realised that the enemy must have broken through and that he had wandered right into the fighting. Leaving Pekkala and the commissar to fend for themselves, he ran for his life back towards the cabin, the only place he could think of where he might be safe.

He did not expect to find Vasko there. By now, Malashenko was convinced that the Abwehr agent had already gone, having accomplished what he came to do. The thought that he had been cheated out of his bar of gold filled Malashenko with barely containable rage.

But when Malashenko arrived at the little shack, with its mildewed log walls and crooked tar-paper roof, he was stunned to discover that, in the few hours he'd been gone, all the windows had been knocked out. 'Vasko!' he shouted. 'Vasko, are you there?'

'Yes,' said a voice behind him.

Malashenko spun around as Vasko stepped out from behind a tree, a Tokarev pistol in his hand.

'I didn't think you were coming back,' the partisan remarked nervously.

'Then you were mistaken, Malashenko.'

'What the hell happened to my cabin?'

'Somebody touched something they shouldn't have.'

'Well, it wasn't me!'

'I know,' Vasko said calmly. 'Because if it had been, you would be the one lying in pieces on the floor instead of somebody else.'

'Pieces?' Malashenko glanced in through the cabin's open door. A headless body slumped in a chair against the wall. The walls were painted with blood. With nausea rising in his throat, Malashenko backed away. 'Listen,' he told Vasko. 'There is something you should know. Pekkala is looking for you. Pekkala, the Emerald—'

Vasko cut him off. 'I know exactly who Pekkala is.'

'Then you know it's only a matter of time before he finds you.'

'That is exactly what I intend for him to do.'

He's gone mad, thought Malashenko. Maybe he was from the start. Malashenko would have shot Vasko by now, but his submachine gun was slung across his back and he knew he'd never get to it before Vasko pulled the trigger on his pistol. Instead, he tried to reason with the man. 'And when he does catch you, after what you've done—'

'Oh, he won't catch me,' Vasko assured him. 'You and I will see to that.'

'You can leave me out of it!' snapped Malashenko. 'I already helped you. I did everything you asked of me.' He held out one dirty hand. 'You owe me that bar of gold.'

'And you will have it,' said Vasko, 'but I require one small additional favour from you.'

'What kind of favour?' demanded Malashenko.

'I would like you to bring Pekkala here.'

'So that you can add another to your list of murders? You don't understand. I have orders to protect the Inspector, as well as his assistant Major Kirov.'

'Orders from whom?'

'From Barabanschikov himself,' replied Malashenko. 'If anything happens to them it will be on my shoulders! In the meantime, I'm supposed to be helping them catch you.'

Vasko smiled. 'Then they will be pleased when you report to them that you found me lying dead in your cabin.'

For a moment, Malashenko just stared in confusion, but as the seconds passed, he began to understand Vasko's thinking. 'The body in the cabin,' he whispered. 'They'll think it's you.'

'When they find the pieces of my radio, along with other evidence, they'll have no reason to think otherwise.'

'And then you can get away clean,' said Malashenko, marvelling at the beautiful symmetry of Vasko's plan, 'because nobody looks for a man they think is lying dead in front of them. Barabanschikov will be pleased, Pekkala will thank me . . .' then Malashenko paused. 'But how will I convince them it is you?'

Vasko thought for a second, then he removed a spare Tokarev magazine from his pocket, pushed out one of the special soft-point rounds and tossed it to Malashenko. 'Just show him this. He'll know what it means. Go now, and the quicker you get back here with Pekkala, the sooner that gold will be yours.'

Malashenko needed no further encouragement. He turned and started walking down the trail to Rovno. Gradually, his walking pace picked up into a steady trot. Then, with thoughts of gold swimming in his brain, Malashenko broke into a run.

*

From somewhere beyond the barricade came the sound of a tank engine. A moment later, a German Jagdpanzer, normally used for destroying other armoured vehicles, appeared from around a corner.

Their faces masked with plaster dust, Kirov and Pekkala began firing at the vehicle, but the bullets bounced harmlessly off its front armour.

With no support, and no anti-tank weapons, the men in the garrison knew it was only a matter of time before the enemy made their final assault on the building. In the room-to-room combat that would follow, there would be no hope of surrender. It would be a fight to the death.

'Why didn't you marry Elizaveta?' asked Pekkala.

'You want to talk about that now?' Kirov asked incredulously.

'There may not be another time,' said Pekkala.

'How can I marry her,' asked Kirov, 'when the odds are I'd make her a widow long before we could grow old together?'

'Do you love her?'

'Yes! What of it?'

'Then let her choose whether or not to take that risk. Your job is to stay alive. Hers is to trust that you will.'

'That's some advice, coming from a man who sent his own fiancée away to Paris as soon as the Revolution broke out! She wanted to stay and be near you, but you forced her to go.'

'And I have regretted it every day since. Do not postpone happiness, Kirov. That has been the most costly lesson of my life.'

The building shuddered as a shell from the tank smashed into the upper storeys of the hotel. Soldiers accompanying the armoured vehicle crouched in the doorways of wrecked buildings, shooting at anything that moved in the hotel.

The Jagdpanzer backed up slowly as it manoeuvred for another shot.

With a sound like a whipcrack, a bullet passed just over Kirov's head and smashed what was left of the light fixture hanging from the middle of the room.

Pekkala watched the barrel of the tank rising as it took aim. It seemed to be pointing straight at him. Slowly, he lowered his gun, knowing it was useless to keep fighting against such a machine. 'I'm sorry, Kirov,' he said. 'I should never have brought you to this place.'

'I would have come here anyway,' answered Kirov.

Then came a deafening roar, following by the squeal of the tank's engine and then another explosion, this one more muffled than the first.

The top hatch of the tank disappeared as a bolt of fire erupted from the turret. Black smoke poured from the engine grille and fire coughed out of the exhaust stacks.

At that same moment, Pekkala caught sight of a small grey cloud sifting upwards from the rubble of a building. A man emerged, still carrying the arm-length, sand-coloured tube of a Panzerfaust anti-tank weapon. At first, Pekkala could not understand why the vehicle had been destroyed by what appeared to be one of its own people, but then he realised that the man was a partisan. Just as he was wondering where the man had come from, and where he could have come by such a weapon, a terrible cry went up from the ruins, and more partisans began to pour into the street.

'Where did they come from?' asked Kirov, who had joined Pekkala at the window sill.

The soldiers, who had been ready to make their final assault on the garrison, began to pull back. But they were quickly overwhelmed by the mass of charging partisans, who seemed to number in their hundreds. In minutes, the SS men were running for their lives, leaving behind the smouldering hulk of their tank.

Deafened and coughing the dust from their lungs, Pekkala and Kirov stumbled their way out into the street. The air was filled with a metallic reek of broken flint from cobblestones crushed by the heavy iron tank tracks.

All around them, Red Army soldiers emerged from hiding places behind the coils of barbed wire which marked their last line of defence.

Partisans milled about in the road. Having driven off the attackers, they seemed unsure what to do next.

Among these men, Pekkala recognised members of the Barabanschikov Atrad. But there were others, many others, whom Pekkala had not seen before. Then he knew that Barabanschikov had somehow managed to do what might have seemed impossible only days before – he had gathered the Atrads together.

The soldiers approached, stepping carefully over the smashed bricks.

The partisans watched them come on, smoke still drifting from their weapons.

Warily, the two sides watched each other.

Just when it seemed as if they might start shooting at each other, one of the Red Army soldiers slung his rifle on his back. As seconds passed, others followed his example. Some even laid their guns upon the ground and, as if driven by a wordless command, walked forward with their arms held out in gratitude to the men who had just saved their lives.

*

When Malashenko arrived at the safe house, he found the doors open and the building empty. There seemed to be only two possibilities, neither of them good. Either Kirov and Pekkala had been killed or captured, or else they had escaped to the Red Army garrison. From what Malashenko could hear on his way into town, the Fascists were attacking the old hotel with everything they had, including, from the sound of it, a tank, against which the garrison had no defences. The shooting had stopped. Which means, thought Malashenko, that everyone inside that garrison is probably dead by now.

But even as these thoughts entered his mind, they were interrupted by the sound of cheering, which came from somewhere over by the garrison. Malashenko listened, mystified. Russian. There was no mistake, and it dawned on him that the Red Army must somehow have repelled the German attack. Malashenko set off towards the sound, his toes half-frozen in his soaked and worn-out boots as they splashed through the ankle-deep slush.

*

In the street outside the garrison, there was cheering, and even music. A soldier had brought out an accordion and was sitting on top of a large pile of bricks, serenading those who stood nearby. The barbed wire had been pulled aside and, in the place where the barricades had stood, soldiers and partisans danced shoulder to shoulder, their hobnailed boots kicking up sparks from the wet road.

The first person Pekkala and Kirov ran into was Sergeant Zolkin.

'Not a scratch!' he shouted, as he wrapped his arms around Pekkala.

'Yes,' remarked Pekkala, as he untangled himself from Zolkin's embrace. 'You were lucky.'

'Not me!' laughed Zolkin. 'The Jeep! I thought it would be blown to bits, but it came through undamaged!' Then he ran back towards the motor pool.

The next person they found was Commander Chaplinsky who, instead of enjoying his victory, was almost in hysterics.

'What is wrong, Commander?' asked Kirov. 'Surely you have

cause to celebrate!'

Chaplinsky held out a scrap of paper. 'I just received this from Moscow.'

Gently, Kirov took the paper from his hands. 'It's an order from Headquarters in Moscow.'

'What does it say?' asked Pekkala.

'The Rovno garrison is ordered to immediately commence liquidating all partisans in the Rovno area.' Helplessly, Chaplinsky raised his hands and let them fall again. 'But if it wasn't for these partisans, none of us would have survived. What am I supposed to do?'

'Do nothing for now,' answered Pekkala. 'Just give me a little time to find out where we stand.'

'Very well,' agreed Chaplinsky, 'but you must hurry, Inspector. They are expecting an acknowledgement of the order and I cannot delay them for long.'

At that moment, Malashenko arrived from the safe house, red-faced and out of breath. 'I found him,' he managed to say. 'The man who killed Andrich and Yakushkin. He was holed up at my cabin in the woods. I went there when the fighting started and couldn't get back until now.'

'He *was* at the cabin?' asked Pekkala. 'Where is he now, Malashenko?'

'Still there, Inspector and he's not going anywhere. He blew himself up with some kind of explosive. It must have been an accident.'

Pekkala paused. 'Then how do you know it is him?'

From his pocket, Malashenko brought out the soft-pointed bullet Vasko had given him and held it out towards Pekkala. 'I found this.'

Pekkala examined the bullet. 'The same kind that was used to kill Andrich and Yakushkin.'

'But you must come now, Inspector,' Malashenko said urgently, 'before someone else stumbles across the body.'

'For once,' said Kirov, 'I agree with Malashenko.'

'You go instead, Kirov,' ordered Pekkala. 'Find Zolkin and his Jeep and get there as fast as you can. Malashenko, you will show them the way.'

'Shouldn't you come too?' blurted Malashenko, afraid that Vasko's plan had suddenly begun to unravel. 'You are the Inspector, after all.'

'You will find the major every bit as capable,' Pekkala assured him. 'I have to find Barabanschikov, before this victory celebration turns into another massacre.'

'But, Inspector . . .' Malashenko's lips twitched as he hunted for the words which might change Pekkala's mind.

'Come along!' Taking Malashenko by the arm, Kirov made his way back towards the motor pool, where Zolkin was still rejoicing at the survival of his beloved Jeep.

As Malashenko allowed himself to be led away, the lustre of the gold was already fading from his mind, replaced now by the fear of what Vasko would do to him when Pekkala failed to arrive.

The two men piled into the back of Sergeant Zolkin's Jeep. Following Malashenko's instructions, they drove east out of Rovno for several kilometres, before turning off the main road and continuing over a muddy trail, passing stacks of mildewed logs, readied long ago for transport to the mill, but left to rot instead.

The condition of the road grew worse and worse until at last it disappeared altogether in a large deep puddle. With water seeping into the footwells, Zolkin knew that it was only a matter of seconds before the air intake flooded, cold water poured into the hot engine and the cylinder head cracked from the sudden change in temperature. Then they would not only be stranded but the Jeep would likely be beyond repair.

'We've gone as far as we can go,' he announced. 'You'll have to continue on foot,' Carefully, he backed up until the Jeep was once again on dry ground.

Kirov and the partisan waded through the deep puddle, leaving Zolkin to guard the Jeep.

Malashenko glanced about warily, knowing that Vasko must be somewhere close by.

'Why are you so nervous?' Kirov asked him. 'The man's dead, after all.'

'If you knew what else was in these woods,' replied Malashenko, 'you'd be plenty nervous, too, Commissar.'

After a few minutes of tramping along the muddy path, they arrived at the cabin, which was so well-hidden that Kirov might have walked right past if Malashenko hadn't told him where it was.

'The body is in there?' asked Kirov, as they approached the door.

'Yes,' replied Malashenko, 'and I hope you have got a strong stomach.'

Inside the cabin, they found the body still slumped in the chair, which was tilted back against the wall. The severed head lay on the floor beside it.

Kirov reached up to the ceiling and plucked a strand of wire which had become embedded in the wood. 'It looks to me as if he was preparing an explosive device and it went off by mistake. But who was it for?'

Malashenko shrugged. 'It doesn't matter now, does it?'

'Perhaps you're right,' said Kirov, turning his attention to the dog tag still fastened around the dead man's neck by a braided piece of string. Kirov removed the tag, scraped away the blood and examined the dull zinc oval.

'SS,' muttered Kirov. Only now did he understand who had been behind the attack on Colonel Andrich. He also understood why. The result of an all-out war between the Red Army and the partisans would have been chaos, giving the German army ample opportunity to retake the territory they had lost in this region. Kirov wondered if the agent had known how close he had come to succeeding.

As he paced nervously around the cabin, Malashenko caught sight of a Walther P38 pistol lying underneath the iron legs of the stove. It had belonged to Luther Benjamin and had been thrown there by the explosion. One of its reddish-black Bakelite grips had been cracked in the blast, but it was otherwise in good condition.

For men like Malashenko, weapons of that quality were hard to come by. When the major's back was turned, he picked up the gun and stuck it in his belt.

By now, Kirov had turned his attention to the severed head, hoping to recognise the man from that night in the bunker, but much of the soft tissue – the ears, mouth and nose – had been blackened or burned away entirely by the explosion. This, combined with the fact that the man had been wearing a bandage on his face when he came to the bunker, forced Kirov to reach the conclusion that there was no chance of making a positive identification.

'We should go,' said Malashenko, peering out of the broken

window into the maze of trees which lay beyond the cabin.

'What is wrong with you?' demanded Kirov. 'If you can't stand the sight of what's in here, then go and wait outside until I have finished my search.'

'You've seen enough,' said Malashenko. 'Now can't we just get out of here?'

'I'll only be a few more minutes,' said Kirov, trying to calm him down. 'You can wait outside.'

Leaving Kirov to rummage through the gore, Malashenko stepped out of the cabin. Maybe Vasko has already gone, he thought to himself. Later, he knew, he would be miserable about the gold but, for now, all he wanted was to leave this place.

Then a figure appeared from the shadows, almost lost among the dark pillars of the trees.

It was Vasko. He gestured for Malashenko to join him.

Warily, the partisan approached, until the two stood face to face.

'Where is Pekkala?' Vasko whispered angrily.

'He stayed behind in Rovno!' Malashenko hissed in reply. 'He sent that commissar instead. I swear there was nothing I could do.'

'That's not what we agreed. You still want that gold, don't you?'

'But how on earth can I persuade him?'

'I leave that to you, Malashenko. Reason with Pekkala. Beg him. Bring him at gunpoint if you have to, or I swear it will be you that I come looking for.' With those words, he stepped back into the forest and disappeared.

In the cabin, Kirov had turned out the dead man's pockets, in which he found a German infantry compass, a wood-handled pocket knife and a cigarette lighter engraved with the word 'Zagreb'.

Malashenko came and stood in the doorway. He looked pale and sick. 'Satisfied?' he asked.

'All right.' Kirov took one last look at the blood-spattered walls. 'Let's get back to Rovno and tell Pekkala what we've found.'

'Gladly,' replied Malashenko.

With feet freezing in their sodden boots, the men returned to where Zolkin waited with the Jeep. Soon they were on their way to Rovno, jolting along over the potholed road.

*

After a short search, Pekkala caught up with Barabanschikov at the wreckage of the Jagdpanzer, where the partisan leader was supervising the removal of a machine gun from the driver's compartment. Through the open hatch in the front hull, one partisan handed out gleaming brass belts of ammunition to another man, who gathered them like a dead snake in his arms and carried them away to Barabanschikov's truck.

'I see that you've wasted no time in gathering the spoils of battle,' said Pekkala.

'With any luck,' replied Barabanschikov, 'we won't need them for much longer.'

'The commander of the garrison would like to offer you his thanks.'

'All I ask in return,' replied Barabanschikov, slinging the belt over his shoulder, 'is that we be allowed to get on with our lives. For that, you can tell him, every partisan in this region is prepared to lay down his arms.'

'Are you sure?' asked Pekkala. 'You have spoken to the other bands?'

Barabanschikov nodded. 'On one condition.'

'Name it.'

'That the promises made by Colonel Andrich will be kept.'

'You will have those promises,' said Pekkala.

'Not from you, my friend,' said Barabanschikov, resting his hand upon Pekkala's shoulder, 'although I do not doubt your good intentions. Let me stand before the leader of this country and hear him make those guarantees in person. Otherwise, they're just the words of other men.'

'Moscow is a long way from here,' said Pekkala, 'and do you really think that looking Stalin in the eye will make a difference?'

Barabanschikov swept his hand towards the crowd of partisans. 'It makes a difference to them. To know that I have actually spoken with Stalin carries more weight than anything that you or I, or anyone sent here to speak for him, could ever say. You know these people, Pekkala. You have shared their suffering. You know they deserve nothing less.'

Pekkala nodded in agreement. 'I will notify Moscow immediately.'

*

'A telegram!' shouted Poskrebychev. As he knocked on the door to Stalin's study, he was already entering the room. 'A message has arrived from Rovno!'

'Finally,' growled Stalin. Although it was a sunny day, he had drawn the curtains, shutting out all but a few stray bands of light which had worked their way in past the heavy sheets of red velvet. 'And what does Kirov have to say?'

'The message is not from Kirov, Comrade Stalin. This one is

from Pekkala!'

'Give it to me!' Stalin held out his hand, snapping his fingers until Poskrebychev was close enough to have the message torn from his grasp. For a while, there was silence as he studied the telegram. Finally, Stalin spoke. 'He says partisans have agreed to lay down their guns, on condition that I meet personally with their leader, Barabanschikov.'

'And will you meet with him, Comrade Stalin?'

Stalin scratched thoughtfully at his neck, fingernails dragging across the scars of old pockmarks. 'Send word to the garrison in Rovno. Tell them to call off the attack. And have a plane dispatched immediately to the nearest airfield so that Barabanschikov can be transported back to Moscow, along with Major Kirov and Pekkala. Tell the leader of these partisans that I will meet with him, if that is the price of their allegiance.'

'At once, Comrade Stalin!' Poskrebychev clicked his heels, then turned and left the room, closing the doors quietly behind him. No sooner had he returned to his desk than the intercom buzzed. Poskrebychev leaned over and pressed a well-worn button. 'Yes, Comrade Stalin?'

'Once the plane is in the air,' Stalin told him, 'have the pilot maintain strict radio silence until they reach Moscow. Air-to-ground messages can be intercepted by the enemy and I don't want anyone shooting them down before they get here!'

*

Ten hours later an American-made DC9, on loan to the Red Air Force, landed at the Obarov airfield. The aircraft had been on its way from Kiev to the Arctic port of Arkhangelsk with a cargo of submarine propellers when, on emergency orders from the Kremlin, it was diverted to the small airfield outside Rovno. The heavily loaded plane landed hard on the short runway, which drew gasps of morbid fascination from the onlookers, followed by wild applause when the aircraft, smoke pouring from its brakes and engines screaming in reverse, finally managed to stop, only a dozen paces from the tree line.

Earlier that day, Kirov had returned from the cabin and reported his findings to Pekkala, who agreed that the assassin, whoever he was, had been killed in the explosion. Now that the case was closed, they immediately turned their attention to the business of transporting Barabanschikov to Moscow.

The pilot of the cargo plane, wearing heavy brown overalls lined with sheepskin, climbed down from the cockpit. Warily, he looked out at the jumbled assortment of clothing, weapons and head gear of this ragged welcoming committee. Some appeared to be Red Army, while others, judging from their uniforms, could have laid claim to membership in half a dozen nations. 'Well, I can't take all of you!' he shouted.

Kirov stepped forward. 'There are only three passengers.'

'Four!' announced Sergeant Zolkin, as he pushed his way to the front of the crowd. 'I'm coming too, on the orders of Inspector Pekkala.'

'Your new driver,' Kirov muttered to Pekkala.

'But what about your Jeep, Zolkin?' asked Pekkala.

Without a moment's hesitation, Zolkin turned and tossed the keys to Malashenko. 'Looks like we both get our wish,' he told the partisan.

Ever since he'd returned to the cabin, Malashenko had been pleading with Zolkin to transport him to Kiev. He had overheard

Pekkala telling Kirov that the case was officially closed and realized there was no hope of persuading Pekkala to revisit the cabin. His only hope now was to get as far away from Vasko as he could. When Zolkin refused to drive him, Malashenko revised his destination to anywhere at all, as long as it was somewhere out of Rovno. In exchange, Malashenko offered the sergeant a lifetime supply of salt, to which Zolkin only shrugged and shook his head.

'Now you can drive yourself!' said Zolkin.

Clutching the keys tightly in his fist, Malashenko bowed his head in solemn gratitude. There would be no gold, but at least he might escape with his life.

Barabanschikov waved farewell to his men and climbed aboard.

Zolkin went next, clambering into the aircraft without so much as a backward glance, as if afraid that his luck might give out before the plane's wheels left the ground.

Now only Kirov and Pekkala remained.

'Be quick!' called the pilot, as he beckoned to them.

Pekkala bid farewell to Malashenko, but as he shook hands with the man, Pekkala noticed the gun which Malashenko had tucked into his belt. 'That Walther,' he said. 'Where did you get it?'

'At the cabin,' replied Malashenko, not thinking fast enough to lie. 'It belonged to the dead man. It was lying on the floor, so I took it.'

'But the gun used to kill Colonel Andrich was 7.62 mm,' said Pekkala. 'A Walther P38 takes 9-mm ammunition.'

Malashenko was barely listening. His thoughts were focused on the idea that Pekkala might try to confiscate the gun as evidence for his investigation. 'If you don't mind my saying so,' he said defiantly, 'it's the least that bastard could part with after blowing my cabin to bits.'

But Kirov understood. 'Do you think there might have been two agents?'

Pekkala turned to Malashenko. 'That bullet you gave to Major Kirov. Are you certain it came from the cabin?'

'Of course I am certain!' spluttered Malashenko, as panic swirled through his mind. Does he suspect? he wondered. Are they accusing me? 'Maybe he had two guns. So what?'

Pekkala shook his head. 'It is unlikely that he would have been carrying two pistols, of different calibres. If there is another agent, the fact that he abandoned his colleague without trying to conceal any of the evidence means that he left in a hurry. He may even have been wounded, in which case he might not have gone far. Whatever the answer, the cabin must be searched again for any sign that the dead agent might not have been there by himself.'

'But, Inspector,' Kirov protested, 'Stalin himself has ordered us back to Moscow and the plane is about to depart!'

'That is why you must be on it,' Pekkala told him. 'Deliver Barabanschikov to the Kremlin. Tell Stalin that I will head for Moscow as soon as I have some answers. In the meantime, Malashenko and I will return to the cabin to search for more evidence.'

Hearing this, Malashenko could scarcely believe his good fortune. 'I will take us there at once!' he said, holding up the keys to Zolkin's Jeep.

Minutes later, with Kirov aboard, the plane taxied for take-off. Its engines roaring, the machine rolled slowly forward, gathering speed until the wheels lifted off the ground and folded upwards into the belly of the fuselage. It climbed and climbed, the sounds of the motors already fading, until it vanished completely in the clouds.

By then, Malashenko and Pekkala were already on their way to the cabin.

The crowd had begun to disperse, walking back along the road to Rovno. The celebration was over now, replaced by a sense of uncertainty about what lay ahead. Soldier and partisan alike knew that, with one message from Moscow, they might all become enemies again.

*

'Another telegram, Comrade Stalin.' Poskrebychev stepped into the office. 'The pilot of the cargo plane has radioed to say that he has taken off and is now en route to Moscow.'

'Good!' said Stalin. 'It's time we had Pekkala back again.'

With a pained expression on his face, Poskrebychev stepped forward and placed a piece of paper on Stalin's desk. 'As you will see, Comrade Stalin, the passenger manifest does not include Pekkala's name. It appears that he is not on the plane.'

'What?' gasped Stalin, snatching up the manifest.

'I'm sure there is some logical explanation,' Poskrebychev said hopefully.

Stalin crumpled up the message and bounced it off Poskrebychev's chest. 'Of course there is, you fool! He has defied me yet again!'

'Surely not,' muttered Poskrebychev.

'Well, radio the plane and find out!' bellowed Stalin.

Poskrebychev swallowed. 'They will be out of radio contact until the plane arrives in Moscow. Those were your orders, Comrade Stalin.'

Stalin smashed both fists upon his desk, causing his brass

ashtray to leap into the air, spilling dozens of cigarette butts and the grey dust of tobacco ash. 'That Finnish bastard! That black-hearted troll!'

'The flight is scheduled to take about twelve hours. Only twelve hours, Comrade Stalin.'

'Only? That's time enough for him to disappear again. No, Poskrebychev.' Stalin wagged one stubby finger back and forth, like a miniature windscreen wiper. 'I have no intention of waiting. Get me Akhatov.'

'Akhatov? The Siberian? The . . .'

'You know who he is. Now just get him, and make sure to have a fast plane standing by, ready to transport him to Rovno.'

'But . . .' Poskrebychev's mouth opened and closed, like a fish pulled from the water.

'Go!' screamed Stalin.

Without another word, Poskrebychev scrambled from the room and shut the door.

Alone now, Stalin settled back into his chair. He rubbed his face, leaving red streaks in the pockmarked skin. The anger he felt was almost as great as his confusion. Pekkala's refusal to return to Moscow was, for Stalin, not only baffling but personal. More than once, he had extended the hand of friendship to the Emerald Eye, but never with any success. Others would have killed for such an offer of comradeship.

That Stalin had tried several times to murder Pekkala was not, in his own mind, mutually exclusive to the friendship he had hoped to kindle. One of the reasons Stalin had remained in power was that he had always been prepared to liquidate anyone. Whether they were friends or family made no difference. For Stalin, power and friendship did not overlap and the mistaken belief that they did had cost many people their lives. He had always thought that a man of Pekkala's intelligence would understand such a thing. Apparently, thought Stalin, I have been mistaken.

Although Stalin could barely admit it, even to himself, he was jealous of Major Kirov and Pekkala, of the cramped office they shared and the banter of their conversations, to which he often listened through the bugging devices he had ordered to be installed. He envied the meals they cooked on Friday afternoons. With his mouth watering at the sound of the cutlery clinking on their plates he would fetch out one of several tins of sardines in olive oil and tomato sauce, which he always kept on hand in his desk drawer. Tucking a handkerchief into his collar, Stalin would eat the sardines with his bare hands, spitting the bones back into the tin. Now and then, he would pause to adjust the headphones with his greasy, fish-scaled fingers, all the while snuffling with laughter at the jokes which passed between Kirov and Pekkala.

In spite of everything, he had missed the Emerald Eye. Yes, it was true that, after the Amber Room incident, he had ordered Pekkala to be liquidated immediately. It was also true that he had commanded Special Operations to begin surveillance upon Major Kirov, in the futile hope that the great Inspector might make himself known to his assistant. But things were different now. Stalin's rage had subsided and, until today, he had felt ready to purge this from the tally sheet that he kept inside his head of the many snubs, real or imagined, but both equally damning, which he had received over the years. In the case of Pekkala, it was a very long list, in fact unequalled by anyone still living. To forgo the satisfaction of punishment was a gift more valuable than any Stalin had given out before, which made Pekkala's disappearance all the more wounding to his pride.

Now, with this most recent news, the anger had returned. Stalin would have his vengeance. Akhatov was coming. He had summoned the dragon from its lair.

A moment later, the door swung open and there stood Poskrebychev, his face a mask of bewilderment, as if his limbs had brought him there against his will.

Stalin fixed him with a stare. 'What is it, Poskrebychev?'

'Why, Comrade Stalin?' he whispered. 'Why Akhatov? Why bring that monster to the Kremlin?'

To Poskrebychev's astonishment, Stalin did not evict him from the room amid a fresh barrage of curses. Instead, he considered the question for a moment before resting his knuckles on the desk top and heaving himself to his feet. 'Come here to me, Poskrebychev,' he said, and in his voice there was an unfamiliar gentleness, almost like pity, like that of a man speaking to an old and faithful animal which he is about to put down. As Poskrebychev approached, his eyes walled with fear, Stalin walked out from behind the desk and rested his hand upon his secretary's shoulder.

To Poskrebychev, the weight of that hand felt like a sack of concrete.

Stalin walked him across the room to the window which looked out over Red Square. As was his custom, Stalin himself stood to one side of the window, unwilling to show his face to anyone who might be looking up from below. 'I want you to understand something,' he began.

'Yes, Comrade Stalin,' replied Poskrebychev, too terrified to speak above a whisper.

'In spite of our differences,' explained Stalin, 'Inspector Pekkala and I have shared one common goal – the survival of this country.

Under such circumstances, old enemies like the Inspector and I can learn to work together, even to trust each other. But there are limits to this partnership. There are only so many times that warlock can thumb his nose at me and get away with it!'

Poskrebychev opened his mouth. He had no idea what words to choose, but he felt he must say something in defence of the Emerald Eye, no matter what it cost him in the end.

But at that moment Stalin's hand, which was still resting upon his shoulder, suddenly dug into the flesh around Poskrebychev's collarbone, causing the frail man to gasp with pain.

'That may not be the way you see it,' Stalin continued, 'but it's the way I see it. And the way I see it is the way it is. Do you understand me now, Poskrebychev?'

This time, Poskrebychev could only nod.

At last, Stalin's hand slipped from its perch. Soundless in his kidskin boots, he returned to his desk and removed a cardboard box of cigarettes from the top pocket of his tunic.

For a moment longer, Poskrebychev remained at the window, looking out over Red Square and unable to shake the sensation that he was being watched. He felt certain that, somewhere out there among the rooftops of the city, the eyes of a stranger were upon him. Instinctively, he stepped to one side, behind the thick red velvet curtain.

'It's out there, isn't it?' There was the rustle of a match as Stalin lit a cigarette.

Poskrebychev turned to face his master. 'I beg your pardon, Comrade Stalin?'

Holding the match between his thumb and index finger, Stalin waved it lazily from side to side until the flame disappeared in a ribbon of smoke.

'You heard me,' he replied.

Back at his desk, Poskrebychev took out a clean sheet of paper and wound it into the typewriter, an American Smith and Brothers model no.3, fitted with Cyrillic lettering, a personal gift to Poskrebychev from Ambassador Davies. Poskrebychev folded his hands together and then, extending his arms, bent his fingers backwards until they cracked. He paused for a moment, fingertips hovering above the machine. Slowly, he typed out the name 'Akhatov' and under the heading he wrote 'Lost Cat', the code word agreed upon between Stalin and the agent, to signal his immediate summons to the Kremlin. And then the room filled with a sound like miniature gunfire as his fingertips raced across the keys. Within minutes, Poskrebychev had completed the message and it was taken by courier to the Kremlin telegraph office for immediate dispatch. He then ordered a plane to be fuelled and placed on standby at an airfield just outside the city. The fastest one available was a Lavochkin fighter, specially outfitted with two seats for use as a training aircraft.

When hours passed without reply, Poskrebychev allowed himself to hope that perhaps the Siberian might have moved on beyond the Kremlin's reach. After all, it had been several years since Stalin had required the services of the notorious Siberian. But just as he was preparing to go home for the day, one of the Kremlin guards called the office.

'There's someone here,' said the guard. 'He won't give his name. He says it's about a lost cat. Should I just throw him out?'

'No,' sighed Poskrebychev. 'Send him up.'

It was not long before a heavy-set man entered Stalin's outer office, which was Poskrebychev's personal domain. He had a mop of curly brown hair, a hooked Roman nose and cheerful, ruddy cheeks. He wore a belted raincoat and old-fashioned black ankle boots which fastened with buttons. Under his arm, he carried a brown paper parcel tied with string.

'Akhatov,' said Poskrebychev, as if quietly uttering a curse.

The man nodded at the door to Stalin's office. 'Should I go straight in?'

'Yes. He is expecting you.'

Stalin was sitting at the small table in the corner of his study where he took his meals and morning tea. The table had a round, brass top, engraved with a prayer in Arabic. Stalin had spotted the table on display at the Hermitage museum and had ordered it brought to the Kremlin. 'It's just the size I want,' he told the bewildered museum curator.

In front of Stalin was a glass of tea, supported in a brass holder. Also on the table was a small bowl filled with rock sugar, which resembled fragments of a broken bottle. Stalin set one of these pieces between his teeth and sipped at the tea as he gestured for Akhatov to take a seat in the chair on the other side of the little table.

Poskrebychev, meanwhile, had switched on the intercom so that he could overhear what was being said in Stalin's room.

'How may I be of service, Comrade Stalin?' asked Akhatov.

'In the usual way,' he replied.

Barely able to make out what was being said, Poskrebychev leaned closer and closer to the dust-clogged pores of the intercom speaker. Then, in frustration, he picked up the whole machine and pressed it against his ear.

'Who is it this time, Comrade Stalin?'

'Pekkala.'

'The Inspector?'

'You sound surprised, Akhatov.'

'I heard he was already dead.'

'That appears to have been wishful thinking.'

'I see,' said Akhatov. 'And where is the Inspector now?'

'In a town called Rovno in western Ukraine.'

'That must be near the front line.'

'It *is* the front line, Akhatov.'

'Then how am I to get there?'

'My secretary will drive you to an airfield outside Moscow, where a plane is standing by. It will fly you directly to Rovno. As soon as you land, you must move quickly, Akhatov. Every hour that goes by will make Pekkala more difficult to find.'

'I understand,' said Akhatov.

'You have come prepared?'

Akhatov held up the parcel. 'Everything I need is here, Comrade Stalin.' There was the groan of a chair moving back across the floor as Akhatov rose to his feet. He was about to leave, but then he paused. 'If I might ask, Comrade Stalin, why not use someone from Special Operations, especially for a mission like this?'

'Because it is *Pekkala!*' roared Stalin. 'And the men of Special Operations all but worship him. I cannot count on them to carry out the task. That is why I called upon you, Akhatov, because you worship nothing but the money I will pay you for your work.'

'But why must it be done at all, Comrade Stalin?'

'Yes,' whispered Poskrebychev in the other room. 'Why? For the love of God, why?' His arms ached from the effort of holding the bulky intercom, but he did not dare let go for fear of missing a single word.

'My reasons are none of your concern,' said Stalin. 'I am not paying you to have a conscience, Akhatov. All I ask is that you do it quickly and cleanly and that you leave no trace behind which could connect your actions to the Kremlin.'

*

The Jeep pulled up outside the cabin. Its stubborn Detroit engine had kept running, in spite of having driven through a series of puddles, which had soaked the driving compartment, as well as the feet of its passengers.

Pekkala climbed out of the vehicle and walked towards the cabin. 'You built this yourself?' he asked, admiring its solid construction.

Malashenko, who was walking just ahead of him, turned and smiled and opened his mouth, ready to take credit for it all.

At that moment, Vasko stepped out from behind the cabin, the Tokarev in his hand.

'Get down!' Pekkala shouted as he drew his gun.

Malashenko turned to face the agent. 'No!' he shouted, raising his hands.

Vasko pulled the trigger.

The first round struck Malashenko square in the chest. Two more bullets had punched through his ribcage by the time he collapsed into Pekkala's arms. The next shot sounded dull and flat. A burst of sparks sprayed from the Tokarev. The gun had misfired. Vasko tried to chamber a new round, but a cartridge had jammed in the ejection port.

Vasko raised his head and found himself staring down the barrel of Pekkala's Webley.

Malashenko lay on the ground between them. He was already dead, the pale blue sky reflected in his half-open eyes.

'Did they not tell you in Berlin,' asked Pekkala, 'that soft-point bullets are a frequent cause of misfired ammunition?'

Cursing, Vasko tried once more to work the slide of the Tokarev.

Pekkala set his thumb upon the hammer of the Webley, drawing it back with a click so that even the slightest pressure on the trigger would cause the gun to fire.

Vasko heard that click. He knew it was useless to go on. Slowly, he breathed out, and then tossed the gun away. It landed with a soft thump upon the pine-needled ground. 'Inspector Pekkala,' he said.

'Who are you?' asked Pekkala.

'My name is Peter Vasko.'

'Who sent you? Was it Skorzeny or Himmler himself?'

'Neither,' answered Vasko. 'My orders come from Admiral Canaris.'

'You killed Andrich?'

Vasko nodded. 'That's what Canaris sent me here to do.'

'Then why didn't you leave when you still could?'

'Because I wasn't finished yet,' he replied. 'I swore to kill you too, Pekkala, before this war even began.'

A flicker of confusion passed over Pekkala's face.

'I don't expect that you recall the name William Vasko. Or his wife. Or his daughter, or his son, who stands before you now? I am all that's left of a family that set sail from America in the summer of 1936, hoping to escape the Great Depression and with a promise of a better life in Russia.'

Vasko, thought Pekkala, as the face of a terrified man shimmered into focus. Pekkala saw him again, sitting on a metal chair in an interrogation room at Lubyanka. His nose had been broken during previous interrogations. Some of his teeth had been knocked out and his scalp was dotted with open sores, the result of being struck by a man wearing a heavy ring. 'I do remember him,' he said. 'He was a spy at the Novgorod Motor Plant.'

'My father was no spy!' hissed Vasko. 'Just an ordinary assembly-man at a car factory.'

'That's not all he was,' replied Pekkala.

'And who would he be spying on, Inspector?'

'His fellow workers at the plant.'

'For who? America?'

Pekkala shook his head. 'Russian Internal Security.'

'You are lying!' Vasko insisted. 'Those men came to start a new life. Why would they spy on each other?'

'That new life they found,' explained Pekkala, 'was not what they had been expecting. There was talk of a strike at the plant, and Internal Security needed a man on the inside to keep them informed.'

'My father would never have allowed himself to be recruited as a Russian agent.'

'He wasn't recruited,' said Pekkala. 'It was your father who approached them, offering to deliver information, for a price.'

'That is all lies!' screamed Vasko.

'What reason would I have for lying to you now?' asked Pekkala. 'Look who is holding the gun.'

'If he was their informant, why would they have arrested him?'

'The Americans at the plant realised that someone among them was spying for the Russians. When your father guessed that they suspected him, he panicked. He went to the local office of Internal Security and requested that they transfer him to another factory in a different part of Russia. But by then he had become a valuable asset to Russian Intelligence, and his request for transfer was denied. Your father was trapped. He couldn't stay, but neither was he allowed to leave. Believing that his life was in danger, he tried the only thing that he could think of, which was to get back to the United States with his family. Unfortunately for your father, his letters to friends in America, in which he described his plan, were intercepted. That's why he was arrested and detained. And because he was acting as a paid informant, and possessed intelligence which Internal Security considered sensitive, his whereabouts were kept secret. Since your father was no longer employed at the factory, you, your mother and your sister were evicted from housing supplied to the workers. Your mother brought you to Moscow and contacted the American Embassy. Following a request from Ambassador Davies to locate your father, Stalin assigned me to the case.'

'And you condemned us all to death.'

'The truth is quite the opposite,' insisted Pekkala. 'When I discovered that your father was being held at Lubyanka, I immediately had him transferred to a proper holding cell. There, I interviewed him personally in order to learn the details of the case. I also travelled to Novgorod and spoke to people who had known him at the plant. What they had to say confirmed his story. I wrote up a report, advising that he be repatriated to the United States, along with his entire family. If my instructions had been followed, you and your family would have been back in America long ago. I assumed that's what had taken place, since my involvement with the case ended there.'

'My father didn't reach America,' said Vasko. 'He probably never made it out of the country. My mother, my sister and I were arrested outside the American Embassy on her way to apply for a passport to replace the ones which were taken from us when we first arrived in Russia. She was convicted of illegal currency possession and the three of us were exiled to the Gulag at Kolyma.'

'Kolyma!' exclaimed Pekkala. 'And how is it that you survived?'

'We never arrived,' explained Vasko. 'We were shipwrecked off the coast of Japan. I was one of only a few survivors. We were taken to a hospital in Japan, but I suspected that it was only a matter of time before we would be handed over to the Russians, so I escaped. I made my way to the German Embassy. When I explained who I was, they offered to smuggle me out of the country and to give me a new life in Germany.'

'But why go to the German Embassy?' asked Pekkala. 'Why not go to the Americans?'

Vasko shook his head. 'I didn't trust them any more than I trusted the Soviets. When I reached Germany, it was admiral Canaris himself who took me in. He trained me. He gave purpose to my life, and I have no regrets for anything I've done in the service of the Abwehr.'

'In spite of that, your mission has failed,' Pekkala told him. 'A ceasefire now exists between the men you hoped to turn against each other.'

Slowly Vasko shook his head. 'It has not failed, Pekkala. All this was only a diversion. The real mission is still under way.'

Pekkala hesitated, wondering whether Vasko might be telling the truth, or if he was just bargaining with lies. 'If you're right about what you say, then tell me what you know and I'll do what I can to protect you.'

'All I know,' said Vasko, 'is that Stalin does not have long to live. Somewhere out there is another agent, and there is nothing you can do to stop him now.'

'Tell me his name,' said Pekkala. 'This might be your only

chance to save yourself.'

'I couldn't help you, Pekkala, even if I wanted to.' Vasko spread his arms. 'So why don't you just go ahead and shoot?'

'I have no intention of shooting you,' Pekkala told him.

'But you will be the one who hands me over to the men at Lubyanka and when, like my father, I am shot against the prison wall, will your guilt be any less than if you pulled the trigger yourself?'

Pekkala tightened his grip on the Webley. 'It does not have to end this way,' he said.

'No,' answered Vasko. 'You could have me shipped me out to Kolyma, and I could end my days in the Sturmovoi goldmine. How long is the life expectancy there? One month? Or is it two? I would rather die here, now, than be led from this place like a lamb to the slaughtering pen.'

'You know I cannot let you go.' Sweat burned between Pekkala's fingers, and his palm felt slick against the pistol grips.

'Then at least have the courage to kill me yourself.'

'You are giving me no choice,' Pekkala answered quietly, as his finger curled around the trigger.

There was no fear in Vasko's eyes. Instead, he stared Pekkala down, like a man who has foreseen his end a hundred times and for whom the emptiness of death could hold no fear.

Pekkala's levelled the gun at the inverted V of Vasko's solar plexus. His breathing grew steady and slow. The muscles in his shoulder tightened in anticipation of the Webley's kick. Already Pekkala could feel the burden of Vasko's death hanging like an anchor chain around his neck and he knew that it would never go away.

At that moment, an image flickered in his brain of the journey he had made to the labour camp at Borodok, in a cattle car so crowded that even the dead remained standing. Once more, Pekkala heard the moaning of the wind through barbed wire laced across the window opening and felt the heat of his body leach out through his flimsy prison clothes until his heart felt like a jagged piece of glass lodged in his throat. As that long, slow train clattered through the Ural mountains into Siberia, the knowledge had spread unspoken through those frost-encrusted wagons that even those who might return would never be the same. For the rest of their lives, the mark of the Gulag would be upon them; the unmistakable hollowness of their gaze, the pallor of their cheeks, the way they slept curled in upon themselves, hoarding their last spark of warmth.

While Vasko stood helpless before him, patiently awaiting his death, Pekkala saw the years fade from his face, like layers peeled from an onion, until he glimpsed a child, frightened and confused, and bound on that same journey through Siberia.

As if the weight of his revolver had suddenly become too much to bear, Pekkala lowered the gun. 'Go,' he whispered. 'Find your own way to oblivion.'

Slowly, Vasko's arms dropped to his side. 'Is this some kind of trick?' he asked.

'Go!' repeated Pekkala, his voice rising. 'Before I change my mind!'

A cold wind shuffled through the treetops, sending wisps of fine snow cascading from the branches. Glittering flakes powdered the clothes of the two men, melting in tiny droplets on their skin.

Without another word, Vasko turned and ran.

Pekkala listened to his footsteps fading softly over the pine-needled earth. Then he sighed and put away his gun.

*

The sun had already set by the time Poskrebychev set out for the airfield in an American-made Packard, the personal vehicle of Stalin, which was garaged at the Kremlin Motor Pool. Its original weight of 6000 lb had been increased to 15,000 lb by the addition of armour plating, which included three-inch thick window glass, able to withstand a direct burst of machine gun fire.

Akhatov sat in the back. With a contented groan, he stretched out on to the padded leather seat. 'Which airfield is it?' he asked.

'Krylova,' replied Poskrebychev and as he spoke he removed an envelope from his chest pocket and tossed it over his shoulder into Akhatov's lap.

Akhatov tore open the envelope and removed the banknotes it contained. There was a rapid fluttering sound as he let the bills play across his thumb. 'One thing I'll say about your boss,' said Akhatov, tucking the money into his pocket. 'He pays his debts on time.'

Poskrebychev did not reply. He stared at the road as it unravelled from the darkness, his hands white-knuckled on the wheel.

Soon they had passed beyond the city limits. Stars clustered above the ruffled black line of the horizon.

The gates of the Krylova airfield were open. Tall metal fences, topped with coils of barbed wire, stretched away into the darkness.

'Why are there no lights?' said Akhatov.

'There is a blackout,' answered Poskrebychev. 'Military regulations.' The Packard rolled across the railyard until it arrived at an empty hangar. The brakes squeaked as Poskrebychev brought the car to a halt. 'We're a little early,' he said, cutting the engine. 'The plane has not yet arrived. You might want to stretch your legs, Comrade Akhatov. You will be on that plane for a while.'

'Not a bad idea,' said Akhatov.

The two men climbed out of the car.

'It's a pretty night,' said Akhatov, staring up at the sky.

'It is,' agreed Poskrebychev and, as he spoke, he drew a Nagant revolver from his pocket and shot Akhatov through the back of the head.

Akhatov dropped to his knees, and then tipped over on to his side.

The shot echoed across the deserted runway and through the empty buildings of Krylova. The station had been closed down six months before, after it was discovered that the main runway had been built over a spring and was prone to unexpected flooding. A new facility had just been completed at Perovichi, and it was here that the plane bound for Rovno waited, engines running, for a passenger who would never arrive.

Poskrebychev stared down at the body of Akhatov. The bullet had exited through the man's forehead, just above the hairline, leaving a hole the size of a pocket watch in Akhatov's skull.

Poskrebychev had never killed anyone before and now he nudged Akhatov with the toe of his boot, as if uncertain he had done the job correctly. Then he squatted down like a little boy, reached out slowly and touched his fingertip against Akhatov's open right eye.

Satisfied, Poskrebychev set to work stripping off Akhatov's coat, which he then wrapped around the dead man's head. As soon as he had completed this task, he heaved Akhatov into the boot of the Packard and drove north towards the village of

Stepanin, where his parents had once owned a summer cottage.

Before he reached the village, however, Poskrebychev pulled off on to a side road and drove into a wooded area where there had once been a slate quarry. The quarry had been abandoned long before, and the deep pit from which the slate had been extracted was now filled with water. As a boy, Poskrebychev had frequently come here with his parents, to swim in the luminous green water.

He backed up the Packard as far as he dared towards the lip of the quarry. Then he stopped the car, got out and walked to the edge. It was a long way down, enough to give him vertigo, and he quickly backed away.

Poskrebychev dragged Akhatov's body from the car, letting it fall heavily to the ground. Then he got down on his knees and, using all his strength, rolled the corpse off the edge of the cliff. Akhatov fell, limbs trailing, until he splashed into the quarry lake, leaving a halo in the blackness of the water. For a while, the corpse floated on the surface, pale and shimmering. Then it sank away into the dark.

Before he got back into the car, Poskrebychev threw the murder weapon into the quarry. The Nagant had belonged to his uncle, who had carried it in the Great War and gave it to his nephew as a present on the day he first joined the Kremlin staff. But Poskrebychev never wore a gun. From that day until this, the Nagant had been hidden in a metal tub of rice in his kitchen.

Before returning to Moscow, Poskrebychev drove to the Perovichi airfield, where he found the Lavochkin still waiting.

'Hurry up!' called the pilot, when Poskrebychev stepped out of the Packard and approached the aircraft. 'I've wasted enough fuel already.'

'I am not your passenger!' Poskrebychev shouted over the

buzz-saw thrumming of the aircraft's Shevtsov engine.

The pilot threw up his hands. 'Then where the devil is he?'

'He's not coming.'

'But I have orders to fly this plane to Rovno!'

'Oh, you're still going there,' Poskrebychev told him.

'Without a passenger?' the pilot demanded in amazement. 'But the amount of fuel this is going to take—'

'Do you presume,' hollered Poskrebychev, 'to question the will of Comrade Stalin?'

'No!' the pilot replied hastily. 'It's not that . . .'

'Then go!' cried Poskrebychev, using the particularly shrill tone he employed on all who were beneath him. 'Take to the sky and be gone and I'll forget your suicidal proclamations!'

Within minutes, the plane had vanished into the night sky.

As he drove back to Moscow, Poskrebychev realised that he had given almost no thought to everything he had just done. There had been no time to consider his actions and to balance out the risks. Poskrebychev had simply made up his mind on the spot that Akhatov had to be stopped. Now he wondered if he would be caught, but these thoughts were vague and fleeting, as if the risk belonged to someone he had met in a dream. There was nothing to do now, Poskrebychev decided, but to carry on as if nothing unusual had happened. He wondered if this was what bravery felt like. He had never been brave before. He had been sly and cowardly and grovelling, but never actually brave. Until now, the opportunity had never presented itself. As he raced along the empty, frozen roads towards the lights of Moscow in the distance, the steady thrum of the V12 engine seemed to reach a perfect equilibrium, as engines sometimes do at night, and Poskrebychev was filled with a curious blur of energy and peace of mind, as if the gods were telling him that no harm would come his way.

After returning the Packard to the Kremlin motor pool, Poskrebychev walked back to his office to collect some paperwork before heading home.

Entering the room, he turned on the lights and gasped.

Stalin was sitting as his desk.

'Comrade Stalin?' spluttered Poskrebychev. 'What are you doing there, alone and in the dark?'

'You drove my Packard.'

'Yes, Comrade Stalin.'

'That is my car! It is not for running errands.'

'But it is the only vehicle whose destination is never listed in the motor-pool logbook, Comrade Stalin.'

Stalin was silent for a moment. 'Yes,' he said finally, 'Under the circumstances, I suppose it makes sense to have used it.' Stalin rose from the desk. 'But if I find one scratch on the paint, you will answer for it, I promise.'

'Yes, Comrade Stalin.'

'The Siberian has been dropped off?'

'I handled it myself,' replied Poskrebychev.

Just before he left the room, Stalin paused and turned to his secretary. 'I know what you think about my decision but, in time, you will see that everything which has been done is for the best.'

'I see it already, Comrade Stalin.'

For a moment, Stalin only stared at Poskrebychev, as if struggling to comprehend the meaning of his words. Then he gave a noncommittal grunt, walked out and shut the door.

*

Pekkala picked up Malashenko, carried him over to the Jeep and laid his body across the rear seats.

By then, the sun had set, and darkness seemed to rise up through the ground.

He went back into the cabin, took up the paraffin lamp, and smashed it against the wall. The fuel splashed over the bare logs, trickling into a puddle on the floor. Afterwards, Pekkala lit a match from a box which he found on the windowsill. When he set fire to the paraffin, pearl-white flames raced across floor and walls and Pekkala backed out of the cabin, shielding his face with one hand.

Quickly, he climbed behind the wheel of the Jeep, turned on its blinkered headlights and raced back down the trail. The wheels spun and side-slipped in the mud and the body of the man who had saved his life jolted in the rear seat as if a pulse were returning to his veins.

As Pekkala drove, he thought about what Vasko had said about the second mission. Maybe the man had been lying, although he doubted it. Over the years, Pekkala had investigated numerous plots to assassinate Stalin. Most turned out to be nothing more than rumours and the rest had been stopped in their tracks long before they turned into actual threats. But Canaris was a formidable adversary. Stalin had confided to Pekkala that the only man who truly made him fear for his life was the admiral. The year before, Stalin's fears had almost become reality when a German plot to assassinate him at a conference in Teheran had only been uncovered by accident. Fortunately, the admiral's powers had been undermined by the ongoing struggle between the SS and the Abwehr, which had weakened both branches of German Intelligence. This bitter rivalry had forced Canaris to undertake operations so secret and complex that not even those within the German

High Command were aware of their existence. Although Vasko had given Pekkala little to go on, the possibility that Canaris could have conceived and set in motion another plot to murder Stalin was very real. There was little Pekkala could do, however, except to transmit a message to the Kremlin as soon as he arrived in Rovno and hope that Moscow took his warning seriously.

As Pekkala drove through the outskirts of the town, he noticed a column of smoke rising from the centre, its blackness blotting out the stars. He found himself wondering what was even left to burn in Rovno. The town had been all but cremated in the numerous battles and air raids unleashed upon it.

The closer Pekkala came to the garrison, the clearer it became to him that the fire was coming from the building itself. Arriving at the barricade, he climbed out of the Jeep and joined a crowd of soldiers who were watching the blaze. No one made any attempt to put out the fire. Instead, they seemed content to stare at the inverted waterfalls of smoke and flames, rolling and boiling from the window frames.

Standing closest to the inferno was Commander Chaplinsky, his sooty face glistening with sweat. Chaplinsky held a bottle of brandy in one hand and the severed receiver of a field telephone in the other. The cloth-covered cord which once attached it to the body of the radio had been wrenched apart and now only multi-coloured strands of wire hung from the receiver.

'What happened?' asked Pekkala, as he went to stand beside Chaplinsky.

The commander glanced across at him, pig-eyed in his drunkenness. 'Nobody knows for sure,' he replied. 'Some of our ammunition stores must have been hit during the battle. By the time we realised the place was burning, it was already too late. It was all we could do to get everyone out of there before the place started falling in upon itself. The partisans helped. Thank God we didn't have to slaughter them. Just before the fire forced us out of the building, we received a message from Moscow, ordering us to cancel our attack on the Atrads.'

He was interrupted by the dull thump of a ceiling giving way. A geyser of sparks erupted through the gap of what had been the front doors of the building. The doors themselves lay flattened on the ground, as if knocked down by a stampede.

'Is there any way that I can contact Moscow?' asked Pekkala. 'It may be urgent.'

Chaplinsky held out the broken radio receiver. 'This is all that's left of our equipment. After that last message from Moscow, everything went up in flames.' Contemptuously, he tossed the receiver aside. 'We're cut off from the world, Inspector, and maybe that's not a bad thing!' he said as he passed the brandy to Pekkala.

Pekkala took the bottle and held it up against the backdrop of the flames. On the label, not quite obscured by the name 'Krug', which had been scribbled across it in black pencil, Pekkala read the words, 'Armagnac Baron de Sigognac', as well as a date of 1940. He wondered what strange journey had brought it to this place. Through the dark green glass he saw the liquid swaying. It had been a long time since he'd been offered anything but *samahonka*, brewed by Barabanschikov himself in an old crow's-foot bathtub, and which Pekkala wisely had not touched. Raising the bottle to his lips, he drank and felt the quiet fire of the brandy spread like wings inside his chest.

'Where is my driver, Zolkin?' asked Chaplinsky, retrieving the bottle from Pekkala. 'Is that him sleeping in the back of the Jeep?'

'No,' replied the Inspector. 'That is a partisan named

Malashenko. He was one of Barabanschikov's men.'

'Was?'

'That's what I said,' replied Pekkala.

'Well, get him out of there before he bleeds on the seats! And where is Zolkin, anyway? Has he deserted? I never did trust that man. I'll have him shot, I swear!'

'Sergeant Zolkin has not deserted,' Pekkala assured him. 'He left for Moscow on a plane not long ago, in the company of my assistant, Major Kirov. He talked his way into becoming my chauffeur. I did not have a chance to tell you sooner.'

'You're welcome to him,' said Chaplinsky. 'Around here, drivers are not hard to find. It's vehicles we don't have enough of, not to mention spare parts for repairs. I guess I can't blame him for leaving.' He raised his bottle at the funeral pyre of the garrison. 'Who wouldn't trade Moscow for this?'

'He said his greatest wish was to shake the hand of Joseph Stalin, and he may well get the chance before this day is out.'

Chaplinsky blinked at him stupidly. 'You must be mistaken, Inspector. Zolkin is the last person who would want an audience with Stalin.'

'Why do you say that?'

'His family used to be farmers in northern Ukraine, but they died of starvation when Stalin ordered the farms to be collectivised. Zolkin is the only one who survived, and if you believe the stories they tell about him, he did so by eating the flesh of his parents. A man like that,' Chaplinsky paused to belch extravagantly, 'is the kind who would carry a grudge.'

While Chaplinsky continued to ramble, one thought blazed across Pekkala's mind. If I were Canaris, he thought, Zolkin is exactly the kind of person I would be looking to recruit. As

Yakushkin's personal driver, he too would have been transferred back to Moscow. Once there, Yakushkin would have been in direct contact with top-ranking members of the Kremlin staff, including Stalin. Drivers regularly accompanied the officers they served to meetings, acting partly as bodyguards and partly as baggage handlers for the briefcases full of documents required at each presentation to the high command. Zolkin would be armed as a matter of course. All drivers were. Perhaps Yakushkin's murder had not been planned. The commander had simply been in the wrong place when Vasko went looking for information on the whereabouts of Major Kirov. Since Vasko did not know the identity of the second agent, or the details of his mission, he had no idea that he had placed the entire mission in jeopardy.

If Zolkin was indeed the second agent, his role in the assassination plot might have ended with Yakushkin's death. Instead, the sergeant had just talked his way on to the plane bound for Moscow, and a meeting with Stalin himself.

And I am the one who made it possible, thought Pekkala, dread rising in the back of his throat. Within a matter of hours, Zolkin will be at the Kremlin. If he is able to carry out his task, it won't just be Stalin who dies. The lives of Kirov and Barabanschikov are also in grave danger.

'Of course,' Chaplinsky continued, 'there are others to blame besides the Boss. Some say it wasn't Stalin's fault at all. Some even say—'

'I must get a message to Moscow!' interrupted Pekkala. 'Chaplinsky, this is very important.'

'I told you, the radios are gone. Burned to ashes. The only way you can contact Moscow is if you get on the plane and go there yourself with the message.'

'What plane?' asked Pekkala.

'The one that landed about half an hour ago, although exactly what he's doing here is hard to say. It's all very strange. He was carrying orders from Moscow to deliver a passenger. The thing is, though, he didn't have any passengers with him.'

'Where is the plane now?' asked Pekkala.

'On the runway at Obarov, but if you want to get on board, you'd better hurry. The pilot said that as soon as his plane has been refuelled, he's going straight back where he came from.'

The words had barely left Chaplinsky's mouth before Pekkala dashed back to the vehicle, started the engine and set out towards Obarov.

'By all means, take my Jeep!' Chaplinsky shouted after him. 'You've already stolen my driver.'

But Pekkala was already gone.

*

Vasko had been running flat out for half an hour, following the dim outline of the forest path, before he finally allowed his pace to slacken. By now, he was deep in the woods and unsure of his location. Not until the moon had climbed above the trees did Vasko even know in which direction he was headed. His only thought had been to get away. To have had his life spared by the man he'd sworn to kill had turned Vasko's mind into a hornet's nest of confusion. But the anger was still there, coiled like a snake in his guts and whispering to him that everything Pekkala had said was a lie. Vasko listened to its patient and familiar voice, demanding blood for blood.

In the strange, gunmetal-blue light of the full moon, Vasko

headed west towards the German lines, passing within a stone's throw of the place where the farrier Hudzik lay naked and frozen among the bones of former customers.

*

The Lavochkin aircraft in which Pekkala travelled, being faster than the fully-loaded cargo plane transporting Barabanschikov, arrived in Moscow only half an hour after the others had touched down.

Scrambling into the air controller's car, Pekkala raced towards the Kremlin, punching the horn as he sped through every intersection.

'Inspector!' Poskrebychev leapt to his feet as Pekkala entered the office. 'I knew you would come back to us!'

Out of breath and wild-eyed with fatigue, Pekkala swiped a finger across his throat, instantly silencing Poskrebychev. With his other hand, he drew the Webley from his coat.

At the sight of the gun, Poskrebychev's expression transformed from one of joy to utter confusion. 'Why have you drawn your weapon?' he gasped. 'You know you cannot do that here!'

Pekkala pointed at the doors to Stalin's study. 'Who is in that room now?' he demanded.

'Why, Major Kirov! And that partisan leader, Barabanschikov. And Comrade Stalin, too, of course. The partisan requested a private audience with Stalin, which has been granted. Major Kirov is just finishing up his report and then he will leave them alone to carry out their business.'

'What about Zolkin?'

'The driver?' Poskrebychev shrugged. 'He came and went.

Kirov introduced him to Comrade Stalin. They shook hands, Stalin autographed the back of his pass book and then Zolkin excused himself.

'He's gone?' Pekkala looked stunned.

'Yes!' insisted Poskrebychev. 'The last I saw of Sergeant Zolkin, he was on his way down to the motor pool, where your Emka has been stored since Major Kirov's departure. I gather that the sergeant is to be your new driver.'

Pekkala slumped back against the door frame. 'I thought...' he began, but his words trailed off into silence.

'Inspector, do not throw away your life,' pleaded the secretary. 'I know how you must feel, but all the good you have done for this country will be squandered in a heartbeat if you shed his blood like this.'

As those words echoed in Pekkala's mind, he thought back to a promise he had made, on a winter's day long ago, as he sat with his friend by the ashes of a still-glowing fire. Then suddenly he knew who he'd been chasing all along.

The double doors flew open as Pekkala stepped into the room.

The three men turned to stare at him.

Stalin was on his feet, sitting on the front edge of his desk with his arms folded and his legs stretched out and crossed, so that only his heels touched the ground. At the sight of the Inspector brandishing a gun, Stalin's eyes grew wide with amazement.

In front of him stood Kirov and Barabanschikov.

At the moment Pekkala entered, Kirov's hands had been raised as he described some event in their journey. Now he froze, his hands stilled in the air, as if holding an invisible ball.

The only one who moved was Barabanschikov. 'Hello, old friend,' he said to Pekkala, and as he spoke, he pulled a small

Mauser automatic pistol from the pocket of his tattered coat. But rather than pointing the gun at Pekkala, he aimed it at Stalin instead.

'Barabanschikov,' whispered Kirov, 'have you completely lost your mind?'

'What is the meaning of this?' roared Stalin, his eyes fixed on Barabanschikov's gun. 'Put that weapon down! This is not some muddy crossroads in the forest, where you can rob and murder to your heart's content. This is the Kremlin! How do you expect to get out of here alive?'

'That was never my intention,' replied Barabanschikov.

'I offered you peace!' roared Stalin.

'I have seen what you call peace. All you gave us was a different way to die. Nothing will change for us while you are still alive.'

Pekkala slowly raised the Webley until its sights were locked on Barabanschikov. 'Why are you doing this?' he asked.

'That day I was stopped at the roadblock in Rovno, at the same time as you were arrested on the other side of town, things did not go exactly as I told you. One of my former students, who had joined the Ukrainian police, was manning the roadblock. He recognised me immediately and I was brought to the German Field Police Headquarters. The commander's name was Krug, and he explained that he knew where we were and that they had already made plans to wipe us out. But then he offered me the chance to work with them, in exchange for which he would spare my life, and the lives of everyone in our group. I had no choice, so I agreed. From that day on, I kept him informed about everything that happened in the Red Forest. And when I told the enemy you had joined us, they gambled that you might one day lead me into the presence of Stalin himself. As you can see, they were right. You once asked me how we managed to survive. Well, there is your answer.'

'Do you remember the oath we took?' asked Pekkala.

'To do whatever good we can,' replied the partisan.

'And to stay alive!' shouted Pekkala. 'Do you remember that?'

'I do, old friend,' said Barabanschikov, 'but I'm tired of treading softly through this world.'

A gunshot clapped the air, deafening in the confined space of the room.

But it wasn't Pekkala who fired.

In the second when Barabanschikov turned his head towards the Inspector, Kirov had reached for his gun. He shot the partisan almost point-blank in the side, so close that the cloth of Barabanschikov's jacket was smouldering as the partisan slipped to the floor.

At the moment of the gunshot, Stalin cried out and shrank away, hands covering his face. Now he slowly lowered his hands and looked down at his chest, searching for the wound which he felt sure he must have suffered. Frantically, he swept his fingers up and down his arms and dabbed his fingertips against his cheeks in search of blood. Finding nothing, Stalin began to laugh. He stepped over to the dying Barabanschikov and began to kick at him savagely.

The partisan was still alive, but he was barely breathing. He kept blinking his eyes, as if to clear the darkness that was closing in on him.

'Comrade Stalin . . .' Kirov said gently.

Cackling obscenely, Stalin continued to jab his foot into the man's stomach where the bullet had gone in, until the toe of his calfskin boot was slick with red.

'Enough!' Pekkala's voice exploded.

Only now did Stalin pause. He whipped his head around and stared at the Inspector, madness in his yellow-green eyes. 'Filthy partisans!' he snarled. 'I'll wipe them all off the face of the earth.'

'The partisans were not behind this,' said Pekkala.

'Then who was?' Stalin demanded.

'Admiral Canaris.'

At the sound of that name, Stalin froze. 'Canaris,' he whispered, and a look of terror passed across his face. He stepped away from Barabanschikov, walked around behind the desk and sat down in his chair. With trembling hands, Stalin lit a cigarette, the burning end crackling as he sucked the smoke into his lungs. Slowly, the madness faded from his eyes. 'You took your damned time getting here,' he said.

Two guards skidded into the room, sub-machine guns at the ready. They looked around in confusion, until their gazes came to rest upon the partisan.

Barabanschikov was dead now, his clawed hands still clutching the wound.

Shouting echoed through the hallway as more guards rushed up the stairs, scrambling in their hobnailed boots.

'Send all the others away,' ordered Stalin, 'and you two can clean up this mess.' He gestured towards the body of the partisan, trailing smoke through the air with his cigarette.

The guards dragged Barabanschikov out by his feet, smearing the red carpet with the darker shade of blood.

'Poskrebychev!' Stalin called into the outer office.

A moment later, the secretary peeked around the corner. As soon as he had heard the shot, he crawled under his desk and stayed there. Only when the guards ran into Stalin's room did he feel it was safe to come out. 'Yes, Comrade Stalin?' he asked in a quavering voice.

'Send a message to Akhatov. Tell him that his services are no longer required.' Stalin took one last drag on his cigarette, before stubbing it out in his already crowded ashtray. 'Major Kirov,' he said, as casually as he could manage, 'I owe you my thanks.'

'You owe him more than that,' said Pekkala, before Kirov had a chance to reply.

Through gritted teeth, Stalin managed to smile. 'I see that your time among the savages has done nothing to improve your manners.'

'Inspector,' Kirov said hastily, 'the car is waiting.'

'By all means go, Pekkala.' Stalin waved him away. 'Just not so far this time.'

*

That evening, after a visit to his apartment, where he took his first hot bath in more than a year, Pekkala returned to his office. As he climbed the stairs to the office on the fifth floor, a wintry sunset cast its brassy light upon the dusty window panes, illuminating the chipped paint on the banisters and the scuffed wooden steps beneath his feet. It was so familiar to him that, for a moment, all the time since he had last set foot in here held no more substance than the gauzy fabric of a dream.

As Pekkala reached the fourth floor, he smelled food. 'Shashlik,' he muttered to himself. The grilled lamb, marinated in pomegranate juice and served with green peppers over rice, was one of his favourite dishes. Then he remembered that it was Friday.

Kirov had not forgotten their old ritual of a dinner cooked on the wood-fired stove in their office at the end of every week.

Pekkala smiled as he opened the door, turning the old brass knob with the tips of his fingers in a movement so practised that it required no conscious thought.

Inside, Kirov was waiting. 'You're just in time,' he said. He had cleared off their desks and dragged them together to make a table. Laid out on the desks, whose bare wood surfaces were stained with overlapping rings from countless glasses of tea, lay heavy white plates loaded with food.

Elizaveta was there, too, clutching a platter of jam-filled *pelmeny* pastries – a gift from Sergeant Gatkina.

'Tell the Emerald Eye,' Gatkina had whispered in Elizaveta's ear, 'that there's more where those came from!'

'I hope you're not surprised to see me here, Inspector,' Elizaveta said nervously, as she laid the platter on the table.

'I would have been surprised if you weren't,' replied Pekkala.

'Before we sit down,' said Kirov, rubbing his hands together, 'I have an announcement to make.'

'You two are getting married.'

Kirov rolled his eyes. 'You could at least pretend you hadn't guessed.'

'You wouldn't have believed me if I tried,' remarked Pekkala. 'Besides,' he nodded at Elizaveta, 'she is wearing a ring.'

'I wondered if you'd notice,' she said, holding out her hand for him to see.

'It's only a small diamond,' muttered Kirov, 'but the way things are . . .'

'Small!' Taking Elizaveta's hand, Pekkala studied the ring. 'I can barely see it.'

Elizaveta snatched her hand away. 'Why would you say such a thing?' she demanded, anger rising in her voice.

'Because I think you can do better,' said Pekkala. As he spoke, he produced a dirty handkerchief from his pocket and tossed it on to the table.

'What are we supposed to do with that?'

'Consider it as a gift.'

'You are crazy!' said Elizaveta. 'I've always said you were.' She snatched up the handkerchief and threw it at Kirov. 'Get rid of that filthy thing!'

'Now then,' said Kirov, as he caught the handkerchief. 'I'm sure there is a logical explanation for this,' adding in a quieter voice, 'although what it could possibly be . . .' He lifted one of the round iron plates from the stove and was just about to toss the handkerchief into the fire when he noticed a knot tied in one of the corners. Returning the iron plate to its place on the stove, he began picking away at the knotted cloth until something fell out and rattled on to the floor.

'What's that?' asked Elizaveta.

Kirov bent down and peered at the object. 'It looks like a diamond,' he whispered.

Now Elizaveta came to look. 'It *is* a diamond. It's the biggest diamond I have ever seen!'

Grinning with satisfaction, Pekkala regarded their astonishment.

Kirov bent down and picked up the gem. 'Where on earth did you get this, Inspector?' he asked, holding up the diamond between his thumb and first two fingers.

'From an old acquaintance,' replied Pekkala and, as he spoke, he thought of Maximov, heading out alone across the frozen lake.

'I think he would have wanted you to have it.'

Elizaveta placed a hand to her forehead. 'And I just called you crazy, didn't I?'

'From what I hear,' replied Pekkala, 'you've called me worse than that.'

Elizaveta turned to glare at Kirov.

Kirov opened his mouth, but the phone rang before he could speak.

Its jarring clatter startled everyone in the room.

Pekkala picked up the receiver.

'Hold for Comrade Stalin!' Poskrebychev's shrill command drilled into his ear.

Pekkala waited patiently.

A moment later, a quiet voice rustled through the static, like a whisper in the dark. 'Is that you, Pekkala?'

'Yes, Comrade Stalin.'

'I thought you might like to know,' said Stalin, 'that Commander Chaplinsky was able to negotiate a ceasefire with the partisans. They have laid down their arms. Those men may not realise it, Pekkala, but they owe you their lives.'

'It's Barabanschikov who deserves the credit,' replied Pekkala.

'Barabanschikov!' Stalin spluttered into the telephone receiver. 'That traitor got exactly what he deserved and I intend to let those partisans know what kind of man was leading them.'

'What makes you think they will believe you?'

'They have to! It's the truth.'

'And when you tell them he was shot in the Kremlin, by a commissar of the Red Army, while under your personal protection – all of which is true – how long do you think it will take before they pick up their weapons again?'

There was a pause. 'You may have a point,' Stalin conceded. 'What do you suggest I do about it?'

'Give Barabanschikov a medal,' said Pekkala. 'The highest one you've got.'

'What?' growled Stalin. 'Have you forgotten that he just tried to kill me?'

'Would you rather that Admiral Canaris knew exactly how close he came to liquidating you,' asked Pekkala, 'or would you prefer to have him think that he was betrayed by a man who had been loyal to you all along?'

In the silence that followed, Pekkala could hear a rustling sound as Stalin raked his fingernails through the stubble on his chin. 'Very well,' he muttered at last. 'As of this moment, I declare comrade Barabanschikov to be a hero of the Soviet Union.'

'Will that be all, Comrade Stalin?' Pekkala glanced at the steam curling up from the food on the table.

'As a matter of fact, it will not. There is something that I need to know.'

'Yes?'

'If you had walked into this room fifteen seconds later, I would be dead now. You knew that, but you walked in anyway.'

'Yes.'

'Why did you let me live, Pekkala, after all I've done to you?'

'Do you really want the answer, Comrade Stalin?'

There was a long pause. 'No,' said Stalin. 'On second thought, maybe I don't.' Without another word, he hung up the phone. For a moment, Stalin looked around his study, at the red velvet curtains, the picture of Lenin on the wall and the old grandfather clock standing silent in the corner, as if to reassure himself that everything was as it should be. Then he opened a drawer in his

310

desk, removed a can of sardines in tomato sauce and peeled back the top with a small metal key. He took off his jacket, rolled up his sleeves and tucked a large grey handkerchief into his collar. But before he began his meal, Stalin lifted the headset, with which he had been listening to the conversation in Pekkala's office. He had waited for the precise moment when they were sitting down to eat before ordering Poskrebychev to place the call. Now, as Stalin heard the sound of cutlery on plates, he slipped one of the greasy, headless sardines into his mouth. While he chewed, he felt the soft bones crush between his teeth. Pausing to lick the tiny, glistening fish scales from his fingertips, Stalin imagined he was there among them in that cosy little room, sharing the warmth and the laughter.

Acknowledgements

The author would like to thank the following:

Walter Donohue, Deborah Rogers, Will Atkinson, Katherine Armstrong, Alex Holroyd, John Grindrod, Lisa Baker, Hannah Griffiths, Mohsen Shah and Christian House.

Also by Sam Eastland

ff

Eye of the Red Tsar

**He was condemned to the Gulag,
now Stalin needs him back.**

IT IS THE TIME OF THE GREAT TERROR

Inspector Pekkala – known as the Emerald Eye – was once the most famous detective in all Russia, and the favourite of the Tsar.

NOW HE IS PRISONER TO THE MEN HE ONCE HUNTED

Like millions of others, Inspector Pekkala has been sent to the Gulag in Siberia. But a reprieve comes when Stalin himself summons him to investigate a crime. His mission – to track down the men who really killed the Tsar and his family, and to locate the Tsar's treasure. The reward for success will be his freedom and a second chance with the woman he loves. The price of failure – death.

'A rollicking debut . . . it's written with flair and has plenty of stand-out sequences.' *Guardian*

'Particularly satisfying . . . Pekkala is a likeable and believable protagonist, and this is a highly promising debut.' *Mail on Sunday*

ff

The Red Coffin

A secret weapon. A suspicious death.
A world on the edge of war.

1939: RUSSIA FACES THE THREAT OF NAZI GERMANY

All Stalin's hopes rest on the development of the T-34 tank – a thirty-ton steel monster nicknamed the 'Red Coffin'. But the architect of the tank is found murdered and Stalin must turn to Inspector Pekkala to find the killer before the enemy reaches the Russian border.

BUT THERE'S ALSO AN ENEMY WITHIN

When Pekkala's investigation leads him to The White Guild – a group of soldiers who also served the Tsar – he realises that the violence of the past still resonates in the present. Will his investigation lead him to the truth – or into a deadly trap?

'Brilliantly achieved.' *The Times*

'A vivid picture of a country still in a state of flux as the storm clouds gather . . . A page-turner of a book with enough neatly resolved twists and turns to keep any thriller fan happy.' Shotsmag.co.uk

ff

Siberian Red

Who can find the Tsar's missing treasure?

1939: RUSSIA TEETERS ON THE VERGE OF
WAR WITH GERMANY

It is also on the verge of bankruptcy. To preserve his regime, Stalin orders a search for the legendary missing gold of Tsar Nicholas II and summons his chief detective, Inspector Pekkala, to find the treasure.

Pekkala's mission is to re-enter the brutal Siberian gulag where he himself was once held captive – and then infiltrate a gang of convicts still loyal to the Tsar. In this frozen fortress he begins to unravel the mystery, and with it the true identity of a murdered inmate whose secrets have lain buried for years. Yet the clues lead to a shocking conspiracy that could decide not only Pekkala's fate but the future of the Soviet Union itself.

'Eastland writes with punch.' *Metro*

'An intriguing blend of curious fact and fiction.' *The Times*

'Eastland has a keen eye for the sensual, brutish, elemental details of the time and place.' *Independent on Sunday*

ff

The Red Moth

Who will discover the Tsar's greatest mystery?

SUMMER 1941. RUSSIA HAS BEEN INVADED

As Hitler's forces roll into Russia annihilating the Red Army divisions in its path, a lone German scout plane is forced down. Contained within the briefcase of its passenger is a painting of a *hyalophora cecropia*, a red moth.

Only Stalin suspects that the picture might be more significant than it appears, and he sends Inspector Pekkala to investigate the true meaning of the red moth.

As Pekkala soon discovers, the real treasure that is being saught is a secret and highly prized possession of the Romanovs, once considered to be the eighth wonder of the world.

But saving the Tsar's treasure may cost Pekkala more than he realises, as his mission takes him deep into enemy lines. Could this be the one case that Pekkala can't win?

'For those who like their tales told in the John Buchan style, with a shot of vodka downed and a fully loaded Webley at the ready.'
Independent on Sunday